THE NUANCES OF LOVE

CELEBRATING 40 YEARS OF ITALIAN-CANADIAN VOICES

ESSENTIAL ANTHOLOGIES SERIES 21

Canada Council for the Arts Conseil des arts du Canada

ONTARIO ARTS COUNCIL
CONSEIL DES ARTS DE L'ONTARIO
an Ontario government agency
un organisme du gouvernement de l'Ontario

Ontario

Canada

Guernica Editions Inc. acknowledges the support of the Canada Council for the Arts and the Ontario Arts Council. The Ontario Arts Council is an agency of the Government of Ontario.
We acknowledge the financial support of the Government of Canada.

THE NUANCES OF LOVE

CELEBRATING 40 YEARS OF ITALIAN-CANADIAN VOICES

Edited by
Christine Sansalone,
Diana Iuele-Colilli,
Maria Pia Spadafora

GUERNICA
EDITIONS
TORONTO • CHICAGO • BUFFALO • LANCASTER (U.K.)
2025

Guernica Founder, Antonio D'Alfonso

Michael Mirolla, general editor
David Moratto, cover and interior design

Guernica Editions Inc.
1241 Marble Rock Rd., Gananoque (ON), Canada K7G 2V4
2250 Military Road, Tonawanda, N.Y. 14150-6000 U.S.A.
www.guernicaeditions.com

Distributors:
Independent Publishers Group (IPG)
600 North Pulaski Road, Chicago IL 60624
University of Toronto Press Distribution (UTP)
5201 Dufferin Street, Toronto (ON), Canada M3H 5T8

First edition.
Printed in Canada.

Legal Deposit—Third Quarter
Library of Congress Catalog Card Number: 2025935356
Library and Archives Canada Cataloguing in Publication
Title: The nuances of love : celebrating 40 years of Italian-Canadian voices /
Christine Sansalone, Diana Iuele-Colilli, Maria Pia Spadafora, editors.
Names: Association of Italian Canadian Writers.
Series: Essential anthologies series ; 21.
Description: Series statement: Essential anthologies series ; 21
Identifiers: Canadiana (print) 20250174677 | Canadiana (ebook) 20250180014 |
ISBN 9781778490064 (softcover) | ISBN 9781778490071 (EPUB)
Subjects: CSH: Canadian literature (English)—Italian Canadian authors. |
CSH: Canadian literature (English)—21st century. | LCGFT: Literature.
Classification: LCC PS8235.I8 N83 2025 | DDC C810.8/085107109052—dc23

Contents

PROSE

2022 AICW BRESSANI PRIZE WINNER

2022 VENERA FAZIO POETRY CONTEST WINNERS

Foreword

It is with pride and love that we present to you this anthology—a vibrant collection of prose and poetry that stem from forty extraordinary years of the Association of Italian-Canadian Writers (AICW). Born in Vancouver in 1986 from the passionate vision of a group of dedicated Italian-Canadian authors—Fulvio Caccia, Antonio D'Alfonso, Pier Giorgio Di Cicco, Mary Di Michele, Genni Gunn, Dore Michelut, Marco Micone, Dino Minni, Joseph Pivato, and Pasquale Verdicchio—the AICW has been a nurturing haven, a vibrant hearth where creativity has flourished and a profound sense of belonging has taken root.

Celebrating forty years of the Association of Italian-Canadian Writers (AICW) is an extraordinary milestone—a testament to the enduring power of storytelling and community. This anthology is a collection of voices that reflect our shared heritage and the richness of our collective experiences.

Over the decades, our members have explored a wide spectrum of themes, from migration and adaptation to resilience and identity. This anthology delves into two universal and timeless themes: love and friendship.

Love, in all its breathtaking forms, has been a form of inspiration for writers throughout the centuries. Here, it blossoms in the tender embrace of familial bonds, ignites in the passionate fire of romantic connections, and whispers through the deep-rooted love of one's heritage and culture. Friendship unites us across the boundaries of generations, genders, and cultures, through shared laughter, shared tears, and shared dreams.

Within these pages, you will encounter stories of immigrants and their children, grandchildren and great-grandchildren. You will hear stories of love and friendships created over shared meals, shared traditions and shared experiences. You will hear voices that explore what it means to be Italian-Canadian today in an everchanging world. Each piece is a window into the very soul of a community that has blossomed in the fertile ground of two cultures.

On behalf of the Association of Italian-Canadian Writers, we extend our heartfelt gratitude to all the contributors, editors, and supporters who have made this anthology possible. Your unwavering commitment ensures that our voices will continue to resonate for generations to come, inspiring future storytellers to cherish this rich literary legacy and build upon the foundation we have laid with so much love and passion.

With gratitude and best wishes,

Diana Iuele-Colilli
Christine Sansalone
Maria Pia Spadafora

POETRY

George Amabile

The Other Annette

Framed by a small window in a small hut that was once
an ice house on a small island among an uncountable scatter
of islands, there is a slant, scant, long view of the dock—
freshly installed cedar that has just begun to darken and shine
with rain. I look up from my work, briefly, and there she is.

It's like a dream, or a fable, but it's neither, it's the woman
I came to rest for, and have been trying to understand
for twenty years, and it's suddenly clear that I don't know
who she is, or what she has learned from a grey afternoon
in a wilderness cabin that drove her out, on a dead run,
to dance on wet wood in a thunderstorm, without clothes, singing.

The Progress of Love

Before we lived
together, we lived
lives so far apart
we could only discover
each other in little huts
of time, in Leaf Rapids
Montreal, or Saskatoon,
until we found ourselves
in the same city of rivers
and snow.
                    Swimming

on Sunday, outside
the law, in a rain fed
quarry, you surfaced, your
eyes, green, your face
breathless and happy
to see me, water
sluicing from your tough
hair, and there, in that
light without shadow
I felt an unmistakable
yes open between us.

VARIATION ON A THEME BY ERICH FROMM for Tam and Tom

Love is a promise. Yes, but it cannot be kept
at full intensity. Like a dazzling moon
it floods the world, thins, goes black and soon
comes round again to brilliance, having slept.

Love is a music that cannot be played
the same way twice. It's a lullaby, a jazz tune
an aria, a ballad we can croon
to the stars, a brass band, a serenade . . .

Sometimes, (who knows how), we are taken and swept
up in a wave that completes us. Then, even
before we can trust it, it's gone and those inept
gestures we make from the deep moods we grieve in
fail to connect us. We back off. But look, we have stepped
again into that *promise* we botch and believe in.

David Bellusci

Sacred Kiss

Stopover in Rome, *Frecciarossa* south,
orecchiette with cousins, my father's side.
Lufthansa again via Frankfurt, Mumbai,
finally, Goa flickers at sunrise.
Classes at our philosophy institute,
adjusting to afternoon drums, monsoon rains.
Short visit to the novitiate, our first encounter,
his smile—and others.
The following year Nairobi on my agenda,
Amsterdam, Kenya Airways hub,
outbound the southern Adriatic, *la famiglia* waits.
Return to Goa; familiar Indian routes.
Now he reappears in my classes. My student.
We spend August together.
His desire to learn Italian, approaching me,
Buongiorno, Lei come sta?
His surname reveals his features: Portuguese and Indian.
He accompanies me to Margau, a town "not far":
details of his mother's pizza,
his love for science, perhaps medicine,
and why he decided not to marry.
An afternoon under the blue Indian sky,
a walk through the rice fields and winding roads,
we find our way to the main street, rainy dark.
Another evening, dinner interrupted, a call from Vancouver;
noticing me without food, he brings beef curry, lentils, and *chapati*.
End of August, "farewell" seems like any other.
I first hear from him on WhatsApp,
then we continue on Telegram,

chats and calls. He sends me packages of masala for tea.
Cities changed for studies, we plan
my visit to Nagpur, another assignment.
A short stay, he arranges to meet me at the airport,
though he doesn't have a car.
And hires a driver to visit the Hindu Temple at Ramtek,
an Indian lunch of chicken biryani, Kingfisher beer at a bar.
At the chapel of his seminary, the two of us pray together.
My student. My brother.
Covid-interruption; travel prohibited.
Our conversations were not frequent
but they lasted longer. Scheduled texts and video calls.
When home, he sends photos of his nephews
on his brother's new motorcycle.
And sipping lemonade at eleven am
prepared by his mother.
Faithful to our appointments during my
summers in Rome, he conveys his love for Italy,
and things Italian, art and history;
perhaps one day, in Italy together.
My friend updated me on his mission to northern India.
Reaching the local people,
though he only speaks Hindi, translators at work.
Monthly Bollywood haircuts, his white t-shirt, and black jackets,
then, I discover his loyalty to John Wick.
Countdown starts, my return to India,
not to teach but at his side.
Sixteen hours nonstop Singapore Airlines,
connecting to Mumbai. And then Mangalore.
Time spent with him—and his family.
His aunt, godmother visiting from Dubai,
another aunt, Sister in her habit, helps with cooking,
and his brother, sister-in-law, and nephews,
together under one roof.
His home stands in the country-side
with fruit I never heard like *ice apple,* clear, soft, and sweet.
We drink milk fresh from the coconut,

and eat jackfruit, mango, and papaya.
Green coriander chutney at breakfast,
his mother prepares pork bafat, spicy squid, and chili chicken,
finally, her famous pizza covered in mozzarella.
Each evening we stand together
before the altar; his father leads the Rosary,
reads from the Scriptures, and everyone
receives a blessing starting with the eldest, "Bless me."
On his brother's red motorbike we ride,
Indian style: without a helmet.
We leave for the Church at sunrise,
my friend puts on his deacon's stole.
Until the morning when the Church is packed
with priests, sisters and worshipers, prepared for his Ordination.
I do not understand Konkani, the language of Mangalorean Catholics,
but I followed the ritual watching the bishop,
until I approach my friend:
I lay my hands on his head, pray,
and kiss his consecrated hands.

Dominic Buttazzoni

Blue is the colour of my Silence

Al cuore non si comanda
E chissà se mai mi penserai

***

Inexplicably,
I miss someone who is not mine to miss.
I dream about someone who is not my mine to dream about.
I love someone who is not mine to love.
But, it is so much easier to act
Like none of this ever happened,
Ever mattered,
And to pretend to wear a smile
Than to confess that my heart has remained blue
From losing someone
Who was never really mine to lose.

Blue colours my silence. It is the irresistible longing of a wounded heart to overcome the distance and time that separate us, and in which you may never return. My solitary blueness recaptures you between the narrow walls we walked together: insanity on one side, desire, and passion on the other.

The day breaks.

The night falls.
And in between,
There is a world of blue.
How mystifying it is to live in a world
Where nothing lasts forever.

One must learn to fall in love with the sad, sweet
feeling that dwells inside the heart.
Only then, will every silent moment
Be worth the remembering.

Vouloir oublier à jamais combien on aime quelqu'un provoque un sentiment d'avoir libéré un papillon qui avait choisi, faute d'une certaine grâce indéfinissable, de faire de mon cœur son refuge. Vouloir faire cela n'est pas possible pour moi. J'aime contempler la couleur bleue, pas parce qu'elle s'avance sur moi, mais parce qu'elle me tracte derrière elle:

Quand le souvenir de tous nos hiers ensemble quittent ton esprit,
Aime-moi alors.
Quand le souvenir de tes amours d'antan,
Et de vieilles promesses s'effacent,
Aime-moi alors.
Quand ton cœur comprendra mon silence,
Et si un jour tu me retrouveras,
Aime-moi alors.
Aime-moi alors, quand tu apprendras la douleur des jours passés
A part.

It is, arguably, a voluntary delusion, a specific, necessary madness. Each blue episode is a secret code meant for a solitary being, or an "X" stamped on the map of a heart too diffuse ever to be unfolded completely, but that contains a recollected universe that can neither never be escaped, nor ever re-possessed. From the physical fact of blue, I draw a poetic truth imbued with an odd and hard-to-describe feeling, with so many recurring overtones and undercurrents beyond the facts themselves, that linger, still, in the heart. What does one actually remember when one listens to the music of such memories? Surely one perceives something greater and beyond the sum total of the specific sounds, something of additional intimacy and meaning, just as in literature one apprehends something more, and other, than the purely literal meaning of words on a page.

And after the silence that is memory, what comes nearest to expressing the inaudible in the music of the heart? Blue. Memory opens a path into the silence, and it lays bare the human soul in stark nakedness, without the customary linguistic trappings. Without memory, love would be a mistake. Without blue, there would be no memory. There would be no laboratory for silenced feelings across Time. Memory and blue, both move in time, sculpting the colour of our love.

E così, ti richiedo; non ti sembra, ancora un'altra volta, che tanto i componenti cerebrali che sensuali d'un amore indimenticabile, come la descrizione obiettiva d'un colore magnifico, emergono in una cosa più grande, più universale, più eterna? Non illuderti però. Non è questione di sublimità. Perfino adesso, e dopo tutto questo tempo, il ricordo di quel rapporto così meraviglioso, così emozionale, sentendo nel frattempo quel piccolo dolore indescrivibile che l'esistere ci dà, mi trovo, ancora senza scelta.

Sei sfuggita
Ma non mi hai lasciato.
Per tutte le notti e giorni ormai
Non mi rispondi più
Chissà se tornerai?
Non so più dove trovarti
Non so nemmeno come cercarti.
Ma nel vento intramontabile, muto così
Sento una voce dolce che
Non smette di sussurrare
Quello che sei ancora per me.
Chiudo gli occhi e penso a te
E per le vie del cuore ti vedo
E nel vederti, esisti dentro me.

But, why blue? I don't know. I don't get to choose what or whom I love. There was simply no choice. And afterwards?—only the unbreakable silence of separation. Perhaps blue is more apt to disturb the soul than to enliven it. I wonder, is it to be in love ... to be in love with a disturbance? Or is the love itself the disturbance? And what kind of madness is it anyway, to be in love with something physically incapable of returning your love?

Many years have passed, I have
Felt the sadness, feigned the laughter.
I know the contradiction of never getting
What the heart searches after.
I have wept over reasons
You will never know,
Felt the pain silently behind the smile, still uncovered.
There will come a time, I know
When you will no longer care
Because no lover ever lingers
When the heart is no longer there.

But whenever I remember you, I catch a glimpse of a particular, barely noticeable glimmer, a sideways gleam of blue. The colour itself is absent as a subject but present as an aura around a feeling. 'Blue' is an ode to the silence born of absence. Blue, is a solitude born of melancholy. Can blue ever resolve itself, or can it at least keep me company within it?—No, not exactly. It cannot love me that way. It has no warm embrace. But sometimes I feel its presence like a sort of wink: here you are again, it says, and so am I.

Still, even now,
You were unexpected.
You unlocked my heart and looked inside my soul,
Like no other love could ever do.
Now, yesterday's world of memories is cached, one by one.

But since you left, mostly I have become the servant of a speechless sadness and a quiet desolation. Still, I search for the beauty in that. To write is memory—or, rather, memorialization—the wish to remember and the desire to forget, the warp thread and weft thread of which the writing-weave itself is woven. Is not "forgetting" an essential element of creativity? Memory more of an act of creative retelling than one of recording? Could the recollection of a love, long-time silent, be perhaps something akin to this type of experience?

Sometimes, blue affects me like an album of personal photographs taken at different stages of life. Each successive image replaces the memory it aimed to preserve. Wishing neither to displace such memories nor apotheosize them, I avoid writing about too many specific blue things. In fact, I would like it best if the writing could empty me further of them, so that I might become a better vessel for a new blue anamnesis. But what if writing replaces the emotion?

Can the memory of love, be love? or does Time freeze the heart to silence? Where does love ever go when the lover exits but does not leave? To wish to disremember while never to forget can feel like too many subtle antagonisms welling up inside. So often it leaves me despairing and forlorn. How often have I wondered, if ever my light can understand this fire? If my searching eye can discern the law by which she filled my heart? If a poetic language exists to interpret my attachment to her? If I could, but I know that I cannot, express the lights and shades, the longings and feelings that dwell in recurring, cold-warm, attractive-repelling remembrances, freezing—hardening into memory, as Time slips surreptitiously into silence.

There is an uncanny uncertainty underlying the question of what is real—the love or its memory? The measure of love is not the quotient of friction between skin and skin, but something else entirely—something of the trust, joy and ease that flow between two beings as they inhabit that private world sequestered from everything and everyone else. All else is a tug of war between the creativity and choicelessness, between memory and the forgetting. And so, I wander about Time's landscape looking for clues, amassing the evidence. But even the highest pile never seems to decide the case.

Perhaps,
This is insane.
Perhaps,
Love is too short
And forgetting too long.
Perhaps,

We just found each other at the wrong moment, in the wrong space.
Perhaps,
Somewhere down the road, Time
Will bring your heart back to mine,
For I can not unlove you, and I know not how again,
To seek and chance upon my place in another Soul.

Quanto ingannevole è che quell'anima così amata un'eternità fa possa rimanere così forte nella memoria. Mi lascia nel cuore una melanconia sia talmente triste che dolce, con lacrime per quello che non può essere mai più guarito. Prima c'eri, adesso no. Prima mi amavi, ora non so più. Spiegami come da quel piccolo dolore che l'esistere ci dà, nascono i brividi d' un amore inesplicabile.

Licia Canton

Ea bea tosa

Ea bea tosa no ghe xe pì
ea xe 'ndà via
par sempre.
Ea ghetto vista passare tì?
Na volta, tanti anni fa, ea xe 'ndà via
distante
ma ea xe tornà ogni tanto,
de tanto in tanto.
Sta volta ea bea tosa
ea xe 'ndà via par sempre
No tea vedare pì.
Pianzi fin che te vo,
ea bea tosa noa torna pì,
ea xe 'ndà via distante,
massa distante.
Ea ga assà qua so gente
che ghe voe ben
Ea assa qua na vita piena,
piena de lavoro e de amore,
Ea assa qua gente
che ghe vorà sempre ben.
Ea bea tosa xe 'ndà via par sempre.
Sì, dai, sta volta noa torna pì.
Ma ea assa qua un mondo de ben,
ea assa qua so gente che farà
queo che ea no ga bu tempo da fare.
Ea bea tosa xe 'ndà via distante,
massa distante par tornare indrio.
Ea prima volta che ea xe 'ndà via,

ea bea tosa
xe tornà na bea femena.
Sta volta ea xe 'ndà via na bea signora
na gentildonna
Ea assa qua na vita piena
de ben.
Ea bea tosa no ghe xe pì
ea xe 'ndà via
par sempre
distante.
Ea ghetto vista passare tì?

La bella ragazza

La bella ragazza non c'è più
è andata via
per sempre.
L'hai vista passare, tu?
Una volta, tanti anni fa, è andata via
lontano
ma è tornata ogni tanto,
di tanto in tanto.
Questa volta la bella ragazza
è andata via per sempre
Non la vedrai più.
Piangi fin che vuoi,
la bella ragazza non torna più,
è andata via lontano,
troppo lontano.
Ha lasciato qui la sua gente
che le vuole bene.
Lascia una vita piena,
piena di lavoro e di amore,
lascia qui gente

che le vorrà sempre bene.
La bella ragazza è andata via per sempre.
Sì, dai, questa volta non torna più.
Ma lascia qui un mondo di bene,
lascia qui la sua gente che farà
quello che lei non ha avuto tempo di fare.
La bella ragazza è andata via lontano
troppo lontano per tornare.
La prima volta che è andata via,
la bella ragazza
è tornata una bella donna.
Questa volta se n'è andata una bella signora
una gentildonna.
Lascia una vita piena
di bene.
La bella ragazza non c'è più
è andata via
per sempre
lontano.
L'hai vista passare, tu?

Questa poesia è ispirata e dedicata a Vittoria Sartori Paralovo, nata a Cavarzere (Venezia) nel 1932 e deceduta a Montreal il 6 agosto 2022. Licia Canton ha lasciato Cavarzere da bambina ed è arrivata a Montreal con i genitori e la sorella nel 1967. Una delle prime persone che ha conosciuto a Montreal è stata Vittoria che le ha poi fatto da madrina di cresima.

Liana Cusmano

Italian Grocery Stores

Italian grocery stores
with their old Italian salesladies
and imported Italian products
are like islands that
time and globalization
are slowly weathering away
the way surf eats
away at cliffs.
When all the old people die
and no longer buy
their *pandoro* and *provolone* here
who will be left
and what will their relationship
to the products be?
How will we be sure that
we are pronouncing their names correctly?
Milano and Berchicci and Euromarché
What does it mean to shop there?
And does it matter?

I still haven't tracked down
the animal cookies
I ate as a child
at nonna's house
the rabbits and chickens and turtles.
The crosshatching on the fish and owls
would crumble beneath my baby
teeth, weathered away in seconds.
She used to call Costco

Club Price
because it used to be called
Price Club
and when she
went to Club Price and
Milano and Berchicci and Euromarché
and then dropped her haul
at our house after school,
we would zip up her winter boots
and tie her scarf
before she went back out
into the snow,
blowing past stop signs
in the GMC truck
that eventually got stolen
three times.

We are too young to know that
it's easy to take things for granted
when you have never wanted for anything.

When my partner and I go to Costco now
I insist that we buy Italian extra-virgin olive oil
because I was taught that it was the best
without ever really knowing or wondering why.

I can still pronounce *sfogliatelle* and *mortadella*
I can still remember the cookies
They have not yet been
weathered away by time.

Adriana A. Davies

A Dialogue with Myself: Home

Only in a place that is not home can I be truly myself.
All of the voices are silent—
Is the work going well?
Will it make a difference?
Will my loved ones be happy?
Will they prosper and succeed?

In unfamiliar streets,
Buffeted by the wind and warmed by the sun,
I feel centred in my skin,
Connected with nature
Through all my senses,
Rather than my reason.

The scents of roses and mayflowers
Come to me on the breeze,
And the songs of birds rise above the sounds of traffic
As if nature were reaching out—
And embracing me—
Since there is no one to whom I am connected.

There is no past or future,
Only the present made luminous
By the motion of wind,
The play of light and shadow
As spring, imperceptibly,
Turns to summer.

It is time to acknowledge
Memories that cause a catch
In the back of my throat
And my eyes to sting with incipient tears.
I do not know whether to let the memories come,
Welcoming them like tame birds.

But I have no choice—
When there is no work to occupy my mind,
They come—
And they are all about loss,
Whether through death, or changed circumstances,
The people I love are no longer here.

In this state of heightened awareness,
I relive those lost times
And know that they will not come again.
I resign myself to that,
Knowing who I am,
Because everything else is unknown.

I am like a balloon
Plucked by the wind
From a child's hand,
And blown hither and yon by eddies of air.
I see everything from a new perspective
Until—one foot touches earth.

In this house of dreams in which I dwell,
The sounds of the world are muffled
By brick walls, double-paned windows and lined curtains.
Light is indirect, filtered, so that it falls, gently, like moonlight
At dusk when the air is cool on the skin as the petals of a vintage rose
Held up to my face so that it releases its unforgettable scent.

Is it withdrawal or moving forward into another state
Where I can take wing with the red-tailed hawk
In a dazzling stillness,
Until, with a swift turn, I go into freefall,
Waiting for the last minute
When fall becomes flight and I lift on powerful wings.

The houses are always impressive and old,
And I wander from room to room admiring the features—
Large windows, high ceilings and wooden mouldings.
I notice fine pieces of furniture, beautiful paintings and colourful ceramics.
But, overall, there is an air of neglect.
The houses belong to old people, who are already dead.

I thought that I was creating the ideal house with every loving touch—
Every day, I made it more comfortable—
I cooked, cleaned, entertained,
Maintained the network of family and friends,
Who were invited to dinners and parties—
The fabric of our daily lives.

But it became more and more difficult
To present the image of an ideal family
When the differences of vision, disagreements
And conflicting aspirations threatened to tear us apart.
The disconnect went on for years because the roles we played were ingrained
And because we were honourable, and there was still some love.

At night, like the princesses who wore out
Their dancing slippers in secret revels,
I wandered through houses belonging to strangers
Questing for the ideal house,
A blend of beautiful things passed on from one generation to the next—
Where, we could be happy again.

Lying far apart in our bed,
You would move into your dream world, where I could not go,
And I to mine where I would wander through rooms which pleased me
Blending past and present,
And bridging generations,
Something I could not do when awake.

Josie Di Sciascio-Andrews

Doll in Blue

Love always finds a way.
It reaches up towards the light
In spite of obstacles,
In spite of darkness

And in my reaching
I have grown tall.
I have closed my eyes
Dreaming of you

My feet dipped in rivers and oceans
Have crossed forests and meadows

I have run in fields of blue grass and daisies
But I have never stopped searching
Stretching my human form to the heavens
My soul is a dove, craving your light.

My hair has become the silken wing of a sleeping raven,
My skin, the powdered hope of a new dawn.
My lips, delicate peach blossoms, praying.

I am the doll in blue, dressed in spring and sky.
Hope is the rose I hold over my heart.

I am a woman spirit rising above the planet.

Gauguin Girls

I love Gauguin girls
In their bright floral dresses
Sunning innocently on tropical beaches
Blue skies as backdrop

These are the women I know
Mothers, daughters, sisters
Women who give true love
Bearing life patiently
Without pose
Simple women
Without pretense
Their innocence
At any age
Shining forth
In hues of red and orange
On plump cocoa skin

I love Gauguin girls
They speak to me of truth
Of life, resignation
These are women I can trust
Faces of friends
Exuding solidarity

Elio Iannacci

La Prima

All breathy and moon breasted
those nasty Italians were working on her
all while she sat and ordered
dipping into her handbag
hunting some off-white tissue under a magazine
scrubbing those home-town lips off her blouse

A half-spoiled *ensalada mista* arrives late
with a tall bottle of mineral water
the thick ceramic edge of the dish brings up
jealous brows from the balcony
they watch her fork pierce and travel
a geography of shiny olives and eggplants
calling between bites and loud music
the pack of dogs holler
billiard sticks pound and clink
distance keeps attention

Coloratura (June 18th)

> "I don't lie lie, I just do some coloratura."
> —Isabella Rossellini, *Some Of Me*

There you go
fighting the devils
in your crispy sheets
walking the street
not a stitch on. There

you go laying around
on a caramel sofa
hiding a man in
your walk-in closet
taking a stroll, screaming
for him, There you

go to the doorway
lean on a panel like
all the world's
a bad blonde wig—
exposing the pulled
black roots under
sexy but vulgar. There

you go blowing the candles
at 69! All the world's
minding your business
watching you come
watching you blow

There in white
and black on film
mourning your cousins,
your mother, crying on caskets
hurting in pearls knowing that
they will go

There you are!
Spraying perfume
waving ciao darlings
from Italy's foot
making New York
feel like it's there

Double Loren

in 1978 her heart's desire was broadcast:
"many, many grandchildren
is all I want"

it simply did not connect
the fire bush of her hair
the half-laugh, the saggy red scarf
the diamond she pet on her throat and those bongo eyes
loaded with makeup for TV
many, many

oh, to be those many
heavy, happy devotees
dragging baskets
soiling with families
stinging with tomato acid
during the long stretch—
grating days of sauce season
flaming every fingernail
every half-moon cuticle
just itching and blazing
oh, to be many, many

to be twenty, three times
to never have anyone leave your selfishness
to give money to children in envelops at Christmas
watch your son frustrate
to be his gagging mother
to be missed, cherished, fussed with
to be sent to the living room
before the offer of help in the kitchen is played

to have twenty, three times
have it curtsey and kiss your wrinkles
oh, to be many, many cheek folds, eye lines
to let your skin show some goddam ego

to see twenty, three times
forget the column bombs, the headlines
to dodge all that silver screenery
to let yourself be literal
shake the masses without prissy English lessons
just seethe on them
seethe
and be that many women before thirty
that kind of woman that fools many

Maria Luisa Ierfino-Adornato

The Traces We Leave

We sometimes question where we belong
We know that the past escapes us, and
We believe that the future awaits us
We are not pure breed or 100% organically-grown, so
We live in perpetual exile; wait our turn in single file
We visit our Grandparent's ancestral home, and
We suffer from collective amnesia, but when triggered,
We go back and warmly remember 'nacatole' with 'anice'
We pour our 'anice' in strong coffee and say amen, then
We fondly envision our mother blessing and kneading the dough
We gather at the kitchen table in anticipation of her Sunday feast
We joyfully consume her homemade pasta with smoky 'ricotta salata'
We devour the traditional 'melenzane ripiene' in honour of San Nicodemo
We listen to Dad singing his latest aria, enjoying his wine and family
We are famished and our parents nourish and nurture

We are obsessed with travel and reverse migration
We leave traces of ourselves in sacred places
We leave secret recipes in the hearts of our loved ones
We leave our footprint and fingerprints
We are not android or devoid
We trust we will all go to a better place, so
We leave androgynous traces of violet flowers
We like to believe they heal and inspire, until we retire
And when those Viola Mammola flowers wither and die,
They simply return to the fertile earth stoically
Where Mother Nature will recycle and defy
So new ones will bloom eternally

I Am My Words

I wined and dined with each word
I ate words with a voracious appetite
I digested the words and I felt light
I was sustained with those satisfying words
I relished them like recurring birds
I would live for those words, however
I wanted those words to live forever
I plunged into the Mediterranean Sea to save the words
I safeguarded those words like the Dead Sea Scrolls
I survived to protect the words which were sacred souls
I swam for my life in that indifferent sea
I held on to all words then let them be
I floated and did not sink,
I fished for each vowel and consonant in the rink
I gathered strength from each syllable, I think
I left no trail or words of wisdom behind
I inhaled each word like oxygen, but never mind
I lifted my head above the water, as I gasped for air
I wiped away the tears and would not declare
I am my words, and now you, I dare.

Engagement Feast

Not a Bohemian-inspired rhapsody but more of a Bocelli-like classical affair
Lovebirds exhausted after painstakingly planning for the last year
Dancing, with Armand de Brignac Gold Brut champagne freely flowing
And Japanese drummers performing, sounding like a sacred haiku
Guests appreciating a Mortlach Scotch Whiskey here, or a fine Cohiba there

Grappling with existential chatter, sipping Nonnino Cru Picolit Grappa, and
Standing tall like the Leaning Tower of Pisa (stuttering Barolo or Bourgogne)
Next to opulent stations, with alcohol-filled watermelons and flying acrobats
Devouring wagyu beef (Brunello di Montalcino sauce, white alba truffle agnolotti),
And appetizers like Moscow Burrata, imported Iberico ham de Bellota;
Luxury knows no borders; no pizza or plain iron band (fédé) for this couple!
Fountain of Bellagio re-created with towering caviar, oysters, and shellfish
Honouring the Roman Goddess Abundantia whose cornucopia was infinite
Guests high on the wow trapeze; parents counting and laying low
Then, the beaming Groom-to-be, on one knee, introduced
The jewel of Italian-Canadian spirits to the Bride-to-be
An exotic vodka martini with an artesian water ice cube in it
Adorned in the center was a diamond engagement ring
A Coster Royal 201 brilliant solitaire diamond ring no less,
The most beautiful diamond cut in the world of course
The ooh's and ahhh's overshadowed the cirque du soleil entertainment
Until the ice-cube was cracked open, she said YES, then fireworks
Like the splinters from fallen stars sparkling in their ingénue eyes
All cheer and shout, Buona Fortuna! In two years, the Destination Wedding!

Josephine LoRe

Le mani della Mamma

Mamma's hands, rolling dough to make *cuddrareddri*
Christmas cookies filled with mandarins and figs
almonds, raisins, espresso
    Nanna's hands, rosary beads slipping
    one by one, her nighttime litany

Mamma's hands, dirtbrown as she tucks *piantine* into the soil
snips stragglers so vines grow strong
    Pipina's hands, flipping through the pages she gifts me
    fostering this wonder of words

Mamma's hands, never at rest
prugne to jam, red peppers to barbecue and peel
    Nanna's hands, knitting needles clicking
    a code of wisdom older than language

Mamma's hands, twisting wet laundry
before passing it through a handspun wringer
    My nanna's hands, using a *stegnatore*
    a four-foot rolling pin my father fashioned from a broomstick
    to create paper-thin sheets of *tagliatelle* and *lasagne*

Mamma's hands, bathing *i miei bimbi*
soaping their skin slippery soft
    Pipina's hands, quiet in the lap of her turquoise apartment
    listening as I read my first poems aloud

My daughter, telling her friends
    about my hands—
What collection of memories
    will these hands hold for her?

a gentle pull

Sicilia smiles back at me in black and white
my mother freshly *fidanzata*
flanked by my father's sisters
skirts flounced high

the smell of the earth baking at 43°
colossal shadows cast
at the Temples of Concordia
of Juno, of Zeus

Agrigento
founded 600 years before *Gesù*
by sailors from Rhodes and Crete
Daedalus and his son Icarus

the timeless intertwine
of history and myth
mystery

echoes, old names—
Girgenti
Agrigentum
Akragas

we sat in greengrey shade
under *l'oliva*
my sister and me
trunk gnarled by the slow blink
of 3000 years

Mediterraneo
the sea
in the middle
of the land

when you walk out of the water
il sole dries *il sale* onto skin
each kiss saltsweet
our nameless origin

one evening *in campania*
ma cuscina asked me
to go with her
to get *nu limuni*

I said *si'*
expecting a car ride
instead she led me
into darkening grove

hanging over us
yellow lanterns
firm ripeness of fruit

Sicilia
a twist and a gentle pull

Carmelo Militano

My Mother's House Beside the Chiesa di San Sebastiano

My mother's house beside the Chiesa di San Sebastiano,
Cosoleto, Reggio di Calabria

You climb the old stone steps to the second floor
Give the door a shove and enter
Hear the sudden hurry and scratch of mice
Note an empty grey swallow's nest in the corner
The only thing left carefully built
Peeled paint on the ceiling, sink stained with rust
From the balcony
You can still look towards the distant blue mountains
See the village of Santa Christiana
Spilled like salt on the mountainside
Under a thin whimsical cloud
Shaped like a long white scarf
Tossed over a shoulder one cold early winter morning in Rome.
Downstairs a bicycle frame, chain, dented rusty fender
Mud on the kitchen walls, smashed empty picture frame on the floor
The chaos of indifference is everywhere.

Forty years ago, I stepped into this same room
It was like entering a symbolic painting called *The Allegory of the Return*
Grandfather smiled his sly toothless grin
Grandmother's hand touched my cheek, proof I was not an apparition
Silver white light poured into the room
Through the half opened wooden door like a revelation
My mother, grandfather, grandmother there
Kissed me cheek to cheek
Under dried garlands of pepper and garlic,

Tomato sauce jars on the shelf
Above the rust-belted wine barrels
Sickle, axe, hoe, the handles worn smooth with use on the wall.

I stand here now as if it never happened
As if my mother never boarded a ship to Canada
And remained sad for the rest of her life
As if her father never rejected her teacher's plea
Her ability to make errorless Latin conjugations irrelevant to him
As if my grandmother never brought me coffee
Mixed with a whipped egg and sugar
Always laughed when I asked her to stop each morning.
Instead, she feared night
Heard the whispers of the departed in the wind and rain
Conjured up cigarettes for me
Left on the table every day.

Time is the other magician
Wears a light brown dress, food-stained white apron
Stands beside the gas stove stirring a pot
Always turns, sometimes smiles
Waves a wooden spoon
Now you see, now you don't
Uses the green mold
On the ancient stone wall
To measure the days.

Cristina Pepe

Vorrei essere una poetessa

Vorrei essere una poetessa
Così potrei esprimere tutto ciò che vorrei dire
con parole magiche
che si sciolgono dalla lingua

Vorrei usare parole come affascinante e meraviglioso
per descrivere le cose di cui scriverò

Che posso mettere a parole …

la luce gloriosa del sole estivo di metà pomeriggio,
che proietta ombre nascoste sui muri di pietra

I suoni allegri dei bambini
quando giocano a calcio
nelle viuzze strette

la vista mozzafiato
dalle scogliere sul mare
e la tenerezza della brezza marina
quando ti accarezza le spalle

la tavolozza ricca di colori brillanti
come il blu oltremare e terra di Siena bruciata
che diventano un dipinto quando incontrano la tela

l'emozione quando uno si trova
adavanti ad un capolavoro di Caravaggio,
con chiaroscuro e luci drammatiche
magnifico da ogni lato

Il profumo indimenticabile
del pane appena sfornato
che fa venire l'acquolina in bocca
e fa brontolare la pancia

Il gusto di un bicchiere di vino profumato e corposo
fatto con un'uva locale
e condiviso con i migliori amici
che valgono più dell'oro

la gioia dell'amore al primo sguardo
e anche la profondità della tristezza
di un cuore spezzato in mille pezzi
per un amore non ricambiato

Per tutti questi è difficile trovare le parole,
o scegliere gli aggettivi adeguati

Vorrei essere una poetessa ...
purtroppo non trovo le parole
e non so da dove e come cominciare.

Giovanna Riccio

Love Circles

1
Nineteen sixty-nine—my debut in a faceless
run-on room laced with greasy, burger'n fries bouquets
the Teachers' College cafeteria spills coffee
with South America thundering in its burgled core,
the pour rouses drowsy disinterest
perks up once-dozy mugs

September sun spanks awake the raw academic year,
lights anew an array of by-the-book naifs, rattled
strangers sieved by grades and guidance counsellors.

In this ruckus of unknowns, Anonymous moves—
an oxymoron, absently present
until attention rewards
a body, intention haloes a face.

A book does double duty as way in, or screen
on buses, in bank lineups, sitting solo at Fran's Restaurant
titles brand me a brainy, raven-haired open book
my left wing flying against a skewed world's headwinds
on this day, sipping java in the caf
Malcolm X Speaks spells out my shield
approach at your own risk

across from me, Anonymous meets
the assassinated Black hero's bespectacled kisser,
our eyes lock—for sure, he's pretty
pivoting
out of neutral territory.

2
I circle the forest of his gaze, navigate
a loop curving on speech, *Are you reading that book?* says he,
a hint of Southern drawl lazes in his rhetorical come-on
Anonymous defines as Christopher, draft-dodger,
former civil rights activist from Atlanta, Joe-jah

anticipation flurries my cool
when luck colludes with spares or lunch
coupled, we bite into the Vietnam war
bond over America inciting another Ginsberg headache
weigh the body bag Chris dodged by enlisting
in the peaceable kingdom of Canada, a three-monkeys-peddler
of phosphorus for Napalm fire bombs, black-marketeer
of Agent Orange—defoliant of commie jungles
and toxic cocktail for Ontario aquifers.

To revive beauty we stuff pockets, mouth,
cracks in sidewalks with poems, friendship
burns holes into elongated school days

our pas de deux merges, kisses linger
body impresses mind, fingers ignite cheeks
so insatiable blushes undercut bruised hearts
in a lust and love union magnetized, realized
in mosquito-crazed fields or slick showers, on travertine floors.

3
Blind to sitcom cliches lurking in setting up house
logistics like rent and grocery-money elude
me, the now-hassled teacher. He?
self-exiled from Labour's ranks
too much a genius to swing a lunch pail
yet, my artless vision casts him as Picasso and Bréton
a myth writ by a slant mystique, so naturally affected
I'm blind to Narcissus bound to mirror and window
poised on a badass pedestal chiselled

from his blarney and my rank naiveté.
Despite our declared egalitarian cosmos
nixing moon ribbed from sun
kitchen, broom and laundry room dictate
my pleasure and, his leisure—library, studio,
intellectual schmoozing with feminists at tony bars
all funded by my proletarian purse,
year after year he banks on an adoring, open hand
galleries no canvas (neither does he try)
when I decline to oversee his underpainted shades,
he ups the charm (no longer winning).

4
We bicker in fields
smithereen endearments on ceramic floors,
cuss in pubs, snarl at roses
draw blood from my shut wallet,
having sussed out his looming loss
Chris seduces a bungalow named Laura—
more than once, I surmise, from inky yearnings
blueing letters tucked into yellowing volumes.

Done, I charge the once-beloved to rent a U-Haul,
refeather my raggèd left wing, and counterclockwise
jet off to Greece.

5
Once
his orbit ringed a torrid obsession
cooled now
to hard-won smarts.
Today
no heat or ache lingers—still
at times I spot him
and uphold his vision
though he sprawls,
fallen, having plummeted
through dream catcher and safety net.

Sante A. Viselli

Cette nuit encore …

Cette nuit encore …!
Faudra-t-il transcrire dans une sensibilité autre,
La Langue pour retrouver l'Aube qui épurée s'enfuit de sa tombe?
Retracer le manuscrit qui succombe sous l'élan de mon stylet plaintif,
De ce Cœur soûlé des sourires de mes magnifiques ensorceleurs?
Cœur errant vers le Pacifique arrosé de flammes et de tendres griefs,
La Nouvelle-Zélande aux impénétrables nuages blancs ?
Les photos noyées dans les tiroirs négligés de ma solitude,
M'habillent les yeux d'inquiétude et de voyance,
Les vains souvenirs des blessures que ravive votre absence,
Le narcissisme de ma poussière réchauffée à votre fontaine de jouvence,
Se nourrissent de votre doux mais dur Amour,
Du désir charmant de vous rejoindre …, purs, légers,
Cette nuit, enragé par un soupçon de plaisir,
Dans les brumes apaisantes de vos loisirs …!

… Je vous offrirai des perles de pluie venues de pays …

En sourdine, languide, le Poème raconte mes fantasmes,
Pendant que les larmes d'un nuage vagabond
S'abandonnent, lentement, dans la paix de la prairie,
Content le chemin de croix de mes arcs-en-ciel,
Le fiel de mes accrocs, les aigus échos de vos naïves comédies.

Adorable, chère enfant aux yeux noirs, perçants et audacieux,
Insondables comme l'océan houleux qui nourrit tes songes,
Voix sonore, colorée d'Espérance et d'allégresse,
Encore une fois, chante avec moi …,
Cette nuit qui …, à voix basse, te bénit …,

Chante entre mes bras qui te bercent, comme jadis,
Quand tu poussais les premiers remerciements à la vie,
La paisible mélodie du jour qui s'éveille à ses bruits familiers
Et chuchote: "*Valentina si.*"

Pascal, toi qui parles, en silence au Cœur de ton *nonno*,
Cœur qui sait lire les litanies de ta jeune âme pensive,
Aimable chevalier de toutes les tables, des beaux contes d'autrefois,
Vole vers moi . . ., ravive mon style anhélant . . .,
Cette nuit encore . . .,
Sans peur ni gêne, sans chaînes ni lois,
Vers nos plaines coiffées de neige et d'aubes boréales!
Oiseau bleu, encre qui efface mes banales lisières,
Sujet et objet de mes élans, de mes prières
Vole léger et secret sur les dunes de ton sourire incertain,
Parfois brusqué, même un peu narquois!
Tu pares nos cieux altérés d'émotion et de chagrin,
De beaux poèmes arrachés aux dégoûts des ans,
De poussiéreuses évocations de ma trop douce enfance,
À l'ombre des cyprès dans ce Latium béni par Rome et par Circé,
Tu traces dans mon jardin poli par le parfum de tes pensées,
Des sillons ensemencés de phénix et de regrets.

Pascal qui dit sans trop parler, les lèvres légèrement crispées,
Qui harangue la haute marée du Pacifique moutonné!
Elle le berce dans les flots mourants sur le sable abreuvé d'or,
Le regard tourné vers l'effrayante nappe insensée,
Vaste linceul moiré moussant sur les écueils vernis de soleil et de sel,
Il s'assoupit sous l'amical nuage opalin des Maoris,
Rejoint dans ses rêves les yeux bleus, profonds et rassurants de papa,
Les cheveux parfumés, ondoyants de maman, son baiser apaisant,
Le sourire généreux, les traits harmonieux de Valentina.
Les lointaines neiges du Canada bercent son réveil
Des couleurs des plaines poudrées à frimas.

Fanciulli diletti, croce e gemme dei giorni miei,
tornerete un dì a ritrovar i vostri affetti,

gelosamente protetti in un quaderno di memorie e di poesie?
Le praterie del Canada e le loro misteriose litanie,
monotone e stanche come i nostri desideri,
le nostre ostiche melanconie?

Per sfuggire all'uggia del muto cinismo che mi acceca,
oso scrivere i lemmi del mio prometeico doglio,
rianimare sulle guglie minate del Cuore,
che impetra perdono,
la violenza, le pene del mio rabbioso abbandono.

Libero, ribelle Pirata che non sa più sfidare l'orizzonte,
oso parlare, gridare, pregare, bestemmiare con orgoglio,
in quella Lingua che asciuga le lacrime avvelenate da quel remoto Scoglio,
dove l'impetuoso, il dubbio, il misterioso e incostante Pacifico
vi rapì, ubbidienti a un volo di superbi albatri,
bianchi come la vostra anima innocente,
grigi come le nubi sul nostro Mare, sulla mia acida ragione,
quando lasciai alle mie spalle la mia mente e la mia gente,
sui ponti di un destino tutto da inventare,
un paese in fiamme, cieli muti, un vecchio, povero casolare.

Questa notte, di nuovo . . ., nella dubbia oscurità dei pensieri miei,
per non sbiadire i fogli sugli scogli senza rime dei miei vaniloqui,
arrendo ai vostri sorrisi cristallini i miei confusi specchi,
dopo avere ascoltato, una volta ancora . . .,
nella quiete della notte che miete certezze e martiri,
le vostre liete voci dipinte dai luminosi colori,
dai tenui germogli dei vostri ingenui sospiri.

Cette nuit encore . . ., avant la fin . . .,
Avant de confesser mes péchés,
Avant que le Soleil ne dise encore une fois adieu à Aurore effrayée,
Avant de narguer le silence d'un autre matin,
La véritable générosité épuise l'égoïsme de mon Amour,
Renoncement difficile à atteindre pour ce "Je" inquiet et sourd:
Il ne hurle que les échos des cafards que bannit la Raison,

Fragile lueur dans les dédales de mon esprit
Soûlé de passé et de l'haleine d'une autre saison.

L'envolée de la Plume qui jaillit des sarcophages,
Arrange des hiéroglyphes sur des pages encore vierges.
Au seuil des mystères, de la nuit des pièges,
Le tapis du silence des premières lueurs de la rage,
Maquille de teintes impressionnistes l'univers en devenir,
Annonce les sueurs d'une autre journée, les métissages,
Les néantises, les caresses, les sépulcres blanchis de délires.

La fumée de cette poussière que le stylet fane de mélodies,
Édulcorées d'obsessions, de belles images et de nostalgie,
Répand, dans la nuit des présages, en gammes mineures,
Une épaisse brume bien sapée de tous les lisérés du Cœur.
Dans le marasme de mes gris souhaits,
La ficelle de l'âme ravie de se soûler de vos folles paroles,
Dresse de calme le jardin qui se complaît dans la torpeur de la terre,
Dorlotée par les rayons de la lune promise en mariage à une nue moins égarée,
Elle empêche l'oubli de vos visages,
Suspend la haine qui noie ces pages.

Dans la faible clairvoyance de ma myopie,
Dans l'opacité de mon labyrinthe,
Je perce le bouclier tyrannique des sombres mythes d'antan,
Les rêves que ma jeune âme subvertit, il y a bien longtemps.
Fripier malade de rancœur, je traduis,
En regardant l'horizon et les signes de ses ravages,
Les mirages, les oxymores de mon enfer,
Je revis le monde à l'envers,
Mais . . ., cette nuit . . .,
Je revois le rire de mes belles, fidèles, insensibles étoiles,
Du printemps qui timidement baille et ensevelit un long hiver
Qui, émondé de sa triste mante, se meurt,
Là où les neiges pleurent le Pacifique en fleur.

Le ris cristallin de deux bijoux si beaux, si magiques,
Jeunes philosophes plus fins que toute une bibliothèque,
Ensevelit un lugubre cri de vengeance sur ma gueule de métèque,
Une dernière, tendre grimace fausse les obsèques du Cœur qui guette
Dans la pénombre de la nuit qui, babillarde, s'apaise . . ., âpre . . ., secrète.

À l'heure où les vagues parent leur vertige matinal d'espérances muettes,
Et cisèlent les côtes dentelées de la Nouvelle-Zélande,
Le Soleil s'anime, tout embrasé de réprimandes,
Des attentes d'une autre journée à réinventer, à retraduire, à réécrire:
La Poésie s'habille d'une mante de douceur plaintive . . ., délicate . . .,
    enivrante,
S'embellit de magie et de guirlandes,
Pendant qu'au-delà de ma fenêtre,
Une folâtre poudrerie,
S'obstine à maquiller, encore cette nuit, les crêtes inquiètes
Des chétives épinettes des prairies.

Enfin . . ., cette nuit en déclin . . .,
Avant les bâillements d'un autre matin . . .,
Apprivoisé, le Poème s'envole vers vous,
Raconte vos yeux enivrés d'avenir,
De manèges enfantins, de sortilèges :
Débarrassé de ses haillons, de son orgueil,
Le Poème perçoit un souffle mystérieux, doux et amer,
La Voix aimable, touchante d'outre-mer.
Elle le soulage de sa haine,
Du lourd maquillage de ses vers,
De sa plume habillée d'obscures peines.

Choyé par les récits du vent,
Le Grand Esprit embrasse le Manitoba,
Ses cent mille lacs, ses grêles forêts,
Annonce sur le seuil du jour,
Les affres de l'éphémère Aurore
Qui, tout en pressant le pas,
Bénit les soupirs d'une ultime étoile,

Le sourire languissant de Vénus
Qui se couche, charmante et légère, après une nuit de rébus.
Insignifiante et splendide, dans le ciel diaphane,
Sa beauté pâlit devant le Soleil qui l'agresse,
Impuissant, il soupire et la blâme de son oubli:
Doucement, elle décline, se meurt …,
Revit,
Encore plus belle, resplendissante,
Dans la plénitude poétique d'une autre nuit …,
Intouchable, dans sa céleste solitude …,
À l'infini.

Le bonheur suinte dans l'autre hémisphère,
Sous le ciel moutonné de nuages blancs,
Chéris des poètes et des amants.
Là-bas, dans la douce terre des Maoris,
Un autre demain cisèle les Alpes du Sud d'éclats arlequins,
Pendant que le Pacifique pare de féérique
Les rêveries de deux jeunes magiciens.

Sur une feuille bigarrée que l'arbre de l'Amour n'ose laisser choir,
Je rédige un Cantique de reconnaissance, de constance, de sage allégresse :
Il est quête, supplique, prière, remerciement et promesse,
Apostrophe touchante qui me relie en sourdine au présent éphémère,
À vous, mes anges, absents de nos cieux,
De cette épave pensante bientôt dans le sapin,
À vous, mes trésors au Cœur de diamant,
Cœur dure et délicat, cristallin, vert et rayonnant
Comme votre tendre printemps.

Cette Lettre, simple et légère, agonisante …, mais heureuse …,
Vous cherche …, outre mes lisières …, outre mon armure …, mes lumières,
Encore une fois …, cette nuit …,
Au-delà des plaintes de la plaine sans falaises, sans murs,
Du Manitoba assoupi dans sa psalmodie …, monotone …, obscure,
Vers Vous, à l'autre bout de la terre, là-bas!
Encore une fois … cette nuit …,

Vers Vous, mes doux phénix,
Phares de la perdrix qui s'échappe, à grand-peine,
De la haine du fier chasseur,
Vous, le prix Nobel de la Raison et du Cœur,
Cœur simple . . ., souvent amer,
Mais toujours fidèle, sincère,
Le Cœur, véritable citoyen de l'univers,
Otage bienheureux de votre Amour,
Vengeur de la tyrannie du Sort,
Des outrages sacrilèges de l'oubli et de la Mort.

PROSE

Gianluca Agostinelli

Suburban Snowfall

"I just can't believe how much we got," he says, as he brushes a fresh dusting off his *Frontenacs* toque.

We haven't spoken enough for me to know if he's being sarcastic, so I play along.

"I know. Definitely didn't expect it. Came outta nowhere, eh?"

We continue pretending we weren't aware of the flurry of weather reports and advisories.

"You got that right, bud," he replies.

I could sense the mandatory, historical reference inching closer.

"You know," he pauses to catch his breath, "this is almost as much as we had back in '77."

He lowers his seasoned shovel into the thick, white blanket, hoping to reclaim his footpath. The worn, wooden handle makes me wonder if it, too, is a relic of the famed blizzard I grew up learning about.

"I used to love the cold as a kid. I was outside all the time. Making forts. Tobogganing. Getting in snowball fights. But I can't stand it now," he adds, gesturing to his right knee.

My nod of lukewarm sympathy confirms that even years of social distancing haven't made me miss unnecessary small talk.

"Yeah, I hear ya. I miss summer for sure," I respond, obligingly.

I don't tell him that my Mediterranean blood yearns for heat, and that I often question why my parents chose to settle here.

"You know what the only thing I like about snow is?" he asks.

I refuse to give in to the inevitable dad joke.

"When it's all gone!"

How many storms have had to weather that punchline?

His chuckle reminds me of my late grandfather. The thought of him trying to pronounce "*Thinsulate*" with his uncompromising accent brings me some warmth.

"I knew you'd like that one," he assures.

I must've been smiling.

"You got me. Never heard that one before."

A skein of fleeing geese mocks me from the pastel grey sky above. Even they know I'm not meant to stay in this land of grocery bagged feet and perpetual runny noses.

For my friends, winter marks the long-awaited start of pond hockey, ice fishing, and snowboarding. For me, it's the numbing return of foggy glasses, frozen fingertips, and opaque windshields.

"Everyone knows this stuff always falls harder on side roads and crescents," he explains.

A long, muffled honk sounds from a nearby snowbank.

"Well, most people," he adds, reapplying his stocking stuffer lip balm.

A snow day used to be a miracle; a prayerful chance to pull off death-defying stunts with my brother on our black *GT Snow Racer*. If we weren't laying on our backs with the wind knocked out of us, we weren't having enough fun.

The phrase, "*Non dirlo alla mamma*," punctuated each journey—and covered up every injury. I'd give anything to hear him say those daring words once more.

Now, childhood nostalgia gives way to the irony of adults celebrating a day off work by working for hours to clean our driveways just so that we can get back to work tomorrow.

A red snowmobile interrupts the crisp silence. The driver waves cheerfully to us as he glides down our street. He probably couldn't wait to get up this morning to clear this shit, I think.

"Bet you wouldn't have to worry about all this back home, eh?" he asks.

I imagine my cousins on pearly beaches, a *granita al limone* the only snow they'll ever have to deal with.

"I wouldn't have to worry about you either ... but where's the fun in that?"

He snickers and shakes his head. I wonder if the welcome banter makes him wish he had a son of his own.

"You want some hot chocolate, bud?" he asks, wiping sweat from his silver brow.

He's too proud to tell me that his back is spasming again.

I contemplate asking him for a *corretto*, but I don't have the energy for a *Duolingo* lesson.

"Would love some. Thanks."

"You got it, boss. Don't work too hard without me," he says as he slowly begins his return expedition.

I listen to the soft crunch of his gingerly footsteps. I fear the day that my father reaches his age—the day when he calls me to ask for help, rather than to offer it.

Snow doesn't care how old you are, where you come from, or how many degrees you have; its humbling beauty demands respect and a hard-earned soreness from all those stuck in suburbia.

I picture what my last moments might look like, lamenting the countless hours spent trying to appease eager dogwalkers and bylaw officers.

Each disingenuous attempt at lifting with my legs makes time more finite and painful.

"You missed a spot," he says, handing me a steaming *Timmies* mug.

He had time to comb his moustache.

"Appreciate it," I reply, before taking a courtesy sip that scalds my tongue.

It's store-bought, but what isn't here?

"Just like my mom's," I lie.

The sputter of a snowblower engine grabs our attention.

"Well, would you look at that? The new guy's helping out what's-her-face on the corner," he remarks.

"What's his story?" I ask, clutching my cup with my calloused hands.

"Retired. Divorced. Moved out here from the city to get some privacy," he answers confidently.

"Good thing he doesn't have nosey neighbours then."

We mask our judgmental smirks with a forced, friendly wave. We claim to have too much dignity to buy such a fancy toy ourselves, but secretly hope that those suckers who own one might take pity on us.

I look at all the fellow shovelers on our block, united in our latitude's struggle to unbury financed sedans and SUVs. My father's annual justification, "*Non c'è bisogno di uno spazzaneve*," seems rightfully out of place.

"Thanks for," he clears his throat, "thanks for helping me out today, chief," he manages.

The see-you-next-snowstorm goodbye befalls us.

"Where else do I have to be? Nothing like braving the wind chill," I wink as I hand him my empty mug.

"Well, it's nice knowing there's help next door," he admits, careful not to make eye contact.

His muted affection is endearing.

"I wouldn't mind you coming back when the snowplow decides to show up. Those poor guys. We curse 'em when they don't plow, and again when they do," he adds.

"Any time, man. You know where to find me. Take care of yourself," I say, with unexpected sincerity.

"Will do. You, too!"

The snow seems even denser on my side of the property line. Every stab, scoop, and toss bring me closer to an asphalt treasure that I wish were storied, Tuscan cobblestone.

I fantasize about one day building a heated laneway. Maybe it would melt my regret, if not the cluster of snowflakes wedging itself beneath my ankle sock.

The paralysis is all too familiar.

As I finally reach the toppled windrow, I turn and admire my due progress. I laugh at myself for wanting to take a picture of the *Instagram*-worthy product of my frostbitten perseverance.

"I can't believe how much we got," another neighbour comments.

There might be something annoyingly quaint about having the same, smalltown conversation all day.

"Yeah, came outta nowhere," I respond, hoping she'll shovel our shared sidewalk for once.

"Well, don't stay out here too long. Forecast says we're supposed to be getting more tonight anyways," she warns, walking back to her brown, brick bungalow.

"Maybe we'll get another snow day tomorrow," I jest.

"Say a prayer!" she teases.

How many more low-pressure systems will this year wield?

I stand my shovel in the garage, knowing that leaving it on the porch would only welcome more snow. I watch a puddle form around its base.

My grade two teacher once asked the class what type of animal we would like to live as. Most students wanted to be lions, eagles, cheetahs, or sharks.

I chose to be a Marsicano brown bear just so that I could hibernate. Escape.

The dreary, afternoon darkness eclipses any reason to remain.

Maybe when I awake from my next slumber, I'll roam the Appennini alone, without a neighbour—or driveway—in sight.

Michelle Alfano

The Hierarchy of Grief

Adelina … long pause … *è la mamma* … *chiamami subito.* The message from my mother was uncharacteristically brief. And unsettling.

Adelina? My mother never called me that. Always Lina. Unless I was in trouble. Was I in trouble? And why so sombre? Usually, the message was playful and a bit aggressive along the lines of: *Why are you never home? I never hear from you [mournful sigh]. When are you coming to visit? I never see you* … And she said to call her right away.

She picked up quickly when I rang back.

What is it, Ma?

Ahh … she hesitated with unusual delicacy … *è Tommaso* … *è morto.*

My heart almost stopped. That was my brother's name.

Tommy died?!

Sì, Bettina's husband. Tommaso. Not your brother. Tah-mee.

I liked the way she said his name, that she was not entirely comfortable saying it in English. Sometimes I would playfully call him that too.

Wait, wait, wait … *what's going on?* I asked her. She explained what she had heard through the family. I promptly burst into tears. No … more like sobbing unashamedly. And loudly.

Ma cara, she patiently reprimanded me, *you can't be more upset than the widow, can you?*

In other words, control yourself Adelina. And then, in Italian, she explained the hierarchy of grief to me. You can't be more upset than the person closest to the deceased.

***

The first time I noticed Tommy, really noticed him, was at my *zia* Regina's wedding and he, *again*, made me cry. Regina was my mother's youngest sister and the baby of the family, barely out of her teens when she became engaged to be married to a boy she had grown up with in our village in Italy. She asked that I be part of the wedding party as the eldest of the grandchildren in our large extended family and my mother's first born. I knew Tommy as our families were close—living in the same neighborhood—but we never spoke really because ... you know ... *ugh, boys* ... which is the mindset of most six-year-old girls I suspect. At least, that was my mindset at the time.

I was the flower girl. I remember being ecstatically happy as my mother pulled the sky-blue dress with its beaded bodice and a layered chiffon skirt over my head. The scratchiness of the fabric, the tightness of the bodice, was made up for by my matching blue satin slippers and a little satin pouch for a "purse" in which I kept exactly nothing. Perhaps a toy or a trinket to make me feel more grownup.

I asked for pink lipstick to match the bride's which I was not permitted to have but eventually Regina relented and dabbed some pink lipstick on my cheeks giving me a rosy glow. My aunt Regina slipped me a tube of flavoured lip balm to pacify me. My mother took over an hour carefully curling my ramrod straight hair into cascading curls down to my shoulders with a curling iron. It hissed and steamed as I sat admiring my dress and new shoes. She gently placed a wreath of baby's breath on top of the curls, securing the wreath with hard, black bobby pins. I felt the jab into my small skull as she applied one bobby pin after another.

Lina, she hissed in my ear, *stai zitta*, as I moaned a little with each jab of the bobby pins.

The wreath kept sliding sideways on my head giving me a bit of a comical look in the wedding photos, like a slightly drunken, tiny princess.

Tommy was chosen as the ring boy because Regina's groom was best friends with his father. He was dressed in a tiny black suit, shiny black leather shoes and bow tie perfectly fitted for a small boy who was just a year older than me. He took one look at me at the reception and told me I looked just like a poodle with that curly hair. My then best friend Bettina, who was standing right beside me the whole time, giggled delightedly as she sucked the cream out of a cannoli from the dessert table, set up after the main meal. I threw my tiny bouquet of pink carnations and baby's breath at him and ran to my mother's table crying.

She asked me what was wrong. Exhausted and overwrought from the day's activities, I told her *I never wanted to get married again!* Least of all to that Tommy, the ring boy.

Tommaso was a common first name in our family and in our small tightknit community. My mother's family—the Pentangelis—and Bettina's mother's family—the Licatos—grew up together in a small village in the *Mezzogiorno*, the name for the southern part of Italy. But my people really don't use that phrase—only fancy intellectuals would, usually from Northern Italy. The village was grim, and life was difficult ... it wasn't Taormina, that beautiful jewel on the east coast of Sicily. It wasn't chaotically vibrant like Florence or Rome. It didn't have the lush beauty of Tuscany. The village was in economic difficulty which pushed hundreds of thousands of immigrants out of the country, and to America or Canada. My grandmother once said that those who wished to be successful either left the country or succumbed to the criminal element to survive and thrive.

Both of our families moved to Canada in the early 1950s into the north end of an industrial city long past its prime. The growing families from our village in Italy had banded together in a cluster of neighborhoods in the downtown core. Bettina's father and my father were best friends and *cumpari*. In southern Italian culture, which was a word used for the godparents of your child, but it also meant a friend, a buddy. It was a term of affection as in *Cumpa ... would you like another glass of wine?* Somehow this was crudely corrupted by *American* Italians into the insult *goombah,* which came to mean something else: an oaf, a clown, a loser. But *cumpa* was meant lovingly. You only used the word with close family or friends.

For a time, Bettina's family lived on the second floor of our house, and we lived on the first. Our fathers, best friends, had immigrated together from Italy and shared rooms in a boarding house when they first arrived in 1956. When Bettina's family was more financially secure, the Licatos moved two or three blocks away into their own house. Eventually the Italian families in our neighborhood moved farther east, closer to the suburbs and farmland or south (to what was euphemistically called "the mountain", a hill really, in the south end of the city which was more prosperous) away from the downtown core. Or, if you had enough money, you moved to a suburb just outside of our city with its postwar houses—McMansions lacking in the flavour and vitality of the old neighborhoods where kids played on the streets until it got dark, and people sat on their porch at night surveying their neighbours' comings and goings.

Bettina and I had our first Communions together at the age of eight—the beginning of your "adult" relationship with God as a Roman Catholic. You were now allowed to have the Eucharist, the wafer that signified the body of Christ during Mass. Our mothers picked out our virginal white dresses which came to just above our knees, sheer veils, white lace gloves and fancy hard shoes at a little boutique that specialized in girls' and women's dresses for special religious occasions—First Communion (at age eight), Confirmations (at thirteen years old), and engagement parties for young brides. Our dresses matched; our shoes matched. We had silk pouches that held a tiny tube of pink lip gloss in mine, nothing in Bettina's. We chose the same rosaries. We held them in our silk pouches for safe keeping until the special photography session in a studio commemorating our communion.

It was customary then to have your portrait taken to celebrate your First Communion. At the studio, the photographer—a wizened, elderly man from the old country with three or four strands of reddish hair rakishly draped over his bald head who knew both of our parents—was entranced by Bettina. She was admittedly a beautiful child with golden skin and perfect teeth.

He was drawn to her and took her photograph first. He delicately puffed on a cigarette which hung from his lips as he urged her into position and adjusted the camera. She stood on a slightly raised dais and a bright light was shone on her face which gave her a slightly beatific look, like the golden halos in portraits of the saints. He urged her to look upward—to fixate on a faded picture of a painting of Jesus, swathed in a blue robe that matched his eyes. He had tactfully placed it at an angle, high on the wall, to catch our eyes during the session. He placed the rosary in her hand and urged Bettina to clasp her hands together and pretend that she was praying.

I was entranced by the rosaries—they consisted of simply made, clear diamond-shaped glass beads strung on inexpensive links of metal, not silver, as I once thought. But the crucifix, with the realistic image of Jesus on the cross, felt solid and significant in my hands. And special. Part of the rosary held a tiny medallion strung along the links of the rosary with the image of the Virgin Mary in silhouette. In moments of stress during the Communion, I pressed my fingers hard on the crucifix to reassure myself. Even though today I can see it was cheaply made, a mass-produced trinket sold in the millions, I thought it beautiful then and now and still have mine today.

Think of our Lord Jesus my dear girls, the photographer cooed to us in Italian dialect. *Today you will become his brides.*

Both of us? I wondered but I was at least smart enough not to utter that thought aloud. All of the twenty Catholic girls in my third-grade class who were receiving Communion that day? Our mothers, mine and Bettina's, nodded approvingly from the sidelines. Did her mother wipe a tear away as she gazed at Bettina?

We may have been thinking of Jesus but clearly the photographer was not. He was fixated on Bettina, who did look, admittedly, like some sort of small supernatural being, bathed in the bright light of the studio. Grey eyes clear and brilliant. Hair perfectly combed in honey curls covered by her short white veil. He touched her chin, raised it delicately, and openly admired her.

È perfetta ... he said, approvingly, as he gazed at her, snapping picture after picture. Me, he patted on the head like an obedient dog he had passed on the street and sent me on my way after one or two photos as he reluctantly took his eyes from Bettina.

***

My mother told me that Tommy had been sick for some time. I had heard some vague rumours that he had had cancer five or six years ago. But I thought it had been treated and that he was recovering. I sent him a text at that time, and he never let on that he was in pain or suffering. I saw him a few Christmases ago at a family reunion organized by a mutual cousin—still as cheerful and upbeat as he always was as well as good-looking (I had long forgiven him that poodle remark and by that time he was married to Bettina). When he got his medical degree he moved to an affluent town north of Toronto, taking my one-time best friend, now his wife, Bettina with him. By that time—they had married and bought a house—we were barely speaking … I noticed that Bettina would not look my way and was busy fussing over her three daughters who sat obediently at their table—like three perfectly formed Russian dolls, each one smaller and more perfect than the last. Beautiful replicas of their mother.

***

Adelina and Bettina, formerly known as "A plus B", a nickname that Tommy gave us in high school, were no more—more like A minus B now. I had not seen her for years. We didn't live in the same city anymore. She was in the suburbs with a growing family. I was in a large city living a very different kind of life: immersed in work and childless. I felt as if a small shadow beside her domestic accomplishments at times if I judged myself by my mother's standards of domesticity.

But as teenagers, we were inseparable. We went to a Catholic high school together—the girls' school was across the street from the boys' school on a main street of the city. We often saw Tommy smoking on the lawn of the boys' school and he waved casually at us, school tie rakishly loosened, neat white shirt cuffs pulled over his wrists, cigarette in his right hand. I waved back enthusiastically, Bettina ignored him, as she usually did. That seemed to work like a charm on him. He knew her through my family and was trying very hard to get to know her better.

Throughout our young lives (who am I kidding it still happens) Bettina attracted the most attention from boys: honey blonde hair, tall, grey eyes and a bit of an attitude … I was her shorter sidekick. Cute, maybe, but … not particularly alluring to teenage boys. Merely tolerated because they wanted to get close to B. I was often sidelined as they tried to get her attention. I had braces then and bad, teenage skin which no amount of charm and quirky humour could offset. She was the one who received longing looks and to which she responded with icy indifference. Total cat nip for teenage boys.

She never really paid attention to Tommy then which was puzzling to me. He was handsome. Very. Some of the boys at the boys' school were cute in a scruffy, puppyish way back then, their long not so clean hair draping rakishly over one eye, often with dirty nails and terrible manners particularly with girls. Tommy was sharp featured in an arresting way with thick black hair and black eyes fringed with thick lashes—a little like a dashing bandit from the old country. With a note of mischief in his eyes. He reminded me of Giuliano, a famous Sicilian bandit who was venerated by our parents' generation and who was mysteriously killed by his enemies in the 1950s while he slept. A sort of secular saint in our household.

But I remember exactly the event that brought Tommy and Bettina together …

At the end of the school year, the boys' and the girls' school had a dance in the girls' gym. Supervised by the teaching staff, which included a healthy allotment of young nuns, it was a bit of a dreary affair in retrospect. Not the stuff that teenage dreams were made of. The nuns were a curiosity to me—as their vocation then required them to dress in a traditional conservative manner although they had recently been allowed to wear dresses that reached only to their calves and not floor length (as I recall the nuns in my grade school did). I briefly contemplated it in the second grade. All Catholic girls have this fantasy where the life of a nun appears appealing and then on further reflection, I determined it wasn't for me.

I often tried to imagine their day-to-day existence. To live one's life wearing one piece of austere black clothing with that little black head dress, no makeup, sensible shoes, no contact with boys or men … was that a life? But really was it that much different as a student in the girls' school where the Principal walked around with a ruler and measured the length between the bottom of your skirt and your knees. If the length was offensively too long between the two, she pulled out a pair of sewing scissors and snipped the stitches of your hem to let the skirt down to a more suitable length.

With the coloured lights softly dimmed in the gym you didn't notice so much the tacky crepe paper ribbons that curled along the beige walls of the gym like a girls' errant curls, or the awkward hand painted signs that celebrated the end of the school year. The music was contemporary but not too wild, no hard rock or metal, something light and popular. The most entertaining part of the night was the teachers' attempts to get boys and girls not to dance so close to each other. That usually involved poking the boy in the back during slow dances to get him to move away from his female dance partner. Was there a ruler involved? (There's that ruler again!) Or is that just something that I concocted in my errant memory—the nuns prodding the poor boys' back with a ruler to make them move?

I was dying to dance but no one asked me. My feet kept up a regular tapping beat on the floor of the gym in tune to the tinny music coming out of the speakers. But my feet and my person were noticed by no one. I was teetering around on black platform sandals to give myself a little more height next to Bettina and had styled my hair into fragile curls that were unravelling in the humidity of the gym filled with sweating boys and girls gyrating furiously. Plenty of boys asked Bettina to dance but she just curled her lip at them, and they slunk away with their metaphorical tails between their legs. I leaned against the wall of the gym and tried to look alluring.

Let's go outside . . . this is so boring! Bettina ordered and pushed past the writhing couples.

The girls' school had a little courtyard that was sheltered from the street where people went to smoke during dances. On regular school days, when the weather was good, the girls sat on the grass in the courtyard, rolled down their knee socks, raised their school kilts to an acceptable level on their thighs, unbuttoned two or three buttons on their white blouses and tried to tan—back then it was still cool and very desirable to be toasted a light café au lait brown. I made the other girls laugh by asking demurely, *Is it blonde yet?* as I pointed to my dull brown hair.

This was a running joke amongst my schoolmates as I told anyone who would listen that my goal was to lighten my dark brown hair so that it was the same honey brown colour as Bettina's. To that end I washed my hair in lemon juice which, it was rumoured, would lighten it, to no effect, except a pleasant citrusy scent followed me wherever I went.

The courtyard was crowded with the usual crew of schoolboys smoking their hearts out. They were laughing, pushing each other, heckling the few girls who had dared to enter their space. There weren't too many out there which made me nervous. I was still a virgin, as was Bettina, and uneasy around boys although I desperately wanted a boyfriend. But they frightened me a bit as, really, did the idea of sex of any kind. They seemed a bit feral, untamed and . . . untrustworthy. And not to mention weird. I didn't understand boys even though I wanted their approval or love or lust or maybe just their attention. I'd take anything at that point. Tommy was there too with a group of friends, winking mischievously at Bettina as we entered the courtyard.

Bettina was unconcerned, leaning against the brick wall of the school, as far as possible from the hordes of boys. She had a pained expression, like she had a headache. They began catcalling us. She always seemed to attract attention—both good and bad wherever we went. I think because she was so cold, so impassive, and so pretty, it seemed to invite approaches from undesirable boys. She just rolled her eyes and turned her back to them, instructing me with a look that I should do the same. I uneasily complied as in everything that B asked me to do.

A clownish blond-haired boy a year or two older than us—Luca—sidled over to where we were standing against a wall. His Italian last name, when translated to English meant *bell*—as in a bell that had been rung one too many times by pot and booze. How appropriate. He had a reputation as a stoner and a lout. He appraised Bettina, looking her up and down with a mixture of desire and derision. Ever the coward in the face of physical danger, I shrank behind my best friend. He looked back towards the crowd of boys he was with, pointed at Bettina and exclaimed loudly with a snort: *This one ...* he paused dramatically *... is the biggest whore in the girls' school!* The boys broke into a snickering laughter. Shocked, I didn't dare look at them.

Bettina was rigid with shock and anger. I saw Tommy come flying out of a corner of the courtyard and sucker punch Luca right in the mouth. Although taller and heavier than Tommy, Luca crumpled like a doll made of paper and remained there, afraid to get up.

Say that again to her face ... No, to my *face*, Tommy commanded, as he towered over Luca with clenched fists. I had never seen him like this.

Luca wouldn't meet his eye and remained on the ground, nursing a bloodied jaw that was already starting to swell. One look at Tommy and Luca's friends knew he meant business, so they kept their distance.

After that ... Tommy and Bettina were inseparable.

They dated for several years after that. He loved her and she had made a coolly calculated guess that Tommy was the best on offer in our 'hood. She was right, he was the best. He was smart, educated, devoted to family (both hers and his) and he clearly adored her. When Tommy was accepted to medical school at McMaster University they decided to marry. She had decided not to go to college or university. She wanted children and she wanted to have them young so that she and Tommy could retire early and, perhaps, move to Florida or find a cottage in the country where they could spend most of their days.

I was the asked to be the Maid of Honour. I felt conflicted about it, uneasy, and not quite sure why. Isn't this what we had all hoped for?

***

But I was an unwilling captive to Bettina's requirements to have the perfect wedding with every detail precisely right. I was forgetful about my duties as Maid of Honour. I was unenthusiastic about the type of dress the bridesmaids should wear. Short or floor length? Accompanied by elegant long-sleeved gloves or no gloves? Hair up or down? Should we hire a salon to do our hair? Heels or flats? Who cared …

I was unwillingly dragged to view options for her wedding dress. I demonstrated no enthusiasm if the colour of the flowers matched the bridesmaids' dresses or the bomboniere. I had no suggestions about who should be seated besides whom (or who shouldn't) at the reception. I didn't care about the first song for the bride and groom or the song for the dance with the bride's father. Never having contemplated that I would marry—these considerations seemed foolish and trite.

But not to Bettina. My indifference enraged her, and she finally called me on it.

You really have <u>no</u> interest in any of this do you? Bettina asked after a particularly trying day where she was barking out orders and I was meekly submitting to her demands.

Um, not really … I said meekly, anticipating a firestorm of abuse but too weary to lie. How was it that I was exhausted when I wasn't even the bride?

I was somewhat nervously looking up addresses for the invites that her mother had handed to me. Beside numerous names in the address book were dollar figures. These, I learned, were past amounts donated to the weddings of the children of friends—presumably as a guide to what Bettina might expect to receive at *her* wedding. I was distracted by the numbers, some of which were quite substantial.

Bettina said more loudly trying to catch my eye, *But it's important to me.*

She placed one well-manicured hand to her chest with passion—she had enlisted another bridesmaid to try different nail polish colours on each of her fingers. Each nail had a different shade of ivory or cream or pearl or alabaster or argent or whatever name was ascribed to the subtly different shades of not quite white to match her wedding dress.

Yes, I know, I said, eyes downcast and focusing on the address book I held in my hand.

Why did you choose me as Maid of Honour? You know I'm not good at these things. I hated the sound of my own voice, whiny and childlike.

Because, she seethed, *you are supposed to be my best friend!*

Bettina had addressed each envelope to the recipients by hand. Her script was, as in everything else she did, beautiful. The ink was lavender, the envelope a very subtle shade of light blue. I was tasked only with the lowly role of verifying addresses before she wrote them down. Now I stared at the envelopes not meeting her eye.

What is wrong with you? she demanded.

When she received no response, she stormed out of the room. I continued collecting addresses and affixing stamps to the envelopes.

I really don't know, I said to no one in particular in a quiet voice.

After the wedding—which at every step I found tortuous—things were never the same. I happily moved out of the city to find work. Bettina and Tommy had their three children. I vowed to have none. She lived in the suburbs; I lived in the downtown core which was grittier and meaner and to which she refused to venture. Henceforth, she avoided me, and it was relief when she did so. We stopped interacting except at family events to which we were both invited but her demeanour was icy and noncommunicative. I kept abreast of her family through my mother's gossipy exchanges over the phone. I told myself stubbornly that we did not want the same things. We did not value the same things.

***

Now I was entering the room in the funeral home where Tommy was placed. Clusters of elderly *zii* sat on various couches and chairs near the casket in the funeral parlour. They cast a baleful eye my way. I imagined their gossip about my marriage-less and child-less state as I passed them although no one spoke to me. Mercifully, the casket was closed. My mother told me Tommy had lost a great deal of weight. Bettina had wanted the coffin closed. Instead, she had posted all these beautiful photos of him—from childhood to adulthood. He was amazingly handsome at any age, and I was relieved not to have to witness the ravages of the disease he had suffered from.

I approached Bettina. She was dressed in black and was rail thin, thinner than I had ever seen her. Her hair had darkened—the shades of our hair colour was now almost identical—mine lightened to look more youthful, hers darkened with age. She was surrounded by her two younger sisters and their husbands as well as their now almost adult children. When her family saw me, they soon scattered to opposite sides of the room. What instinct told them to move away? I had not seen them in years ... they likely did not know what had passed between us except that we rarely saw each other. Or did they?

She watched me approach. Her brows narrowed as she surveyed me and with a curt nod gestured that we should move into a quiet corner of the parlour. She folded her arms on her chest and surveyed me.

You know ... you have always acted as if he was too good for me, she finally said.

He was ... I was thinking. But I had no business thinking that.

Is it because he chose me?

If only she knew how far from the truth that was.

But why did I resent their coupling? What *was* Bettina's crime? That she wasn't as smart as he was? Neither was I but was it that I thought I was more his equal than she was? And why had he fallen in love with her and not me? No, it wasn't that. When I didn't answer she turned from me and left the room with a disgusted look on her face.

Later I went to my mother for consolation as I usually did. She was particularly good at advising me on thorny issues relating to Bettina. I was inconsolable, my heart full of rage and hurt. She poured me an espresso in the tiny perfect cups she had kept and cherished since the early days of her own marriage and brought the obligatory plate of biscotti that we shared during my visits, pushing it towards me. I slid the plate back wearily.

Dimmi cara … did you love him? Did he break your heart? she asked gently in Italian, putting her arms around me. They were fleshy and warm and felt so reassuring wrapped around my shoulders.

I said nothing, wiping my eyes on the sleeve of the expensive black dress that I had chosen so carefully for Tommy's funeral.

Is it her? Is it how you feel about her?

I looked up at her sharply.

I … I can't say, I finally said, feeling the tears dry up and something hard solidifying inside me.

I could never say what was locked in my heart.

Domenico Capilongo

Parents' Night

She kicked me out of the house on parents' night. I've always hated parents' night. It's so awkward. You never know exactly what to say and no one ever really tells you. It's not discussed or taught in teacher's college. When I first started teaching, I used to try and tell them what they wanted to hear but now I like to lay it all out on the table.

It's the in-between-time that can really drag the whole event out: between the end of the school day and the arrival of the first parents. When times were good the powers-that-be would lay out a huge spread of food in the staffroom or a group of us would go and see a movie. Those days are gone now with all the recent cuts. And the more years I teach the more tired I seem to get. At the end of the day, I feel as drained as a squeezed out lemon. I usually head home to have a quick nap and a bite to eat before the madness begins.

We don't live that far from the school. I hated the idea but Maria wanted to be close to the office. You know, have only one car, save the environment, get me on my bike for exercise; which is marriage code for honey, you're a fat ass. What I hated was seeing my students everywhere, the grocery store; restaurants, sometimes they'd even drive by honking while I mowed the lawn.

Our house is a classic two-storey suburban home: light brown brick, single garage, nothing special, but lately none of it was good enough for Maria. We put in new floors, curtains, furniture and fresh paint. I couldn't help but think she was trying to fill the space that we decided we wouldn't fill with children because she wanted to focus on her career.

When I turned into the driveway all I could do was think about sleep. Yes, I won the battle to keep a second car: emergencies I said. I knew something was wrong when I saw the curtains closed tightly. Maria never did that when she left for work. My suitcase was on the front step. It was the dark green suitcase we had just bought for the cruise that we ended up cancelling because her sister got sick.

Sitting in my classroom at night never feels right. It's mostly the silence. It feels so strange, especially for a math class. I can never get over how much noise students make when I try to teach them math. I don't understand what they could possibly have to say to each other. For me it was always about the numbers. I just focused on the numbers. I walked over to the cupboard at the back of the room and opened it to put on my all-purpose tweed sports jacket, a gift from Maria. She said I should look nice for parents, or when the principal came in to observe my class. I slipped it on and moved closer to the windows to use them as a mirror.

I've aged so much in this job, in this one room. I can barely count the number of students I've taught to love math right in this very spot. I noticed how much grey hair was taking over my thick mop of brown at my temples. I could never be bothered to figure out when it was time for a haircut. Maria was always on top of things like that; always looking after me, the absent-minded math teacher. I tried to button my jacket and felt how much my belly had grown. Okay, so I've been letting myself go, she could have found a better way to tell me.

Maria and I met in a grocery store parking lot. No, I wasn't smooth enough to say something charming while she stepped out of her car. The store was having some promotional launch of their summer products. They had loud music playing, tents set up and free samples. I wandered over and she was managing the whole set up. I noticed her right away. She was dressed in a dark skirt suit; her short black hair was slicked back tightly. It brought out her features more, her big brown eyes and round little girl cheeks. She was short and a bit overweight but curvy. This was before she moved up the managerial ladder, before the working out obsession, the personal trainer, jumping on the yoga bandwagon and trying to save the planet. It was when I could just strike up a conversation about the weather, and she said it was the little dimple in my left cheek that made her fall for me.

"Mr. Thornton?" The first parents arrived and that's when it hit me. I had my marks with me but I had forgotten my parents' night schedule at home. I could see it in my mind on the kitchen counter, the counter Maria had been complaining about. I had no idea about the order in which parents were coming and when.

There are a few kinds of parent visits for me. You get the ones where only one parent, usually the mom, comes and sits in the chair in front of you as though she were being interviewed for the job of mother-of-the-year. The next is the mother and father, where the wife does most of the talking and the husband is just sizing you up for the final question; something like, "So, what does my son need to do to get an 'A'?" The subtext here is: you know I am a better man than you, I make more money and I could kill you if I wanted to. And finally, my favourite, the parents that think their kid is an idiot and stop just short of bribing you for a passing mark.

Most of my interviews that night went well. I introduced myself, the parents introduced themselves, which made it easy for me to find their child's name on my list and I told them the mark and proceeded with discussing areas for improvement. The problem came at the end of the night. The last couple just stood at the door like shadows or as if they were waiting to be seated at a fancy restaurant.

I knew I was in trouble right away because they did not introduce themselves. I stood up like a good maître d, "Please, come in and have a seat." The mother was a small Asian woman, Korean I thought or Japanese or Malaysian. I couldn't quite place her because she had no accent at all; just a very soft smooth voice that reminded me of Maria or at least the young Maria who barely spoke on our first date. She just listened to me babble on about how I wanted to eventually buy a sailboat and live in Florida. "Thank you, Mr. Thornton. This is my husband." She just tilted her head slightly toward him as they entered my classroom. The dad was a tall man. He must have been about six-four or so with the brightest red curly hair I had ever seen. He burst into a big toothy smile and power squeezed my hand which gave me a weird flash of lumberjacks working in the forest. I had no idea who their child was and instead of asking, all I kept thinking about was where I was going to sleep that night. I imagined Maria finally being able to read her novels all night without me complaining about the light or drowning her with my snoring.

The mother folded her hands in her lap, gave me a gentle smile with warm eyes while her husband decided to stare at me as though I was a fresh cut log that he'd like to see how far he could toss out the window.

"Well, this year I have really concentrated on making math more engaging for the students and hands on." What else could I start with? It was the first thing I remembered from our last staff meeting. "I don't know if you've heard from …" I didn't know if I should guess or not, so I switched, "I don't know if you've heard anything about what we have been studying lately?"

"No," came the booming voice of the husband. "He doesn't tell us much." Thank God, I thought, at least I know it's a boy.

"Yes, well most teen boys are like that."

"No, he doesn't like to have any conversations anymore. We used to have so much fun talking." With that the mom locked eyes with me and all I could hear was Maria. We used to have fun and now nothing. We barely even spoke. I looked down at my hands. My simple wedding band bounced the light back up at me. It was so hard to take off now. It was like the flesh of my finger had been growing over it. We did have fun but was it my fault that I didn't know how to talk to her anymore?

"Oh, he'll come around. Give him time. He probably has a lot of things on his mind, school, work, his future …"

"Yes, maybe but I'd just like to see him show more of an interest and show how much he really cares about things. I tell you, it's like pulling teeth sometimes." The husband sat back, happy having made his point; he folded his arms and sighed. I did care about Maria but it was like she needed to hear it every day. Since getting in touch with her yoga stuff she always wanted to talk about how she felt, how I felt or how we felt about us.

"You know, I think you have to trust that you already know how he feels without asking him to show you all the time. This kind of pressure might make him distance himself even more or make him go deeper into himself." The constant nagging and pressure made me pull further away wasting evenings watching television until she was asleep. I'd fool myself by thinking that I was really interested in the show but it dawned on me during that parents' night that I was avoiding her and myself.

"So, wait a minute." Now the husband leaned forward. "What you're saying is that we should just leave him alone and somehow he'll just come around and start talking to us again and start studying and doing better at school?" It's always some miracle answer, a quick fix secret formula that they ask for. What should my child do to be a star or successful? It's not that simple.

"I don't know." I didn't feel like I knew anything anymore. I felt like a cloud just floating aimlessly over an endless parking lot.

"What do you mean you don't know? Aren't you the teacher? What does he need to do to get better?" The husband's hands were now holding all his weight on my desk between us. I wanted to reach out and hug him, wrap my arms around his big shoulders and squeeze him. I wanted to cry into his massive chest and tell him that the world doesn't work the way he thinks it does. That it doesn't matter what we believe or feel, in the end things are just going to happen the way they're going to happen. That tonight I will go and sleep in some dingy motel close to the airport, buy myself a bottle of whiskey, call my wife and beg her to let me back into her life.

Instead, I took a slow deep breath, "Look, there's no magic to math. If your son focuses on doing the textbook work and makes sure he asks me for help with the parts he doesn't understand, everything will be fine."

Maria Giuseppina Cesari

Chi trova un amico trova un tesoro

"Attenzione, sta per entrare il Presidente della Repubblica, tutti in piedi," annuncia il cerimoniere del Quirinale, moderno mazziere e custode dell'antico retaggio dei Re sabaudi, mai tanto vicini come in questa cerimonia di apertura dell'anno giudiziario presso l'alta Corte di cassazione. Il consigliere Antonio Pariello, seduto alla penultima fila del palco d'onore dell'Aula Magna, proprio vicino al podio, sta ribollendo di indignazione, ma si alza insieme agli altri magistrati per omaggiare il Capo dello Stato. Finge di non sentire i risolini di scherno dei colleghi e i commenti espliciti delle velenose colleghe: "Ma non si vergogna?!" "Ma dove crede di essere?" "Mai vista una cosa più oltraggiosa!" E pensare che l'oggetto di tanto dispetto, non è nient'altro che la sua enorme toga di ermellino, di tre taglie più grande, che lo avvolge come una coperta e che lo fa sembrare un topolino affogato in un bicchiere di mistrà. Solo spunta il naso romano, sovrastato dagli occhiali di tartaruga Gucci. La lucida pelata è nascosta dal feltro, ma dai lati scendono rivolini di sudore che il consigliere cerca invano di asciugarsi con la manica della toga. Il caldo opprimente e il rubizzo della vergogna fanno un tutt'uno con il rosso amaranto dell'ermellino. "Come ho potuto fare questo a me stesso, perdere la faccia così, proprio quando sto per essere nominato Presidente di Sezione ...," riflette il meschino. "E poi con la Presidente della Quarta Sezione, Gina Amaiello, seduta proprio dietro a me! Ho perso credibilità ancor prima della nomina," si dispera. "Tutto è cominciato ieri mattina, il giorno più sfortunato della mia vita," rimugina il magistrato, masticando fiele e perdendo il filo del discorso del Presidente.

In realtà, la mattina precedente è iniziata bene per il Pariello, con ben dieci processi definiti solo alla prima udienza. Passando nel cortile d'onore, al centro della Corte, per recarsi nel suo studio, nell'altra ala del palazzo, riceve distrattamente i saluti dei colleghi e gli omaggi untuosi degli autisti, appostati nelle vicinanze. Di tutta quella banda informe, riconosce solo vagamente un ometto ben vestito, dall'aria modesta e, come lui stesso, scuro di pelle, con i capelli grigi, le fattezze pronunciate e la parlata campana. "Buongiorno dottò e buona giornata," gli fa l'ometto. "Buongiorno", risponde il magistrato, sorpreso dal tono sincero. "Questo lo conosco, ma non mi ricordo come e perché ...," mugugna tra sé e sé.

Raggiunto il suo studio al secondo piano, vi trova sull'uscio il Consigliere Luciano Frivoli, suo amico-nemico da oltre trent'anni, che lo sta aspettando. "Ehilà Antò, sei pronto per domani? Sfili anche tu, quest'anno?" esordisce il perfido Frivoli. "Ti serve qualche consiglio da un veterano della sfilata come me?" "Certo che sfilo, sono proprio in prima fila," ribatte stizzito il Pariello, "ecco qui la mia toga, bell'è pronta!", e per chiudere la bocca al collega, si gira e apre il vecchio armadio di noce traballante ad un'anta, dietro la scrivania. "Ma dov'è la mia toga di ermellino? L'hai presa tu Lucià, è uno scherzo?" "Ma che dici, Antò, non ne so niente", risponde il Frivoli che se la fila di corsa con un sogghigno stampato in faccia.

Il Pariello si precipita per le scale fino al suo vecchio studio al quarto piano, di cui ha ancora le chiavi, e guarda nell'armadio: niente. Poi corre di nuovo al secondo, incredulo e concitato, passando in rassegna tutti i colleghi del corridoio. "Colletti, hai visto la mia toga?" "Ma no, Pariello, che dici?" "Marziali, hai per caso preso in prestito la mia toga?" "Ma figurati, che vuoi che ne sappia io della tua toga!" "Fiasconi, dimmi la verità...sei stato tu?" "Sei impazzito!! Io non ne so niente!", nega il Fiasconi, e aggiunge: "È inutile che cerchi la tua toga di ermellino. Se non la usi da tempo, è stata riassegnata dalla Corte a qualcuno che ha sfilato negli anni scorsi. Vattelappesca dove è andata finire." "Quindi la mia è scomparsa. Ne hai una da prestarmi, Fiasconi?" chiede affannato Pariello. "Certo che no; ne ho solo una." Mentre Pariello esce lo sente dire al Colletti: "E se anche ce l'avessi una toga in più, figurati se la darei a quello lì." Distrutto dalle parole del Fiasconi, vede arrivare nel corridoio un suo collega di vecchia data, tale Giuseppe Battaglia: "Peppì, buongiorno, puoi prestarmi la tua toga di ermellino, visto che quest'anno non sfili?" "Assolutamente no, Antò. Lo sai che io ne ho una personale, fatta su misura dal mio sarto, non uso quella della Corte."

"Ma, Peppì, per favore ..." "E comunque l'ho mandata a pulire a Caserta, non è a Roma," lo interrompe il Battaglia. "Mi dispiace, Antò, non arriverebbe mai in tempo."

Il Pariello, disperato, decide di chiedere aiuto alla sua vecchia fiamma, il consigliere Maria Del Faggio. Si precipita, quindi, trafelato, attraverso il cortile verso le due rampe che danno all'ala est della Corte, dove si trova la stanza della collega. "Buongiorno dott. Pariello e buona giornata," gli fa di nuovo l'ometto al suo passaggio "'Ngiorno, 'ngiorno," risponde lui col fiatone, senza dargli troppo peso. "Maria, scusami. Sono qui a chiederti un grosso favore: puoi prestarmi la tua toga per domani?" esordisce senza preamboli. "Antonio, mi dispiace, ormai l'ho restituita, non sfilo più," risponde mesta lei. Pariello, ormai fradicio di sudore, riscende nel cortile e si appoggia allo scalone per riprendere fiato. Prende il cellulare e, come estremo tentativo, chiama la sua ex-moglie, Luisa. "Pronto, Luisa. Sai se avevo portato una toga di ermellino a casa nostra qualche anno fa?" "No, Antonio, non me la ricordo per niente, e se l'avessi trovata, l'avrei bruciata," gli appende il telefono in faccia la ex Signora Pariello.

"Mi scusi, dottò, posso aiutarla?" Appare il solito ometto, questa volta al fianco del magistrato che non si è accorto della sua presenza fino a quel momento. "Solo se avesse una toga da prestarmi," butta lì Pariello. "In effetti ce l'ho, è la vecchia toga del Presidente Sgrolli, pace all'anima sua," E prima che Pariello si possa riavere dallo stupore, l'ometto sparisce e ritorna in pochi minuti con la gigantesca toga dentro un sacco di plastica.

"Grazie, non so come ringraziarla, Signor ...?" "Sono Ciro Palumbo, dottò, davvero non si ricorda di me?" Come una meteora che colpisce il suolo con una deflagrazione improvvisa, quel nome scuote il Pariello, che sente rimbombare nelle orecchie la voce del suo maestro elementare che fa l'appello: "Paccioni, Palumbo, Pariello." E si rivede bambino, con il grembiule blu e il fiocco bianco al collo, seduto al banco dietro ad un piccoletto di nome Ciro Palumbo. Sessant'anni cancellati in un attimo, mentre intorno a lui si ammassano sfocate le immagini delle partite di pallone nel campetto dietro la chiesa, le corse fino al mare nei pomeriggi assolati, e le lotte con le biro e le palline di carta. Una sensazione di benessere lo pervade, come un'ondata di calore che lo raggiunge, inaspettata, in una fredda mattina di gennaio.

"Ciro, sei tu, amico mio?!" salta su il Pariello abbracciando il commesso di slancio, sotto gli occhi stupefatti dei rari passanti. "Sì, sono proprio io, Antonio," si commuove Ciro, "sapevo che non mi avevi dimenticato."

Il Presidente della Repubblica ha finito il suo discorso inaugurale e tutti si alzano. Mentre gli altri magistrati lo attorniano con battute, commenti di politica giudiziaria e ancora malevolenze sulla sua toga sproporzionata, il consigliere Antonio Pariello, magistrato dell'alta Corte di cassazione, futuro Presidente di Sezione, si scrolla di dosso la toga e si avvia all'uscita, senza voltarsi indietro. Sta già pregustando il caffè che prenderà tra poco al bar, subito fuori dal palazzo, con Ciro, il suo compagno di scuola, l'amico di ieri e di oggi. Un caffè ristretto, napoletano, senza zucchero e senza fiele.

Nella Cotrupi

The Quiet One

Dedicated to Richard Wagamese

He was always soft-spoken and did not say much. There was stillness in his long slender body, and even in his unobtrusive gestures. The only outward signs of energy were the movements of his shoulder-length ink black hair and the occasional dart of a raised glance. When he spoke, he used very few words: a short direct answer when questioned by teachers or by one of the other students, and then silence.

As usual, he was walking some meters ahead of me on Major St. one early October day after school. Unlike some of my other classmates, he never waited for me to catch up so that we could chat along the walk home. His lumberjack shirt of red and black checks made a strong note in the early autumn scenery.

I decided to bite the bullet one day and called out, "Hey John, wait up!"

He turned to see who was calling and then stopped, waiting for me to close the distance between us. Silently he reached out, took my heavy stack of books and moved to the street side of the sidewalk, measuring his long-legged steps to my own much shorter ones.

I was suddenly at a loss for words so we walked along in silence for a time. Softly, his voice breaking into bass, he asked if I had far to go.

Nervously I replied that it was not too far, just near the Catholic high school; and then I clammed up again. He nodded his head once and on we walked. The sun was strong on our faces and the leaves caught its fire.

As we approached the turn off to my street, just past St. Jerome's High School, I made a gesture towards my books. He shook his head, then tipped his chin forward and turned into my street too. I didn't know what to do: too shamefaced to say that it was better I go on alone. We walked on, past the brick and aluminum-siding houses that preceded mine, and then I stopped in front of the yellow stucco house with the wrought-iron clad veranda and the terracotta pots filled with still blooming geraniums.

He stopped too and after briefly looking up at the house, handed me my books, being careful not to make physical contact. Turning back the way we had come, he said, "See you tomorrow." I watched his departing figure for a moment and then went inside.

It went on like this for many weeks, except that now he waited for me outside the school. The one or two times I emerged in the company of a friend he silently turned and walked in the opposite direction. I began to feel more comfortable with his silence—his stillness. He would occasionally point to a vector of migrating birds or offer me a particularly colorful maple leaf he found lying on the ground. I never saw him in the cafeteria at lunchtime, but we did have one class together, English. He was no slouch, and when called on to answer always had something interesting to say. Without fail, he had read the books, and when we covered English poetry in class, I could see a strong light in his eyes, especially when we were studying Emily Dickinson.

One day, as he was passing my books to me in front of my house, he said, "I want to show you something. Can we sit on the steps for a minute?"

By now, I had explained a little bit about my background. An Italian immigrant family, we had arrived to this northern Ontario railway hub during my early childhood. I was part of an extended clan, very close knit and old fashioned, protective and strict. There was no dating for me, even if I was soon to be eighteen and graduating from high school.

I looked at my watch and, thinking we had some time before my parents arrived from work, I said, sure, and sat down on the steps, cleared now of flowerpots and blooms. Sitting down a few steps below me, he pulled a piece of paper out of his pocket, unfolded it and passed it to me. This is what I read:

Autumn
A leaf
Brushes my brow
And leaves me
Laughing

I raised my eyes and met his intense gaze. No words came to me, just a smile that he immediately returned.

A car pulled up in the driveway and I jumped up, letting the paper spiral to the ground. My father came barreling out of the car, slamming the door. Rushing around the car, he ignored John, came up to me, lifted his callused hand and hit me, hard, across the face. John made as if to grab my father's arm and I pushed him away saying, "Go. Now. Please. I'm fine."

He looked at me, saw the pleading in my eyes and turned away, just as my father hissed, "*Via*, go!"

I saw John's hands clench into fists, but he did not look back, just kept walking. I picked up the paper and went inside, knowing I would never see him again.

***

I was wrong. Some twenty years later at a Toronto literary reading, I sat in the back row of the room as a tall, dark man with short, slightly greying hair, read from his first best-selling novel. It was a meditative alleluia on a return to traditional indigenous life on James Bay after years struggling to make it in the big city. When he finished the reading, I went up to the book-signing table to ask for a signature, and smiled as he greeted me by name.

"Hi Nina, did you see the dedication?"

I nodded, tears threatening as my husband came up and, after thanking the author for the reading, led me to the exit. I turned and looked back just as we reached the door. John's gaze met mine and he nodded slowly, once. I raised my hand and, for a fleeting instant, brushed it across my brow.

Domenic Cusmano

Zoom Cocktail

"Unmute, unmute," Brian says. "Roger, unmute, please. We can't hear you. You need to activate your mic."

Roger is mouthing soundless words.

"Roger, unmute please," the host repeats. His voice is a notch higher and on the verge of exasperation.

Roger and the other eight people in the meeting appear as miniature headshots encased in squares on my laptop screen in varying shades of clarity. We are volunteers on the board of an NGO which shall remain nameless to protect the innocent. (The names of the people being described have been changed for the same reason.) We wait patiently for Roger to internalise the physical laws of the virtual reality into which we have been thrust by the Covid pandemic.

Roger's lips stop moving. His grey-bearded face freezes, except for his eyes, which dart from side to side, top to bottom. They finally come to rest on the bottom of his screen. He brings his face in closer.

"It's the icon that looks like a microphone. Click on it," Brian instructs.

Roger looks up and smiles, the picture of triumph. His face disappears. A black square with his name in big white letters replaces his image. "Can you all hear me now?" Roger's voice comes through loud and clear.

"Yes, we can hear you, Roger. But we seem to have lost you …" Brian's voice is resigned.

Roger's "Oh …" encapsulates sorrow, confusion and frustration all at once.

"Go back to the bottom left of your screen, where you were before, and click on 'video,' just 'video'," says Brian.

I am taking this in stride. As a volunteer, there is no point in stressing. Besides, the fact that we can "attend" meetings from the comfort of our homes procures a great many advantages, not least the fact that we can multitask. Several in this bunch are taking full advantage of this.

Valerie, a retired bank manager and new grandmother, is knitting a pair of baby slippers. Sam, a stockbroker, is definitely focussed on something else, probably the stock market ticker on his browser, judging from the way his eyes don't move. Rob, a lawyer for thirty years whom I've known for almost as long, is in his leather chair with a whiskey tumbler by his side—perfectly understandable on a Friday afternoon. I send him a private message of a clinking-glasses emoji via the chat. He replies almost instantly with two thumbs up and a full-toothed smile. Liz, an attractive, 40-something travel consultant sidelined by the pandemic is comfortably lying on her sofa in a nightshirt, her back against the armrest, looking like she just woke up.

Roger finally comes online, voice and video in harmony, and begins his financial report. He shares his screen, surprisingly, without a hitch. His desktop window reveals his bookmarked browser tabs, one of which says Pornhub. I wonder if anyone else notices.

I'm about to send Rob a message, but he beats me to it. It's a big-eyed-flushed-face emoji. I reply with a thumbs-up and sunglasses face. The rest of the meeting is more presentations, questions, answers, and votes on resolutions, thankfully, without additional delays.

Just the same, the meeting carries on longer than planned, which makes me late for my next commitment of the day: a Zoom literary reading I am really excited about. I belong to a writers' group which meets every Friday. I don't always attend, but this week's featured member is someone I admire, and she's also a friend. I hope I don't get turned away like they do at the opera or the theatre. It's not like my arriving late will disrupt the proceedings.

I already have a reputation for being late—in physical reality, I mean. Lately, I find myself arriving late at virtual events, as well. Funny how our nature seems to carry over from one dimension to another. I am inclined to believe that some things are cosmically out of our control.

Take my doctor, for example. Just this morning I had an appointment with him booked for 8:30. But, of course, he was late. Not his fault, I'm sure. Just his nature, like all doctors. I logged in on Zoom as scheduled, only to have his secretary come on and say that Dr Z was running late due to a high volume of patients. He would see me as soon as possible.

I went to the kitchen, made myself another espresso, and read the *New York Times* on my phone while I waited. He called me 90 minutes later, but on FaceTime. "This Zoom thing isn't working for me. Too many layers of technology," he said without the slightest bit of irony.

I told him about the migraines and pain around the eyes I've been getting. He asked how much time I spend in front of a screen—computer, smartphone, tablet, TV.

"Too much, lately," I said. "What else is there to do?"

"You're suffering from digital eyestrain. The blue light of your screen is searing your eyeballs."

For a moment, the thought of having to give up my channels to the outside world or go blind made me feel weak.

"Easy solution," Dr Z continued, interrupting my grim thoughts. "You need to get reading glasses with a blue-light filter."

I called my optometrist as soon as I wrapped things up with Dr Z. The secretary gave me an appointment for next week. I kind of figured it wouldn't be on Zoom, but I decided to ask her anyway. She paused for a second before confirming.

When I click on the Zoom link for the literary reading, a window opens and a message appears: "Please wait, the host will let you in soon." I am relieved. Sure enough, my screen comes to life within seconds, transformed into a checkerboard of tiny faces in myriad colours. There must be more than thirty people.

The checkerboard is quickly replaced by the image of Dave, the organiser and host, standing behind a podium as if onstage. He is, in fact in his living room. I'm glad I haven't missed the start of the actual reading.

"Now, it is my privilege to turn things over to this week's featured writer," he says. Hand-clapping emojis fill the checkerboard. Dave's image is replaced by an extreme close-up of the writer. (Let's call her Jenny.) Her rosy face covers my entire screen. The top of her head is cut off, as is her chin.

Jenny smiles and looks into the camera. Silence. Jenny continues to smile. More silence. The silence seems to last forever. Jenny's smile begins to fray.

"Oh, is it me?" she says finally. "Can I start? Now? Dave? Can I start?"

"Yes, Jenny," Dave's disembodied voice replies. "Actually, if you can," he continues over-politely, "maybe you can move back a little. You're too close to the screen."

"Oh." Jenny's image shakes and wobbles as if projected by a hand-held camera. "Is this better?"

"Perfect!"

Jenny is sitting in a plush armchair. Her red, long-sleeved sweater and pearl neckless contrast beautifully with her dyed raven-black hair that encircle her face like an aura. I sit back, ready to absorb the imagery that her words and the sound of her voice will evoke.

Jenny clears her throat, ready to begin, when a black cat saunters into the shot completely blocking the view. It stops and stares into the camera. Giant translucent cat eyes fill the screen.

"Oh, Bella!" Jenny stays cool. "This is Bella, my cat. I guess she wants to share the spotlight." Jenny chuckles. If she's flustered, she's not showing it. She leans forward and tries to scoop the furry beast by the belly with one hand and by its hind legs with the other. But Bella (her real name) has other ideas. The screen wobbles and shakes, and pivots. A quickly receding image of Jenny's living room ceiling is followed by a thud. Then Jenny's screen goes black. I mean completely black—not even her name in white letters.

"Well folks, it looks like we've lost Jenny," says a slightly anxious Dave. "I'd ask you all to be patient while we restore the connection."

Fifteen minutes later, nothing. Only about half the attendees remain. I decide to log off, as well, and give my eyes a much needed rest. I have one final Zoom this evening, so I want to be fresh.

My friends and I have been getting together on Friday nights for cocktails and banter for years. The place matters less than the company. As long as there's a table and something to drink, any café or bar will do. But Covid has put a stop to this, at least for the time being. We've kept in touch by phone, text and email, all in agreement that Zoom cocktails are downright silly. You cannot replicate the humour, hyperbole and verbal jousting of a face-to-face social on a computer screen, or can you?

After wave upon wave of curfews, quarantines, and isolation, we are ready to give it a try, essentially out of desperation. Tonight is the night we agreed to pretend that it's normal to pour yourself a glass of liquor alone in your house, turn on your computer, and watch your friends do the same thing.

When I log on to initiate the social (on time, I might add!), my three buddies are already in the "waiting room." I let them in simultaneously. Unlike my earlier zooms, my screen fills with friendly, if nearly forgotten, faces. There is Nat the accountant, André the Phys-ed teacher, and Frank the psychologist. The first word we all utter in unison is "hey"—as in, hey, what are we doing here?

We've all got our drink in hand. Nat is in his customary foulard, a half-empty bottle of brandy within easy reach. Clearly, he has gotten a jump on things. Frank is sitting in quasi-darkness, perhaps trying to replicate the bar ambience. He is nursing a glass of red, while André is looking rather sulky in his beige turtleneck and dishevelled hair.

"Cheers," says Nat, raising his glass to the screen.

"Cheers," we all reply. Then, silence.

Maybe this wasn't such a good idea. It occurs to me that business or event zooms are structured, with speakers lined up in succession. A zoom cocktail that tries to recreate the atmosphere of an informal gathering may be too tall an order.

Nat breaks the ice. "What kind of wine are you drinking," he asks me.

I tell him the truth. "I felt a migraine coming so I'm having apple juice."

The fact that he was fooled draws a laugh from the others. Frank comes clean, as well. The rosé in his glass is cranberry juice. He's been getting headaches too.

"It's digital eye strain," I blurt out. I'm about to tell them all about Dr Z and blue-light filter glasses, but Nat cuts in. "Am I the only one drinking real booze?" He feigns indignation.

Soon, the banter starts to fly, and we talk and laugh late into the night.

It's early morning when I finally turn in. I think about what I have read about past pandemics and wonder how humans survived without the internet. I connect my phone to the charger, turn off the light and pull the sheets up to my chin. For the first time in a long time, I go to bed feeling like I did more than just survive another Groundhog Day.

Liana Cusmano

Nonna Goes to the Club

The best translation you can think of for *club* is *discoteca*, which is not exactly accurate. You haven't heard disco in a club since ... ever. You explain to nonna that first you have to line up outside in the cold. *Why don't they just let us in?* nonna asks. You don't really have an answer for her. Young men walk through the slush in sneakers while women brave the icy wind in stilettos, their arms and legs exposed to the wind and snow. *Aren't they cold?* nonna asks. *Why are they dressed like puttane?* You tell her that that's just the style, and that we don't use that word anymore. At the bar, one shot is ten dollars. Nonna tries to haggle. You explain that that's not how it works here. *Why is it so expensive?* Because of inflation, you say. Nonna scoffs. *Why not have wine or Vecchia Romagna at home?* Because here, you get to dance, and be with your friends, and it's loud. *Why is it so loud?* It's fun, you say. *What?* nonna shouts. The DJ spins his records. Couples grind up against one another and nonna covers her eyes. In the bathroom, there are tampon and condom dispensers. *What are those?* she asks. You do not know the Italian words for them. One is for when you have your period. The other is so you don't get pregnant. *Why would you need both at the same time?* nonna wants to know. *And why are those girls dressed like that if they don't want to get pregnant?* You try to explain consent. Nonna stares blankly. You want to avoid that sad feeling that appears when all the lights come on at once when the club is getting ready to close, everyone's smudged faces and wilting outfits outlined in the glaring white light. To get ahead of the crowd, you leave the club and head up the street to Chez Mein. Nonna watches as someone drizzles peanut butter generously over piles of noodles in Styrofoam containers and gives one to each of you. You hand over two toonies. *Why is it so cheap?* Because of all the business they get here, you say. *You get what you pay for*, nonna grumbles, and you finish what's left of her peanut butter noodles. You hail a cab that will take you home. So what did you think? Nonna stares out the window and shrugs. You young people, she snorts, waving her hand. With all your nonsense. *Viva la gioventù.*

Sonia Di Placido

Our Lady of the Saugeen Grotto

I look onto this same horizon, standing on this same rock, my eyes squinting out onto the expanse of Huron's peninsula in the high noon sun of July. Four years later, I find myself here, again, with my wife, Cathy, the fourth year in a row we bicker, keeping the anniversary that's become more important than our own.

"It's no lake. It's more than that," her attempt to make a point weighed on me as if she imposed her conviction between command and commandment. Cathy was never pensive nor so meticulous before. Each year she became more obsessive.

"See the grooves, these jutted out edges, slabs over slab with all this cave-like formation? It's all Karst—smoothed over limestone with bedrock underneath, the softer stuff just being slowly run down and pulled away. I don't know if the water is higher or lower this year. It's hard to tell, but everyone just loves this side of the scarp. The great edge of everything." Cathy surveys the landscape, attempting to find some resolve.

"Yeah, there's no sand, no sediment."

"Not on this side. Just floods of water that ran through here between huge ice making giant holes and scrapes. That's what made this crazy mouth over here.

"The Grotto?"

"Yup."

"It's so cool," I caught myself. "Aha! My glacial pun. Yeah, an Ontario haven."

I just wanted to lighten her up a bit. I was starting to feel like she was going to turn into a feminist Moses atop the edge of the trail.

"A haven? I don't think so. Not anymore, Mark. Not with so much rock that you have to climb up, down, so much to get to the water. That? A real cave? It's a water cave, I guess."

"The best ones are."

"Well, you can't understand the cave unless you get inside it."

"C'mon Cathy."

"What!?" She smacks at me incredulous.

"That's enough. Don't put this on me. You know we can't do that anymore. The Park rangers are on patrol. There's always something happening here, and if we're found on the grounds after hours, we'll be fined thousands. Besides, it's too dangerous at that hour."

"I'd like to know what went on here before the park."

"Yeah, sure. Who wouldn't?

***

Everyone from the GTA is all over visiting at least once now that we have one of these at the peninsula. In Canada, of all places. Ha! It has become a fancy feature now considering it's not an ocean edge or some rocky island jutting out from a seabed. Nothing like Bay of Fundy, but still, it's the tail end of the escarpment and a massive great lake entry into ginormous fresh water. And so many shades of blue from aquamarine to deep cobalt. Seems no different than some jungle grotto with all the cedars jutting out from the cliffs. All the year-round visitors make it comparable to the exotic ones in Phuket or Greece and Capri. This one looks almost the same. Not as deep. Not as scary. Maybe a few centuries ago. There's not that many in the world, apparently. The place to go in summer and anyone who comes to Ontario wants to visit. I've never seen any bears, coyotes. A few jays. Cars lined up bumper to bumper all the way up Hwy 6 from Owen Sound. No one can get into Tobermory now. Highway they call it, it's a little road, one that they trotted over at some point, needs a serious makeover. It wasn't like this fifty or sixty years ago. Doesn't matter the weather, it's not the 1920's at the Bruce anymore, but it still feels wild and possessed after dark.

***

It wasn't until we stopped hearing from Rowena that we knew something was weird about this place. This is no safe peninsula. It's a fathomless wormhole at the edge of a peak connecting lakes at times worse than a sea. I don't tell Cathy what I think of these towns. We've never been really sure about the month it happened. Ro came up here and stayed for a few years. That's when Cathy started to really get freaked. After a year passed, she understood her best friend wasn't coming back to the city. It's one thing to disappear for a while; it's another to know when a friend is seriously gone. Real gone. Forever missing. And we know she went out around the whole peninsula at night sometimes.

"We keep coming back. What's the point, Cath? We're not going to find anything."

"I don't care."

***

I have no idea why she did it. To think she was here all alone in the cold. What makes some young lady go out and do that? She was sick. She needed help—some fuckin' trauma. The Saugeen would never call it that. They'd say what happened was spiritual. I want to believe it's both. The police, the locals—everyone's right. We heard she was almost killed by her boyfriend soon after they showed up here. Some neighbours said it was her baggage—they kept telling Cathy that it's what she was going through and Ro had to figure herself out. Now, she'll never forgive herself for not confronting Ro. Then there's the possibility of something else that was going on—what I saw of Ro's attitude before she left the city. She wanted to do it, maybe disappear, and something made her go there. We can call her missing or whatever we want. For those folks who wanted answers, to see her, find her, talk to her, hear her, or pick up on whatever happened, a lot of them all say she became something else and that just before she went missing she started to know stranger things about this place.

***

The Light and Life Chapel said that she was a smart, sweet, and very pretty lady. "Glorious red hair! She had some special aura; she belongs to the light now, I guess," the pastor's wife put on a solemn face.

When the fuck did that start? We just smiled and nodded. When I think back about it like this, I kind of wish we'd have come up to see her here a few months after we married. I knew she'd change a bit, become different or was it indifferent? But then again, if I'd known she would disappear or possibly die, wouldn't I be more horrified than I already am now? Haunted. As if we weren't already. She became part of the rock; we came to understand that well enough. The pastor's wife called her Romina a few times. I wanted to correct her.

"It's Roweena," I muttered under my breath. Cathy stopped me, brushing my elbow the second my lips twitched.

We got into the car soon after. It was a warm afternoon. A great day to take the Chee-cheemon and get over to Manitoulin. But no way that was going to happen today or tomorrow or the next and I'm the worst for even thinking it. That was the second year we came up here after Ro was reported missing. I'm driving as my wife looks out the window. I swerve into the motel lot, and she utters another one of her commandments, "She *did* change her name when she got here."

"What makes you say that?"

"She hinted at a new identity when she told me she was leaving, sort of."

I gave her a squinty look insinuating she was going off as I put us into park.

"Mark, c'mon. A year we were married, and I could tell she wanted a change."

"What's that supposed to mean?"

"C'mon?! Really? She was my maid of honour, Mark! We were best friends before I met you."

"Ok. I get what you mean. Why did she have to move here for that?"

Cathy was quiet. She lifted herself from the low-slung seat of our Impala, swung the door open and, just before she slammed it shut, cried out, "She must'a been looking for a way out."

***

The second year we visited a Saugeen elder they called Mindimooyenh. She spoke sparse and knowingly about how there's too many souls to count on fingers and toes five times over. She said, "They drift between the edges of the rocks and their crevices, each whispering their sorrows anywhere as far off from turtle island for over a thousand years." Cathy wants to know if she can do a ceremony or annual ritual. She offered to compensate her. I was embarrassed at her presumptuousness. Cathy reminds me, "I want to believe ... no, I actually do believe she found her spirit and became one with it."

***

Tourists come and go. It doesn't hit the news anymore, but folks have been reported to drown around here more than we know. It gets busy. No one really cares when accidents happen except the immediate family. We were Rowena's family, but I guess we took that for granted. We'd only been married over a year when all contact stopped. Ro left a month after the wedding. Everyone's careful on the rocks during the day. I get it; it's fun. Midnight has gotta be so dangerous on the east edge and so fucking gorgeous with the night sky up here. A flashlight isn't enough light in the forested park, even if you're following the paths. Fuck, three flashlights aren't enough light. What the fuck was she doing?! Her boots in the freezing water of that cave, never to surface. I wouldn't be surprised if some folks from the reserve might have an accurate suspicion on something about it. There's gotta be someone, something to blame. Cathy has brought flowers and a new blessed rosary every year we've come to visit. Cathy says Ro is like *Our Lady of the Grotto* and she prays when not too many visitors are around. The pastor at the chapel tells us that she's now praised with a rite and well-remembered. "She's *Our Lady of the Bruce.*" Really? I thought at the time. She's now just a lost damsel. Gone. He seemed refer to Ro's happening in a blessed way. This makes me very uncomfortable. And I find him and his wife both creepy. We're heading back to the city tomorrow morning. By nine-thirty Cathy brushes her teeth and I'm on the bed looking at the chapel pamphlet I grabbed on the way out, skeptically.

"We should find out more about them," I tell her.

Cathy looks at me with big round, glaring eyes from the bathroom sink. I stick my head out to her and bulge mine out too glaring back. She thinks I'm wacko for about 20 seconds. Then, she makes a low moan, nods her head up and down slowly, bulging her eyes back, toothpaste all over her mouth. She gets my hunch.

"We're coming back before next July," I say.

M. Verbena Donati

1956—KITIMAT

Excerpt from Memoir, UNSETTLED

I took a boat from Naples to Genoa and then to Halifax. I was very fortunate in that the Second Class section was overbooked and there were two empty spaces in First Class. Myself and another teacher were upgraded to First Class. So, the trip was fantastic. I spent a lot of time on the deck lying on the comfortable deck chairs because it prevented me from feeling the churning of my stomach brought on by motion sickness. The dinners were served in a large banquet room and my travelling companion and I were surrounded by interesting people. We were treated as royalty and the captain would sit at our table for some meals.

On arrival in Halifax, my trunk was taken to customs to be inspected and the border services officers asked me if I was an actress because of the beautiful clothes they found inside. Next, I took the train to Montreal. It was a terrible experience. People were eating and the aisles were littered with food wrappers as well as broken bottles. I had never seen anything so dirty. They should have been taught to respect public property.

When I arrived in Montreal, I was approached by a social worker asking if I needed a shower and rest. I said yes and after felt renewed.

In Montreal, I transferred to a train travelling to B.C. Fortunately, I had a window seat. The rhythmic movement and sound of the train across Canada sang a lullaby over the six-day trip, but I slept only for very short periods. As well as the excitement of being reunited with my husband, I was fascinated by the wonder of so much space and so much snow. Snow, snow, and more snow. Now and then little colored roofs would appear among this immense white. Miles and miles of land dotted by little doll houses. I was accustomed to Italy, where there was little empty space between cities.

It was dawn when finally, the rumble of the train made me close my eyes and go to sleep.

When I arrived in Terrace, Leo was waiting for me. My heart was beating wildly. I had not seen him for four years. We embraced, and I didn't know what to say.

We boarded another train. And it was frightening, because there was no road yet between Terrace and Kitimat. We were surrounded by mountains and forest, travelling on rails that were still being laid, over bridges as they were being constructed. At times the train slowed to a crawl, and when I looked out the window, I could see steep cliffs beside the track.

We were headed for Kitimat, a company town that had been built by ALCAN in 1951. It was an aluminum smelter town set in a flat valley, bordering an inlet and deep-sea port. It advertised itself as "The city of tomorrow, today."

Leo had been living in a bunkhouse in Smeltersite—one of the four camps where men lived. He rented a room for the two of us in the only hotel nearby. The town itself was still under construction, and consisted of a neighbourhood called Kildala, made of prefab houses assembled in Kitimat, as well as a hospital. They were building a new neighbourhood up on a hill, called Nechako Centre.

Once I was there, I said to Leo, "I am not going back until I find a job and we can call the girls." So, I decided to apply for a position at the hospital, given that I had a social worker degree.

In the employment office, the man in charge, Mr. Fossum told me, "I can't give you a job for two reasons: you can't speak the language, and the only job available is in the kitchen washing dishes and preparing meals. You are over-qualified for this."

I said to him, "Please give me this job, I'm willing to try. I need to practice and learn the language."

I must have impressed him because he wanted me to meet his wife, Beatrice. She was a wonderful person. She also tried to discourage me from taking the job, but I insisted that I wanted it, and didn't want to go back home to Italy to get the girls until I was sure I wanted to remain in Canada. I took the job and started working the night shift.

Most of the women working at the hospital were German so they spoke their language amongst themselves; if I had thought that by working here, I would learn English, I was disillusioned. I knew only a few words of English: how are you and thank you, etc.

In the early morning, we had to prepare all the trays for the patients and had to remember what to put on them. When my shift was over, I had to face the northern British Columbia weather: snow and ice that I was not accustomed to.

It was so hard to go back and forth to the hospital. The streets and sidewalks (if there were any) were not plowed. I had bought a pair of boots that reached my knees and still, when I lifted my feet as I walked, the snow would enter my boots. Every step I made was a torment; the snow was almost three feet high, my boots were full of snow and there were moments that I wanted to sit and cry. My feet were almost frozen, I could not breathe, but I carried on as I had made my choice and Leo was waiting for me with a warm cup of coffee, and his arms to hold me and transfer some of his warmth to my frozen body.

By the time I would arrive home, my hands were cold. The index and middle fingers of both my hands were often painful and almost frozen. Nowadays, if my hands get cold during winter, they ache: a souvenir of my first few days in Canada.

In the mornings at the hospital, the workers were allowed to have breakfast in the dining room with the doctors and nurses. The doctors always asked me to sit at their table and Dr. Duncan helped me learn some English words to the envy of the German women who started to hate me. I was treated differently; I had an education, and this made my colleagues jealous. I remember one of them; she was a small girl who really defended me and who would often sit with me and say, "Don't worry, don't pay attention to their rudeness, they are always like this."

We bought a house in Kildala on Kootenay Street, a two-storey house with a lovely garden. I was happy to be in Kitimat, with my Leo, who now was gentler than when we were in Trieste.

Then, one day, Leo played a kind of joke. He went to another room and whispered through the heating grate, "*Eterno riposo dona a loro,*

Signore." (Lord, grant them eternal rest.) I was struck by this as I thought suddenly about Gino—a duke I had been seeing in Italy when Leo and I were split up. And I cried and cried. Later, when I returned to Italy, I heard that he had killed himself. He didn't have money, had debts, and had become involved with art thieves. Afraid to go to prison, he killed himself. I always wondered if Leo's chant was in fact an omen marking the death of Gino.

A friend of Leo and his wife were very kind to us. They taught me some English expressions. I remember that she had no teeth, only dentures; I couldn't believe that she would have had all her teeth removed. She was very young! She said to me that this way she only had to see the dentist once.

We missed the girls, but we felt they were too young to travel alone.

At the bunkhouse, Leo had made a friend called Mr. Savorgnan. This man was strange. He would talk about his wife, their sex life, and how great she was in bed, and how he longed for her to be there with him. Soon, he began to make arrangements for his wife to join him in Canada. We decided that it would be a good idea if the girls could come with her. She was a peasant from Friuli.

Genni and Ileana travelled with Mrs. Savorgnan and her child on an ocean liner, arriving in Halifax on July 15th 1957 and then took the train to Kitimat. Seeing the girls was such a joy. I was trembling from the emotion. We went home. The girls were very happy to see their father and I was happy for their joy. We enrolled them in the Kildala school in grades 3 and 5. I kept working as we needed the money to pay our mortgage.

We were so thrilled and thankful for Mrs. Savorgnan's actions that we offered to have the couple live in our home until they could find one of their own.

I was still working the night shift. Mr. Savorgnan was also working night. One morning I arrived home earlier than usual. I kept quiet as I did not want to wake the children. My bedroom door was half open; I heard a little noise coming from the open door. I thought that my heart would leap out of my body. Was this history repeating itself? I thought: Leo, Leo how could you forget your promises? I remained silent so I would not disturb the two people in our bed. With my arms around my breasts to keep my heart inside, I withdrew into the garage where no one could see me.

I remembered Leo's words: "If a woman makes a pass and the man refuses her, she would think that he is impotent. So a man cannot refuse her."

I knew that Leo would soon come out to go to work, and that Mrs. Savorgnan's husband also would be returning from his shift, so I waited until the coast was clear.

I decided that when I was alone with Mr. Savorgnan, I would tell him that it was time to take his family and find another home.

I think he knew. With his head down he answered, "Yes, I know." I wonder if he kept telling his friends how great she was in bed, to advertise her.

We had enrolled the girls in Kildala Elementary school a block away from our house. Genni, being younger, had little trouble learning English, Ileana on the other hand struggled somewhat. My English was poor. However, as I had studied French in school, I was able to help Genni with sentence construction; Ileana refused any help.

After a few months, Leo started to say that he wanted to go back to Italy, but not quite yet.

Thinking of what had happened in our bedroom, I felt the same, but I wanted to go back right then, not later.

I had agreed with him that I would give him my paycheck and keep fifty dollars for myself to purchase personal items. I did not realize how expensive everything was. No matter how much I wanted to return home I could not do it. I did not have any money for our tickets. So, I waited. Leo, being influenced by his mother, had been sending our money to his father to keep it for him and to invest it.

The Savorgnans suddenly found a place to stay. Two months went by and our relationship became tense. I wonder if Leo was aware that I had discovered his indiscretion. The thought of wanting to go back to Italy and leave Leo forever churned though my mind but how could I take such a step? I was tormented.

Eufemia Fantetti

Lushing it in the Bush: Friendship, Fine Food and Flights of Fancy

I went to the woods because I wished to write deliberately—to alter Thoreau's famous quote—and to front the essential elements of writing life. This locale was an unusual choice for a dedicated urban woman: take me too far from a cappuccino-based business and I begin to fret. I'm used to the hectic pace of Toronto life, falling asleep to the sounds of sirens and waking to the whirr of early morning streetcars. There's an unnerving serenity in the stillness of the countryside that often makes me wonder, "How can people live like this?"

Then again, for over a thousand years, my people lived like that, dwelling in the mountainous region of Molise and specifically the municipality of Bonefro, a place I mistakenly referred to as a village until an internet search revealed the language mishap as another Grand Canyon of misunderstanding. Then also, tired as well as distracted, I searched for a writing retreat away from the hullabaloo. For five nights, I slept in a cabin next to the French River (ponds are passé), attended three workshops on craft, pondered the power of prose and met with others willing to share their words and wisdom—an author's Arcadia.

Day 1: Fire

The first morning, I rise to stoke the woodstove and find the fire has gone out. I imagine my long-departed Nonna Femia aced this chore throughout her life, starting in childhood. She cooked delicious meals over open flames whereas I would have frozen my family to death. I stare at the ash and shake my head, disappointed in myself. On arriving at Champlain cottage the previous afternoon, I'd received basic instructions for fire-keeping: don't use kindling for burning, keep adding logs, and open the air vent for the wood to ignite.

My roommates, Suzanne and Barbara, woke to the cold. Thankfully, everyone packed sensible clothes for the chilly first week of a wet May. We're determined not to let this minor setback dampen our mood. A breakfast basket filled with warm croissants, organic raspberry spread, yogurt, fresh fruit and homemade granola delivered to our door is a soothing balm. We discuss our writing goals and interests over coffee before crossing the bridge to the main lodge.

At the first session, "Influential and Exacting Editors and Why We Need Them," by *The New Quarterly's* Susan Scott, I take copious notes and compare anecdotes with other participants. Behind every great writer, or more appropriately—beside every great writer—there is a gifted editor. Hallelujah, the self-made genius myth is exhausting. The remainder of the day involves sitting by an enormous hearth in the Main Lodge, eating chicken satay with rice pilaff, workshopping with my group members and dining on seafood penne with chocolate mousse dessert.

This is luxury: my stomach is full, and I didn't lift a finger. I almost hear the whispering voices of my female ancestors in the burning, sputtering, glowing heat: *How can anyone be this lazy*?

Day 2: Air

The breeze at Pine Cove is fragrant with smouldering oak, maple and birch. Dawn breaks and I feed the fire a few logs. By breakfast, the flames are crackling. I wish the creative spark was blazing. Beyond their writing abilities and passion for craft, both my cabin mates are considerate and well-read souls. We each start keeping a list of recommended books and writers. The downpour from the day before tapered off. The rain turned into a light drizzle. We're in the signature cottage and want to spend time on the screened porch that overlooks the waterway.

Caffeinated and ready to soak up more wisdom, I ask a question about the intersection of memoir and disclosures that could cause unnecessary harm to loved ones in Don Gilmour's session "Using Your Own Experience". His compassionate response about finding another way to reveal a similar truth helps put puzzling pieces into perspective. Another member of my workshop, Laura, deems the process "writing about the cloudy business in your heart."

For me, this is the crux and the crucible of creative nonfiction. With apologies to Caesar: I wonder. I worry. I write. Telling true stories frequently means revealing what others would prefer to keep hidden. Writing about my mom's schizophrenia and my dad's depression feels like a Faustian bargain. Late at night, I remind myself that —beyond monastic retreats and staying calm through life's swirling chaos—silence serves nothing and no one.

Day 3: Water & Wood

The sound of rain on the roof lulls me. I'm grounded in the ambience of evergreen trees. Transformation might be underway. I could grow accustomed to warm pain au chocolat appearing as I'm brewing java. The flow of fire-keeping is a waltz I respect. I'm so enthralled by gathering wood from the porch, re-filling the indoor container and re-fuelling the woodstove that Barbara names me Mistress of the Fire.

I think of a story my father told once me. He was fifteen and freezing, stuck on a mountain pass in a snowstorm with a stubborn mule refusing to budge. They were returning from another fourteen-kilometre round trip for firewood. My journey is less than five steps from the front door.

Early May 2017 is a particularly damp spring, double the average rainfall, with floods occurring in Quebec and Eastern Ontario. Inside Champlain Cottage, situated on a point, a panoramic view unfolds of the river winding past.

I write and make more notes. I read. I watch the flames crackle and flicker. I listen to the downpour. I talk with Barbara and Suzanne. Writing is a solitary act, a craft that requires patience, faith and much time spent alone. I'm cheered by their company. As a solitary book-worm in a family of mathematicians, this is paradise. Walking back to the cottage at dusk, I finally hear the call and response wail of loons. I stop to listen: the sound is comforting.

Day 4: Earth

The sun is high in the sky, warming the ground beneath our feet as Suzanne and I set off for the Birken Lake hike early in the morning. She knows the route, having hiked a few afternoons with the other intrepid retreaters when it rained.

I chose to wait for the clouds to part and a trumpet blast from a divine being announcing, "This is perfect weather for walking." I feel guilty about not taking advantage of the pastoral beauty of Pine Cove, and my tendency of admiring nature from indoors.

The hike takes under an hour and is stunning—the greenery of spring available in every shade of emerald and lime, in every leaf and blade of grass.

During the final workshop, we discuss and decide on reading selections for the last evening. An emerging essay risks derailment if the initial response is negative.

After the banquet meal, I cheer and clap loudly when Barbara and Suzanne read, feeling fiercely proud of their lyric power. We'd practised our pieces together.

I read about my first visit to Bonefro as an adult, a trip that took thirty-six years. I'd written about experiencing the destructive 2016 earthquake as tremors in Rome and the dreadful symptoms of heatstroke: "Italy was a haunted house, shouting at me to leave."

Later, another participant will comment, "Maybe that was Italy's way of saying, *welcome back, we missed you*."

Standing up and speaking the story given to you alone to tell, in whatever form it appeared (a poem, some fiction, an essay) requires courage. In this way, we compare insights and offer each other collective knowledge. What allows a human to thrive or survive, to endure or flourish? People have always gathered—near fire, away from home, in grief or joy—to share in communal wisdom.

Day 5: Ether

I'm a walking cliché: I hate saying goodbye. This is why the Italian "Ciao" is brilliant, used in greetings and goodbyes; there is much mileage in a word that represents both "see you again soon" and "lovely to run into you." The term simplifies leave-taking. We pack up our belongings and set them on the porch.

After marinating in great company with enthusiastic readers and vocabulary aficionados, finding the right way to say farewell is pressure. I want to be witty, wise, and memorable but feel full of platitudes. I think this can't simply be me but the many pastries I've consumed. Emails and phone numbers are exchanged. Plans are made to reunite in the city. Future writing feedback trades are promised. The retreat was an inspired combination of making new friends, re-imagining the shape of my memoir and reconfirming the value of creativity in an internet-drenched world.

Receding in the rearview mirror, I spot swaying pine trees, the bending riverway, authors hugging and snapping photos.

An auspicious convergence—this opportunity to only connect.

Tessa Floreano

Friuli è nell'anima mia

Gente coming and going all day long, stopping at the wrought-iron gate,
entrance to the aged family compound
Tractors firing up and heading out to plow fields where rows upon
rows of sweet *blave* will soon reach the sun
Light breezes waft in through open windows, where some stop to read,
author books, or let *panettone* rise
I gaze up at the *čhisčhel* on the hill; the occasional toll of the *campanile*
draws parishioners to it like a beacon

Orchards of twisted vines *vecchie e nuove*, providing fruit for winemakers
and wine lovers alike to imbibe galore
Neatly stacked firewood leans on tool sheds, required fodder for the
warmth a *spolâr* or *fogolâr* willingly gives
Lovingly tended *giardini* offer up abundant greens for the mid-day
meal; hungry *contadini* await *cena* at the *tavola*
I draw in calming breaths of country air, some as close as the mountains
of *Carnia*, some as far as *il mare Adriatico*

Dogs and cats wander aimlessly under *il sole di primavera;* happy just
hanging out, eating a treat, or watching life go by
La dolce vita is tranquil in this quaint hamlet of Friuli where the locals
speak *Furlan*, a millennia-old dialect in these parts
Kilometers of terracotta roofs as far as *l'occhio* can see; pre- and
post-earthquake stone houses dot the landscape
I paint the familiar surroundings onto the canvas *della mia memoria;*
photographs a poor substitute for the richness I see

From atop Muris *alla Chiesa di San Giovanni* in Monte, the impressive
winding course of *il Tiliment* cuts a wide swath

Il terremoto wreaked havoc among the long-time residents here, the
fear of it not yet a distant memory for most
In the piazzas, I spot the remnants of the elite mountain infantry
proudly wearing their distinctive *cappello alpino*
I smile, thinking of *il nonno*, one of their own and a survivor, for whom
I am named and take after in large measure

Famiglia in Rive d'Arcano, Pignano, and Mels; they are a journalist,
bankers, nurses, farmers, *un poliziotto,* and a former priest—
The best in their chosen professions, and also La Nicchia, *un piccolo*
ristorante in centro Udine nell'università; *lavori per tutti*
L'albero genealogico: a weighty task, begun in earnest, reaping success
in *parocchia* as far back as the mid-17th century
I come to see and smell and taste and feel and touch all things *friulane*
and *italiane*; *questa regione* is my second home

On the *ponti pedonale* admiring my reflection in the Livenza River in
Sacile, holding no candle to Cividale's infamous Devil's Bridge
Oohing and aahing at the razor-sharp *Dolomiti* as we climb steadily
toward the valley-nestled ski resort of Cortina d'Ampezzo
Mulberry trees stand like sentinels throughout the *comune*, remnants
of the once-thriving silkworm industry, Mom's nemesis
I imagine enrolling in *La Scuola Insieme* in the seaside port of Grado,
immersing myself in the *marilenghe* of my ancestors

O Palmanova, fortress city of yore, your stony star-shaped walls invite
the curious onlooker, forgetting its first settlers—criminals
Roaming the cobbled streets of restored Venzone—*una città*
medievale—ignoring the preserved mummies (crowd pleasers)
Hungry, I long for *cjalsòns*, that sweet and savory specialty, followed
by a thick slice of *gubana* pastry and steaming *tè caldo*
I have started to make *amici* of my own in town, pleasing me to no
end and tenderly will I cultivate those friendships from afar

The *Benandanti* once had tenure here, where suspicion still runs
rampant and *streghe* of all stripes are best consulted at night

While many foreigners come seeking *amore o spiritualità*, the Italians
follow a wayward path trying to live *una vita cattolica*
In the land of the Veneto, *La Serenissima* takes hold of even the most
hardened of hearts, bewitchingly I might add
I, too, sought solace in Venezia's crumbling *palazzi* and tourist-infested
piazze until Friuli beckoned me back for good

Scrittori have sway here: Ippolito Nievo, poet-as-hermit tucked away
in Colloredo, Pier Paolo Pasolini in the bosom of Casarsa
Mauro Corona in the hinterlands, Umberto Saba and Italo Svevo
holding court with James Joyce in the Hapsburg enclave of Trieste
Brovada, frico con Montasio, trota, or *gnocchi* on the menu when they
dropped their quills long enough for sustenance
I pay them tribute from my side of the Pacific, toasting in absentia
with '*il rit del tajùt*': *Schioppettino*, *Ramandolo*, or a little *grappa*

Traipsing over to the knives of Maniago and the roar of jet engines
above me to observe American *soldati* at Aviano's base
Then, the behemoth chair rising over Manzano—a relic of the many
one-industry towns here, forced out by overseas competitors
Reminders of the *pantofole* factory in Majano where Dad used to work;
closed now, the buildings decrepit yet looming large
I maintain hope, for the resiliency of the Furlan people is legendary,
spanning centuries; they will live on and rise again, higher still

The tambourine performances in the ancient borgo of Cordovât in
Palazzo Cecchini during the Night of the Peasants; nary a revolt
Il territorio di Coseano, a medieval municipality, its stately *ville* sit
reverentially on either side of the square, like grand dames
A few stray *zingare* parade themselves with outstretched hands, an
eyesore, or worse, nuisance to passersby and citizens alike
I crave *le tradizioni folkloristiche* the rituals of yesteryear, the *sagre*
held in every corner of this province, rotating place to place

Fiats, Alfa Romeos, even a Ferrari or two, pass us on the *autostrada*,
as we traverse the roadways from Tolmezzo to Bassafriulana

Plates of *prosciutto* and *polenta;* Slow Food at the ready at the many
frasche—old woodland bars—we find on our varied travels
Marvelling at *bella arte* at the Villa Manin, *mosaici* at Spilimbergo and
Aquiliea, mass in *il duomo*, and *terme* in Bibione
My passion for *libri* is sated during Pordenonelegge, the festival where
the *litterati* converge and sip prosecco at every turn

Sono canadese e italiana and now, a pseudo-American; I say *mandi* not
ciao, but always *il mio cuore* is here because *San Daniele*
O bel *Sant Denêl* . . . you are in my blood—paternal, maternal, eternal.
San Daniele . . . *ti voglio bene . . . molti baci da me!*

Anna Foschi Ciampolini

L'ingenuità delle margherite

Mi chiamo Rita Vallesi e oggi è il mio compleanno. Forse l'ultimo dei tanti già trascorsi ma questo in fondo non mi preoccupa troppo. Sapete chi si è ricordato di me per mandarmi gli auguri? Sono state soprattutto le grandi aziende proprietarie dei negozi dove di solito faccio acquisti, suadenti nel definirmi una preziosa cliente e mi hanno mandato buoni sconto da spendere per ulteriori compere. Non sarò ingiusta, anche un paio di anziane amiche hanno proposto di andare insieme a prendere un caffè per celebrare e ne sono stata felice perché se guardo indietro alla lunga galleria di amicizie e amori fioriti e disseccati in tutti questi anni, o peggio ancora, se ripenso ai miei cari ormai tutti sepolti dall'altra parte del mondo, avere ancora qualcuno che ti è vicino è consolante. Non mi lamento, senz'altro c'è gente che sta peggio di me, ma la verità è che non riesco ad abituarmi ad essere vecchia, anzi, scusatemi, *senior*, un termine molto più garbato. Ci sono dei vantaggi ad essere senior, pochi e per piccole cose, ma ci sono. Ad esempio, la mattina poter prendere tutto il tempo che si desidera a sorseggiare il caffè, in vestaglia e pantofole, curiosare alla finestra invece di strangolarsi e precipitarsi al lavoro. Anche l'avere una ricchissima collezione di ricordi e la saggezza di selezionarli, quelli cattivi vanno ricacciati subito, a quelli piacevoli ci si può aggrappare. Parlando di ricordi, e vi assicuro ne ho una miniera, proprio qualche giorno fa, mentre ero in palestra a pedalare sulla bicicletta del *Rec Centre,* involontariamente e senza un perché ho rivissuto un momento della mia infanzia, con immagini nitide come fossero davvero gli anni '50 e io fossi a Firenze, ai giardini della Fortezza da Basso dove mio nonno o la tata Teresa mi portavano a giocare. Noi bambini ci divertivamo con poco, giocando a nascondino o correndo sui prati della Fortezza dove giovani coppie abbracciate si stendevano al sole fra le margherite. In quegli anni, molte ragazze lasciavano la campagna per lavorare in città come domestiche per farsi la dote, mentre i ragazzi dovevano partire per il servizio militare obbligatorio e facevano la "naja" in regioni lontane dalla propria, ovvero se eri del Sud ti mandavano al Nord e viceversa. Era inevitabile che quelle due solitudini si incontrassero, che ragazze e ragazzi, spaesati e lontani dalle proprie radici, cercassero un conforto nelle braccia dell'altro. Guardavo quei corpi avvinghiati sul prato, quelle bocche ansiose e sentivo la gente ridacchiare: "fanno all'amore!" Non ne capivo molto ma pensavo che il mondo era pieno di amore. Sì, credevo davvero che tutti si amassero con tutto il cuore e questo amore traboccasse sui prati, dietro i portoni dei palazzi e dappertutto. Non ci sarebbe stato nulla di male in quella ingenuità infantile se non avessi continuato per tutta la vita a voler credere che il mondo fosse pieno di amore e che l'amore, l'amicizia fossero lo scopo dell'esistenza di ognuno di noi. Lo so e lo sapete che non è vero ma preferisco credere ai ricordi o alle illusioni piuttosto che soffermarmi sulle tante delusioni subite o quelle che forse io stessa ho causato.

Quando sono arrivata in anni lontani in questa città d'acqua e di alberi, un puntino sulla carta geografica chiamato Vancouver, ho compreso l'assoluta necessità dell'amicizia perché qui non conoscevo niente e nessuno. Quando ti senti sola e nuda, anche i piccoli gesti da parte di sconosciuti, di gente che non si incontrerà mai più, ti rimangono dentro. Come quel portiere anziano e corpulento che lavorava al motel dove capitammo appena arrivati come *landed immigrants*. Era la vigilia di Pasqua e non avevamo nessuno con cui trascorrere la festa. Il portiere venne a invitarci: "Venite a pranzo a casa mia, abito qui vicino. Siete benvenuti, abbiamo birra fresca e starete in compagnia. Appena arrivati in Canada non è giusto passare la festa da soli." O il passante che mi sorresse e mi offrì un caffè quella volta che in una strada del centro d'improvviso mi sentii quasi svenire. Piccoli sprazzi di luce. La stessa luce, ma più intensa e duratura, che ha accompagnato le poche, vere amicizie che ho incontrato. Per questo voglio raccontarvene almeno qualcuna. Vi chiederete perché insisto a parlare di amicizia invece che di amore, visto che in fondo sono sentimenti quasi identici. Non lo so, forse perché dall'amore ci si aspetta di più, ma anche l'amore ha i suoi inganni e da quelle ferite non si guarisce.

Ho incontrato Liliane solo una volta, a un caffè sulla West Broadway durante una sua visita a Vancouver per partecipare a una conferenza.

Scoprimmo una comunione di spiriti, una magica alchimia e riconobbi in lei una sorella, una guida che apriva e condivideva la ricchezza della sua anima senza riserve. Non la vidi più ma iniziammo una corrispondenza che durò fino alla sua morte. Fu Liliane a incoraggiarmi a scrivere, a infondermi fiducia di poter liberare qualcosa del mio vissuto attraverso la parola. Liliane era una donna assorta, intensa, che viveva l'esistenza su un piano di profonda spiritualità, con gioia, con intensità olistica e panteista. Era luce.

Non potevamo essere più diverse, io e Adriana. Lei era dotata di una energia senza fine, scalava montagne, si inerpicava per sentieri perigliosi, viaggiava avventurosamente in paesi lontani e malsicuri, niente la fermava. Veniva da un piccolo paese in Toscana, la incontrai poco dopo il mio arrivo a Vancouver e stringemmo un'amicizia lunga quaranta anni. Nei miei momenti più oscuri, l'ancora di salvezza mi venne dalla sua profonda bontà d'animo, dalla sua vocazione ad aiutare e anche dalle sue sferzate volutamente crude. La pensavo immortale ma in quella stanza del St. Paul's Hospital lei combatteva con furia una battaglia perduta. Ogni giovedì andavo a trovarla e quella mattina mi richiamò mentre stavo già avviandomi alla porta. Mi strinse forte la mano, ci guardammo per un lungo momento, senza parole.

Aida insegnava *Social Sciences* a Douglas College. L'avevo conosciuta durante un incontro dedicato a donne immigrate. Iniziai a frequentare la sua casa dove viveva con il marito, un uomo intriso di lucido pessimismo che prima del loro esilio era stato ai vertici del potere nel loro paese. Furono una presenza importante: in quelle conversazioni cominciai a costruire una conoscenza più profonda e critica della società canadese e di quello che veniva allora chiamato *the vertical mosaic.* Li rividi dopo molti anni, poco prima che scoppiasse l'epidemia di Covid-19 del 2020. Lui era confinato a letto, lei faticava a muoversi e mi offrì dei dolcetti comperati, scusandosi di non aver potuto fare la *muhallabia.* Gli anni trascorsi avevano inflitto loro pesanti limitazioni fisiche che sopportavano con dignità ma l'acutezza intellettuale, la lucida capacità di analisi erano rimaste intatte.

Non so se qualcuno un giorno scriverà due righe anche per me. Non lo nascondo, mi farebbe anche piacere. *Non omnis moriar,* non morirei interamente. Sarebbe una prova che per qualcuno ho contato qualcosa. Io non ho figli né famiglia, non lascio niente dietro di me, solo quanto ho fatto di buono nel mio lavoro e le storie vere o meno che ho scritto e che nessuno ha letto ma va bene lo stesso, scrivere mi ha aiutato a vivere. E poi, sapete cosa vi dico? Anche se non succederà, non importa. Sui prati di margherite, in qualsiasi altra dimensione essi esistano, forse tornerò a correre come la bambina di ieri o riprenderò le conversazioni interrotte con le persone amate.

Lucia Gagliese

The Lonely Goatherd Redux

Prologue. This morning, I finally might manage to write about Albert and Donny. The idea came yesterday, watching The Sound of Music. No spoilers. I'll only say it's a musical starring Julie Andrews set during World War II. There are nuns, Nazis, crypts, singing kids, and yodelling marionettes. Nonna, Ma, and I used to watch it on TV every year. I know all the songs, always sing along. Yesterday, mid-whiskers-on-kittens, I decided to try writing favourite things. The first is Holy Name School putting on *The Sound of Music.* Fifty years ago. Unbelievable.

Setting. Donny, Albert, and I were classmates from junior kindergarten to Grade 8. It was Canadian multiculturalism's heyday, and most students, including us, were children of immigrants. We'd have these multicultural pot-luck lunches. I brought lasagna, Albert spaetzle casserole, and Donny shepherd's pie. Our moms warned against strange food, guaranteeing that was all we ate.

See this picture? Eighth grade. Kids form a triangle up the schoolyard stairs. Here's Donny and me on the bottom step, the base. That's Albert, alone, at the top, or as he'd say, vertex. Last summer, I sat where I sat in that picture, tried to write about Albert and Donny. I was thirteen again, reliving schoolyard games, fights, laughs. Impossible to write. Today may be better with *The Sound of Music.*

Cast. The marionette show features the song, "The Lonely Goatherd," about said goatherd yodelling for love, connection. In the movie, the final stanza is a boy-goat yodelling for a girl-goat. That's the stanza we used in our play. Donny and I played the goats. I don't remember auditioning. Probably, the teachers assigned us. Ma, Papà, and Nonna were proud, although Ma wished I had a starring role. Truth is, we only got our parts because we were the smallest second graders.

See the class pictures? Donny and me, sitting in the front row, grade after grade. In the upper grades, when he was the only boy small enough for the front, he stood next to us, where the teacher usually stands. My favourite is Grade 7. That's me, sitting at the end of the row. That's Donny standing beside me. See how he's leaning towards me, like he's just whispered something? He has. That's why I'm laughing, mouth wide open, eyes crinkled shut.

And that's Albert, the tallest boy, always standing back row centre. He was tall enough to play a soldier, to march with the older boys, including my big brother and Donny's, too. I suddenly realize they cast the blond, blue-eyed boy whose parents emigrated from Germany as a Nazi, made him wear a swastika. Wish I could ask him about that.

Anyway. Point is, Albert was tall, and Donny was small. The reason's irrelevant (genetic disorder). Today, the play's the thing.

<u>Rehearsal.</u> We waited in the gym for our turn. Donny, in his fuzzy goat-body, and Albert, in his uniform, played war with wooden rifles. I sat cross-legged on the floor, in my fuzzy goat-body, reading (Beverly Cleary, probably).

"Goats!" Miss Stables snapped her fingers. I marked my page, grabbed my goat-head, coarse brown face, floppy ears, tan horns, pink ribbon. Donny dropped the rifle, donned his goat-head, like mine except for a goatee and green Alpine hat. We climbed onto the stage, took our places behind the heavy blue curtain. Me stage left, Donny right. The music started. "Enter goats!"

Finally, our moment had arrived. We marionette-walked from behind the curtains. We'd practiced for weeks in the classroom, schoolyard, walking home, jagging our arms and legs as if controlled from above by puppeteers. Albert coached us, made sure we were perfect. At home, my family pleaded with me, in vain, to stop marionette-walking and yodelling.

"Where is your head?" Miss Stables pressed stop on the tape deck. "This is a dress rehearsal."

"I can't breathe with it." I held out the head.

"Can't sing neither," Donny mumbled. "Can't open my mouth. It's too tight."

"Heads on this minute! Snap, snap." She pointed off stage, pressed play. "Enter goats!"

At centre stage, we faced each other. On cue, Donny tried to yodel. A muffled groan.

Miss Stables pressed stop. "I've had quite enough of this nonsense."

She rewound, pressed play. Donny inhaled, tried again. Even worse, a groaning yodel. We looked down to hide our laughter.

"Girl goat!" I tried, but between laughing and the tight mask, I couldn't get a good breath, let alone yodel. Miss Stables stopped the tape. "What is wrong with you?"

I yanked off the head. "Can't breathe."

"Me neither." Donny worked his off.

"Give them here." She snatched them away, sparks dancing between our fingers. "Bodies, too." We stood in shorts and undershirts. "You will stay after school tomorrow. And you will rehearse until you get it right. No more excuses. No Italian class or other foolishness. *This* is the priority. Tell your parents." Now, I'd protest, but then I was seven and Miss Stables was scary. Besides, my parents always sided with the teachers.

"Static electricity from your hair," Albert explained the sparks later. Back then, everybody thought he'd be a scientist. Instead, he became an artisan woodworker like his dad. This desk, slant-topped secretary with little drawers, cubbyholes, shelves, Albert made it, his last present, to celebrate me quitting my hospital job to write. "A proper writer," he said, "needs a proper writing desk."

A digression. Forgive me. Too many memories. I tell one and remember another. Ma does that, too. Her stories branch and weave through Italy, Canada, and generations of family and *paesani*.

Where was I?

Opening Night. Costumes fixed. Gym packed. On cue, we marionette-walked to our spots. We must not make mistakes. We must impress our parents, teachers, friends. I scanned the audience for Ma, Papà, Nonna, but beyond the spotlight, only darkness.

The music started. I faced Donny. On his cue, he yodeled, "*Lay-ee-odl lay-ee-odl lay-hee-hoo*?"

"*Lay-ee-odl lay-ee-odl-ooo!*" I responded, forgetting Miss Stables' direction to "be flirty."

We marionette-walked to centre stage. A toy baby-goat dropped from the rafters and thumped onto the stage. I jumped away from it. The audience laughed. I stared at the baby-goat, wondering what to do. The refrain repeated, our cue to dance. Panicked, I stooped, grabbed the baby-goat by the horn, and marionette-walked toward Donny. We marionette-danced, baby-goat swinging between us. Here's a blurry yearbook picture of that dance. The song ended. The audience burst into applause. They kept applauding as I dropped the baby-goat and we exited, marionette-walking, stage right. The curtain closed.

"Hear that?"

I pulled off the goat-head. "Sounds like thunder."

<u>Epilogue.</u> Years later, Donny said that was the moment he became a singer. "A star was born. Nobody'd ever listened to me like that. It was the first time. Still get that feeling, can float on it forever. When I sing, someone finally hears me."

I heard Donny sing many times. That's what he did, Irish folk music mostly, in noisy pubs. Always, he closed with *Turaloora,* his family song, learned from his father. Listening made me wish for a family song. Our closest might be *Tu scendi dalle stelle*, sung every Christmas Eve at midnight. Really, only Ma, Papà, and Nonna sang. We kids mumbled along, eyeing our unopened presents. Ma and Papà still sing it when their grandchildren place Baby Jesus in Ma's *presepio.*

Another digression. A distraction, probably, from telling about my favourite Donny performance. Favourite but sad. *Ave Maria,* when he sang it at Albert's funeral (leukemia). I'd never heard him sing how he sang that day. Love woven with loss.

Donny's funeral (multiple-organ failure) was almost exactly three years later. Same church, our parish church, also called Holy Name. It's where together we received first communion, confession, confirmation, and probably, eventually, where my own funeral will be.

I tried writing there, too. Father Leo gave me permission. I lit a candle, sat where I sat for their funerals. The longing was too intense, I couldn't write.

When the friends die, when the heart aches,
When the words won't come,
I simply remember Julie Andrews' advice ...

Another favorite thing. Donny's album. That's the music you hear. This is *Turaloora*. Seems my writing needed Albert's desk, Donny's voice.

How to end this? Reference the movie, the yodelling? Predictable. Describe Donny and Albert as brother-friends alive in my heart? Sentimental. No matter, the ending will arrive. Today, I wrote this draft, full of digressions and dips into darkness. A start. Another day. I'll revise it into an approximation, a fictionalization of grief-tinted nostalgia.

Time for lunch. I won't leave you (or me) feeling sad. Maybe one last favourite thing. This picture. I took it, gave Donny and Albert framed copies one Christmas. We're twelve. Our end-of-grade-seven trip to Sainte-Marie Among the Hurons, an excavated and reconstructed seventeenth-century village. Kids crowd around a wigwam. Albert's at the back, towering over everyone. Donny's in front of him, on tiptoes, turning towards Albert, saying something, making Albert smile as he looks right at me.

Connie Guzzo-McParland

Up Côte-des-Neiges Road: Chapter One of a Novel-in-progress

This is the first chapter of a semi-autobiographical novel-in-progress, still untitled, set in a beauty salon in 1966–67 Montreal, exploring the search for both personal and national identity during the heady period of Montreal's Expo 67 and political unrest in Quebec.

Of all my trepidations while waiting for the 165 Côte-des-Neiges, fear of a mailbox bomb explosion had not been among them. It was mid-October, but it felt like winter weather already, and I shivered in my light fall coat. As I paced back and forth to keep warm together with a crowd of other passengers waiting impatiently for the bus, I did not pay any attention to the ubiquitous Canada Post mailbox nearby, anxious as I was for what awaited me up the hill named after Montreal's infamous snows.

I had spent a sleepless night stewing in my own bile after having spoken to my friend Antoinette. She and two of my other friends had begun their training at St. Joseph's Teacher's College. If I had had my way, that same bus I was waiting for would be taking me downtown to join them. Instead, I was headed to meet my brother at an empty store location, a former laundromat that would soon become our own *salon de coiffure pour femme*—not a prosaic little beauty parlour, mind you, according to him, but a *salon de haute coiffure*, appropriately named, Louis Haute Coiffure. Well, my brother was still called Luigi at home, but on Côte-des-Neiges Road, he had become French.

"Finally, we'll be our own bosses," he had promised me.

Change or the prospect of change always excited me, but this new venture left me cold. I was only eighteen years old and couldn't have been less excited about starting a business in partnership with my brother and in an unfamiliar part of town. Waiting to board the bus had felt as fretful as when in the summer, I had crossed the American border for a day trip to a beach in Plattsburg, and a stern border agent questioned my name, my citizenship, and place of birth. The information was written on my passport, yet he stared at me longer than it felt necessary. Did he doubt I was a Canadian citizen because the town where I was born was unpronounceable to him? Or was the identity of someone who showed both Canadian and Italian credentials too confusing to process? Truth be told, at times it was confusing to me too. I was now venturing into yet another new surrounding and an unwanted family obligation.

I had remained in bed in an almost semi-comatose state that morning while listening to my brother complain to our mother that he was leaving without me and I'd have to take the bus. "It's half her business. She'll be working there too. She can show a bit of interest."

When my mother came into my room to coax me out of bed, I mumbled, "What's the rush? I won't be doing anything there today, anyway. I'll take the bus," and snuggled tightly under the blanket. Louis then left in his second-hand 1963 Chevrolet bought a few months earlier. He was to be handed the keys to the store and he had lined up a plumber and an electrician to get quotes on the renovations. He had wanted me to go with him and look over the space, but I had already seen a rough draft of the floor plan he had drawn based on his first visit there without me.

"This is his dream more than mine," I whispered as my mother left the room. If she heard me, she didn't respond.

As I got dressed an hour later and then walked along Delormier Street where we lived, I could not shake off the sense of incapacity and futility I often got after one of my recurrent dreams, the type where you're stuck in one place while trying to run away from someone or something. I hopped on the 92 Jean-Talon bus, still pondering why I was going somewhere I did not want to go, yet being unable to speak up for myself. I was too much of a people pleaser and compromised too easily. That's how I explained it to myself. Or was mine some psychological disorder, this need to comply with other people's wishes and then feeling resentment? The uneasiness about the somewhat imposed new phase in my life enveloped me like a dark cloak that weighted me down yet did nothing to keep me warm. I had succumbed to my family's wishes, and could not turn back.

With the cold now biting into me, I decided to walk up Côte-des-Neiges Road, or at least partway, to warm up and release all that bottled-up tension. I walked to the corner, and as the traffic light turned green, I started crossing the street. Suddenly, an ear-piercing blast burst out above the sound of the car traffic—a sudden, deafening boom accompanied by a blaze of light, like fireworks, followed by a hair-raising silence. I stopped in the middle of the street and looked back. A few yards away to the left of the bus stop, where a red mailbox had been secured to the sidewalk, what looked like tiny metal shards and paper fragments were flying up in the air and falling onto the heads and clothes of those standing closest to the bus stop. How unnatural! The flying debris looked like a sudden shower of dirty snowflakes. It missed me by mere feet. I stood still for a few instants, then my survival instincts kicked in and I ran across the rest of Jean-Talon Street. Once on the other side, I looked back and watched other witnesses run away in different directions, furiously brushing debris from their clothes. One woman lay on the ground, with a dog circling her as if wanting to help her get up. Cars had stopped at all intersections and the traffic stood ghostly still. I remained glued in place stunned and confused. Should I run back to help the woman get up? Then I saw a man run to the woman. Luckily the mailbox that had been blown to pieces had been a few yards away from the people waiting for the bus, and behind it was a park, so it didn't seem as if anyone was seriously hurt, except for the woman on the ground who had probably been walking her dog and was nearest to the mailbox as the bomb detonated.

Fearing other explosions, I started running up Côte-des-Neiges Road past an underpass. Along the way, I saw pedestrians stop in their tracks, looking around for the source of the noise, which had come from the other side of the underpass, and asking questions of the people running uphill.

"*Qu'est-ce qui se passe?*"

"*C'est une bombe?*"

I kept answering, nodding my head, "*Oui, une bombe, une bombe.*" Finally, I stopped at the next bus stop, joining in the conversations of other nervous-looking commuters.

"*C'est sans doute le FLQ,*" someone said. It had to be the work of the FLQ. Most of the other people nodded in agreement. How many explosions had there been since the early 60s when the *Front de libération du Québec*–a Quebec terrorist group, fought to establish an independent Quebec through violent means? There had been a long series of mini-bomb incidents that had filled the newspapers and created angst amongst locals everywhere. Could this be a message to the mostly affluent Anglophone residents of the charming Town of Mount Royal that the FLQ was still a force to contend with? Montreal was gearing up for an international world's fair in the coming spring, Expo 67, a global gathering meant to put the city on the world map. Was the FLQ recharging its forces to get world attention for its cause? A lot of speculation was thrown around at the bus stop by those standing nervously and impatiently around me, but all attributed the act to the FLQ.

Soon, police cars, an ambulance, and a firetruck sped downhill, sirens blaring. Then, the uphill traffic stopped while cars driving downhill piled up bumper to bumper unable to move. It seemed police had stopped all traffic at the five-corner intersection.

It became clear to me that no bus would be passing by anytime soon, so I started walking amidst the honking of cars whose drivers had yet to know the reason for the traffic gridlock. The street was one of the most commercial and congested thoroughfares of the city. The walk became more strenuous the further up I climbed. I had to stop a few times to catch my breath, wondering if it could be another one of my dreams where I'm running but going nowhere. But the street looked all too real—a tangible urban hill made of cement, storefronts, and commercial buildings. Oddly even in the confused and fearful state I was in, I mused that the street had been named after not merely neige/snow, but neiges/snows. I imagined that in the deep of winter when it was still farmland and devoid of its current tall grey buildings, its trees and bushes must have howled in the gales of Quebec winter snow storms. In the hilly town where I was born, it rarely snowed and when it did for a few hours, we children jumped for joy.

Since our arrival to Canada, eight years earlier, my family lived in the east end of Montreal, and rarely had I ventured west of Boulevard St. Laurent—a street everyone called the Main, which served as the dividing line between east and west, French and English, rich and poor. I was neither English nor French and had never considered myself dirt poor, though I had had to quit high school early on my family's insistence to become a hairstylist and earn my keep. Before that, I had spent the first ten years of my life in a hill-top Calabrian village which could be traversed from tip to tail in less than thirty minutes and no one doubted that I belonged there.

As I walked up the hill, I reconstructed that morning's itinerary before the explosion and remembered the sensation of wonderment I had felt after the 92 had sped past Boulevard St. Laurent and the blue-collar neighbourhood of Park Extension, and veered through the residential and bucolic Town of Mount Royal, a town within a city that felt like a village. Treed, luxurious but old-world-quaint, and a reality far apart from the one I was living in, it had reminded me of the make-believe Victorian-era snow-covered scenes depicted on Christmas greeting cards we used to receive from Canada. It's how I had imagined life in Canada, living in one of those gracious houses, homey and warm, with the snow covering the evergreen trees on the lawns, enveloping the homes like a cozy blanket in the stillness of the night. Instead, on traffic-heavy Delormier Street, the minuscule lawns of my apartment building betrayed the lack of care that neither renters nor building owners could dispense. A row of duplexes owned and inhabited by other Italians flaunted tomatoes and green vegetables in their backyards in the summer, and the only visible flowers spurted from zucchini plants. My mother, brother, and I had moved to a minuscule unit of the apartment building after my father's sudden death which happened merely three years after our arrival to Canada.

After what seemed a sightseeing detour, the bus had swerved back onto Jean-Talon and dropped me on the five-cornered traffic-heavy intersection, another world apart from what I had just ogled with wistful eyes. And then the mailbox went up in the air, and I ran up the hill!

I was still only halfway to my destination. When I eyed a red Canada Post mailbox in the distance, I instinctively ran across the street, navigating amid the bumper-to-bumper cars blaring their horns, the blast of the detonation still in my ears, my fear and anger rising.

Exhausted and out of breath, I finally reached the semi-basement of an apartment building, cornered by Côte St. Catherine and Côte-des-Neiges roads. I was further reminded of the area's connection to snow when I saw the image of Snow White and her dwarfs reproduced on the neon sign—*Blanche Neige Restaurant*–next to the former laundromat. On setting foot in the empty locale, I found Louis in animated conversation with a heavy-set man and a miniskirt-clad woman smoking a cigarette and holding a coffee cup in her other hand.

Louis ran towards me and hugged me, "I've been worried sick about you. Did you get caught in the explosion in TMR, near the bus stop?"

"Yes," I blurted out, "I just escaped a bomb explosion to get here. Happy?"

Louis made the sign of the cross. "Lucky you! A good omen! Thank you, God."

I wanted to laugh. My brother and I saw things so differently!

Then he turned to the couple, "*M. et Mme Gagnon, voici ma petite sœur.*" They were the caretakers of the building I had been hearing about already.

"*Mais oui, vous êtes bien chanceuse!*" Mme Gagnon said extending her hand. "*Bienvenue a Côte-des-Neiges.*"

I shook hands with the caretakers. My throat felt parched, and I was exhausted from the running and long uphill walk, but I managed a smile. If a bomb explosion was my first sign of welcome, what else could I expect in the days to come from this noisy, dusty, treeless, cement hill?

Nicole Haldoupis

Two Eyes, Shining

i

Toni walked into the first-floor bedroom and saw two dimes on the floor near the door frame. She panicked for a moment, wondering if the coins were a sign of ghosts, her dead loved ones sending a message. She left the dimes on the floor and stripped the bed, threw everything in a pile to the right of the dimes. She carried the pile of bedclothes down to the basement, stuffed them into the washer, and started the load. She walked up to the second floor, to the second dirty room, and opened the door—two dimes sat on the floor a few feet in. She blinked and tried to remain calm, touched her palms to her thighs and took two deep breaths. Perhaps both guests had two extra dimes that fell out of their pockets, both near the door? Toni did not look at the dimes again, stripped the bedclothes, tossing the sheets into a pile close to the bathroom door away from where the silver pieces sat, then gathered up all the linens in her arms, giving the dimes a wide berth. She scurried up the stairs to the third floor.

Toni walked back down to the first-floor room after the sun went down. She intended to pick up the coins. This was the last thing left to do in each room before they were clean, ready for new guests. She kept her eyes low through the second floor. She opened the door and switched on the light. Quickly scanned the room, which was still empty. She looked down at the coins. Two eyes shining up at her, each piece heads up. She turned off the light and ran back upstairs.

ii

Toni bit her nails. A splotch of red polish was left on only one pointer, the rest chipped off into the floorboards, the carpet, the shower. She tried desperately to scratch off the last bit cemented into the grooves, not allowing her the luxury of a new colour. She would go to the store to buy remover if she could get out of bed and put a shirt on.

Her plants withered around her, bits of fern leaves littering the shelf they sat on. If she got up, the leaves would crumble under her feet. If she stayed in bed, she would avoid dirtying her feet and therefore her sheets more than they already were.

She flailed her limbs in an attempt to shake out her crumpled blanket and sheets and felt something cold. She paused, pulling the sheets apart more slowly. A shiny dime revealed itself. She hesitated before picking it up and placing it on her bedside table, watching its face glint in the lamplight as she slid into its former place in bed.

Maria Luisa Ierfino-Adornato

Words Of A Writer

I don't remember a time when I didn't love books or reading, just like I don't remember a time that I didn't exist. I loved writing and it was part of my DNA. My parents passed on their folklore and customs. Their dialect was rich in proverbs and parables. The history of Reggio Calabria, Italy (their homeland), was interwoven with ancient Greek mythologies which nurtured my inquisitive imagination. They always had a family story or trilogy to share with us. We devoured every word and we vividly imagined all the dramatic scenes, as though they were describing a play performed at the Centaur Theatre.

There was the real world in Montreal and there was this imaginary world of my forefathers that contained such captivating tales. In the latter world I could create new worlds with powerful word combinations and visions. Words were magical and they danced before me, with coupled letters doing the tango, and syllables soothing my soul. Words had tremendous energy and like eagles, they were sharp, laser-focused, and could soar across the skies. Words would land safely and comfort me through good times and bad. Their aura was ever-present and visible to me. Words would become lifelong companions; partners for life.

In the real world (approximate age, 5), my Godparents gave me a 'Suzy Smart' doll. This doll was no ordinary one. The gift came with a blackboard and a desk. Suzy Smart was a bright student and a quick study. I would pull the magical strings and she would spell out loud and simultaneously write the words in a mechanical fashion on the cosmic blackboard. I would pretend that I was her teacher and I would teach Suzy Smart to read. Here was someone I could totally share my passion for learning and for books with! She never interrupted me, and I could speak freely and fluently. Suzy Smart had all the time on the planet for me, in my microscopic fantasy world.

I also remember acting as a librarian (approximate age, 10) when I would play with my siblings. If they wanted to borrow a book of mine, they had to sign an index card that I had prepared, stating that they would return the book by such and such a date. I would ask them to summarize the book to determine whether they actually read it. They played along grudgingly and thought I was severe. I chuckle in retrospect and sincerely hope that I didn't ruin their image of books and of reading. This librarian business was serious and entertaining for me at the same time, and the books were absolutely sacred. I was careful in handling each book and I took great pleasure in actually reading every line. Once I started reading a book, I had to finish it at lightning speed. Of course, my brothers and sisters enjoyed teasing me about my obsessive reading and meticulous word-smithing. Yes, they called me a bookworm and said that someday my children would be born with glasses. (Not I nor my daughter wear glasses to this day, as of the writing of this story-LOL ... but definitely, both of us are avid readers and writers).

Books throughout my life, were absolutely priceless to me and I looked upon them with the deepest reverence. I was ecstatic when my parents bought me my first typewriter and set of Encyclopedia. The feeling was better than getting your first car (approximate age, 16), in my estimation. I will never forget that moment. It validated my desire to become a writer and it was my dream come true.

In all those types of books I quietly escaped and spent countless hours travelling the world in awe of every country and fascinated by Greek mythology. In particular I enjoyed the pastoral English world that Jane Austen opened up to me. I appreciated the work of Charles Dickens and was sensitive to the 'tale of two cities,' the rich and the poor, especially the latter, who were struggling from generation to generation, always hungry, destitute and discriminated against. They suffered all the injustices of society, but I believed that the meek would inherit the earth. The world needed the great writers who would acknowledge their existence and lift up their spirits. Words have power. The writers and artists, are the unacknowledged legislators of the world, according to Shelley and others. A great writer holds up the mirror of society and is a trail-blazer. Often times the writer is banished for telling the truth or for opposing war and lives in exile or a self-imposed exile. Great works of art have been created from silence and isolation. The words of a writer are mighty. I would lose myself in a novel for hours on end. I learned so many universal truths from the classics and literature.

I loved the 'portrait of the artist as a young man' and its stream of consciousness, by James Joyce. I admired the Italian landscape (as well as the depictions of paradise), through the writings of Dante Alighieri and I mourned his exile in Ravenna. I treasured the French countryside and *Les Misérables* as depicted by Victor Hugo. My love of Canadian history and literature blossomed and when I travelled across our vast nation, it felt like **déjà** vu. I had lived every life possible, every adventure, and I had travelled everywhere, through space and time. Those books were my salvation in a home where I was lovingly overprotected and where house and school were my strict boundaries. Those books were my escape into the multiverse.

I was determined to write my own books one day. Eventually, I had stories to tell too. Relatives told me when I was a pre-teen, that I would be a good teacher. Career choices seemed limiting as a young adult, and no one in our circle was a writer, but I was not deterred. I knew that one way or another, writing would be my anchor. It was the medium most natural to me, to express myself. I was not as comfortable speaking, because I was basically an introvert. I was sixteen when I declared to the world that I wanted to be a writer. My full-time career would be totally different, but I always kept writing to stay grounded and connected.

I stopped to think about who encouraged me to write. Yes, there were the English teachers who helped me discover and acknowledge my talent. They supported me from a scholarly and clinical perspective. 'Write properly, check spelling, grammar and syntax,' I heard them say, but the poets were the ones who truly fired me up. I recall with excitement, the poetry readings of such towering rock stars like, Margaret Atwood, Leonard Cohen and Irving Layton. I admired Leonard Cohen's musical talent and the fact that he started writing poetry before he became a performing artist; how cool that he could hypnotize us with poetry and with song!

For me, no other concert could ever compare. My love for poetry emerged as a result, and I secretly wished to be like the literary giants of the time; except that I was excessively shy. I would picture myself on stage, singing Bob Dylan-like songs such as "Like a Rolling Stone," so meaningful and deep I thought, but it was not me, just my alter-ego. I continued writing for my own sanity, despite having an exciting career that monopolized my time and existence. One lifetime is not enough.

My admiration for the written word and for history remains unchanged. I would still like every person in the world, to borrow a proverbial library book, to learn from it, to laugh or cry, and to treat it with total deference; (approximate age, 65), and I would still act as that old-school librarian, even though I have officially 'retired,' but not from writing or travelling ... one can only watch so much Netflix!

Where would we be without history and all the stories of mankind? Where would writers be without the written word? The written word is sacred and the history of the world is the memory of our collective past experience. I believe in everyone's story, not just the story of the literate, the social media influencers, the powerful, the billionaires and the elite. Social media is important but so is oral tradition, popular folklore, the family story and even the cave drawings. The written word is for everyone and is meant to be inclusive. Every medium of expression is priceless and every individual has a preferred and distinct voice. I love writing and it is part of my DNA. Let's celebrate each other's story!

I thank the AICW for being my SHERPA and cheerleader as I continued to write throughout the decades. Congratulations on your 40th anniversary and for promoting all of our stories. I am so grateful to you, for being my Suzy Smart, always listening to our voices without interruption and providing literary spaces for our free expression.

Diana Iuele-Colilli & Christine Sansalone

La lezione di Zoom

"La lezione di Zoom" is one of the vignettes in the play *Zoomiamoci* that Diana Iuele-Colilli and Christine Sansalone wrote and staged virtually in March of 2021 in the midst of the Covid-19 pandemic. It illustrates the touching relationship between grandparents and grandchildren and the lengths that people had to go in order to stay connected with loved ones during the global pandemic. One of the main goals of the plays written by Iuele-Colilli and Sansalone is the formal documentation of *Italiese*, the patois that Italian immigrants created when they landed in Canada. Therefore, the languages used in all the plays are Italian, Calabrese dialect, English, and *Italiese.* All *Italiese* terms are *italicized.* These terms have been spelled with the Italian alphabet and should be read as such.

La lezione di Zoom

La scena si apre nella cucina di Giulia che prepara il pranzo per suo marito, Matteo. Squilla il telefono.

Giulia: (*strillando al marito*) Mattè! Prendi il telefono che io sono *bisì*.
Matteo: (*gridando*) Sono al gabinetto. Rispondi tu!
Giulia: (*seccata, asciugandosi le mani*) *Gésos Cráisti*! Devo sempre fare tutto io! (*risponde al telefono in maniera brusca*) *Alό*?! (*pausa, cambia a un tono dolce*) Oh, Ivano, bello di nonna, come stai? Come stanno mamma e papà? (*pausa*) *Notubéddi, notubéddi*! (*pausa*) Veramente, Nonno Matteo *mécca mí crési*, ma *uaraiugonadú*? È la mia croce. (*viene interrotta da Matteo*)
Matteo (*urlando*) Giù, chi è?
Giulia: (*gridando al marito*) È Ivano. (*ritornando al nipote*) *Só*, bello di nonna, *uazzaméra*? Perché *iu cólla mi*? *Somatínga rónghi*?

(*pausa*) *Iú néve cólla mí* la mattina presto!(*pausa*) Una *sorpráisa*?! (*pausa*) *Formí*?! (*pausa*) Ah, *formí* e nonno! (*pausa*) *Dázza náisi*! (*pausa*) *Ochéi, ái cólla ímma*. (*gridando al marito*) Mattè, esci da quel gabinetto maledetto che Ivano ha una *sorpráisa* per noi.

Matteo: (*gridando*) Vengo, vengo!

Giulia: (*gridando*) *Ariáppa*! (*ritorna al nipote*) Tuo nonno, quando va al gabinetto ci mette cent'anni! *Í técca forévera*! (*pausa*) Come *livalónna*? È la verità! Passa giornate intere in quel gabinetto!

Matteo: (*entrando e interrompendo la moglie*) È l'unico posto nella casa dove sto in pace!

Giulia: Smettila di fare lo *smárti*. C'è Ivano al telefóno e dice che è qua sotto con una *sorpráisa* per noi. (*pausa e poi ritorna al telefono*) Come devo fare? (*pausa*) Ah, *ochéi* (*al marito*) Ha detto di prendere una *baschétta* e mandarla giù che ci ha portato qualcosa. (*al nipote)* *Ochéi* bello di nonna. La mando adesso.

Matteo: (*seccato prende un cestino con una fune attacata dal tavolo*) *Aghénni*, con sta *baschétta*!

Matteo si avvicina alla finestra.

Matteo: (*avviandosi*) *Ochéi*, ma vieni pure tu che io ho mal di schiena e non ce la faccio a tirare su. *Ái brécchi mái bécca* l'altra volta a tirare su tutta quella maledetta farina.

Giulia: (*sarcastica*) Come siamo delicati!! (*Matteo esce*)

La scena si sposta alla finestra della sala da pranzo. Matteo apre la finestra e manda giù il cestino al nipote.

Matteo: (*gridando*) Ivà, ti mando la *baschétta*. (*gesticolando con le mani*) Spostati altrimenti ti prendo alla testa. (*voltandosi alla moglie*) Giulia, vieni qua che Ivano sta riempiendo la *baschétta*.

Giulia: (*gridando*) Metti tutto nella *baschétta*.

Si vede il video del cestino che sale alla finestra.

Giulia: (*urlando dalla finestra*) *Tenchiú*, bello di nonna! (*si rivolge al marito*) Guarda Mattè, guarda che bel *presénte* che ci hanno mandato Ivano e Chiara.

Matteo: Che è questa cosa?

Giulia: (*stringendosi nelle spalle*) *Aronó*. (*parla al nipote al telefono*) Ivà, amore della nonna, ma che *presénte náisi* che ci hai mandato. (*pausa*) Ma che cos'è? (*pausa*) Un *compiútero*? (*al marito*) Ah Mattè, è un *compiútero.*

Matteo: (*sorpreso*) Ma che cazzo ci facciamo noi con un *compiútero*?!

Giulia: (*coprendo la cornetta del telefono*) Shhhhhhh, non fare il maleducato che ti sente Ivano!

Matteo: (*seccato*) Ma *plíssi*! Manda giù 'sto *compiútero*!

Giulia: (*dolcemente al nipote*) Ivà, amore della nonna, ma noi che ce ne facciamo di questo *compiútero*? (*pausa*) Cosa dici? (*pausa*) Ah! Dobbiamo aprirlo? (*al marito*) Mattè, *uí gára ópena*, dice Ivano.

Matteo: (*toglie il computer dal cestino, lo mette sul tavolo e lo studia*) Ma come si fa ad aprirlo?

Giulia: *Aronó*. Tu sei quello *smárti*, che dice sempre che sai fare tutto! (*ritorna a parlare con il nipote al telefono*)

Matteo: (*seccato*) Ma porca misera! *Fa sciaráppa, plíssi*!

Giulia: (*al nipote*) Ivà, ma come si *ópena* il *compiútero*? (*pausa*) Oh, è già aperto. (*pausa*) Oh, oh, ok. (*al marito*) Mattè, *púscia* così (*mostrando come aprire con le mani*) *Ochéi*, Ivà, *ízza ópena*. (*pausa*) Cosa dici? (*pausa*) Mi chiami col *compiútero*? (*pausa*) *Iú énghi áppa náu? Ochéi*, bello, *bái, bái.*

Matteo apre il portatile e l'immagine si sposta interamente su Zoom. In un riquadro vi sono Matteo e Giulia e nell'altro vi è Chiara. Nel riquadro di Matteo e Giulia si vede solamente il soffitto della cucina e si sentono le loro voci.

Chiara: (*chiamando*) Nonna! Nonno! Mi vedete? You see me?

Matteo: (*sorpreso*) *Omaigádda*, Giulia! Chiara è nel *compiútero*, Giulia, guarda!

Giulia: (*contenta*) *Lemisí*. Oh ciao Chiara. Ma sei veramente tu? (*gridando*) Mi puoi sentire?

Chiara: Ciao nonna! You don't need to scream. I can hear you, but I can't see you.

Matteo: *Uaraiumínna iú nó chénni sí mí? Ái sí iú*!

Chiara: I know, but the camera is showing me only your ceiling. Push the screen down.

Matteo: (*confuso*) Il *silíngo*?

Giulia: E come si cambia? *Áu uí céngi*?

Chiara: Nonna, move the screen down and centre the camera.

Matteo: (*sarcastico*) Certo! Facile per te!

Giulia: (*al marito*) Chiara dice di *pusciáre dáuni* così.

Chiara: (*interrompendo*) Not too far, not too far because you're gonna close the computer.

Matteo: (*aggiustando piano piano*) Láica díssi? (*adesso si vedono solo la fronte di Matteo e Giulia*)

Chiara: Yes, perfect. Just a tiny bit more, because now I can only see your fronte. Ma piano, piano.

Matteo: *Íssa béra náu*?

Chiara: (*con enfasi*) Yes, yes, stop! Don't move the computer. That's perfetto.

Giulia: Ma Chiara, Ivano dov'è?

Chiara: I guess he's on his way home. He was supposed to drop off the computer to you and then leave.

Giulia: Ah, viene a casa tua?

Chiara: No, nonna. He's going to his place and he's gonna login from there. And then when we're done zooming, he'll come over again to pick up the computer from you.

Matteo: (*confuso*) Che deve fare Ivano?

Chiara: He has to login to this Zoom call.

Giulia: (*completamente confusa*) Bella mia, io non ti capisco per niente! (*al marito*) Questi giovani di oggi parlano così moderno.

Chiara: You'll see, don't worry. Oh, he's logging on now. (*indicando*) You see that box dove c'è scritto connecting?

Sullo schermo appare la casella di Ivano che sta cercando di collegarsi.

Matteo: (*indicando*) Questa qua?

Chiara: Sì, quella. You'll see che arriva Ivano.

Giulia: (*contenta*) Guarda, Mattè, c'è Ivano.

Ivano: Ciao Nonna, ciao Nonno!

Matteo: (*contento*) Uei, Ivà. Come sei *fésti*! Prima eri fuori la nostra finestra e adesso sei già a casa!

Ivano: Sì, nonno. Ho guidato *fésti, fésti* per vedervi. Nonna, you see, you can work a computer. Non è così difficile.

Giulia: Grazie, bello della nonna! Ma, Ivà, come sei dimagrito! *Uái iú só schiní*?

Ivano: (*guardandosi*) What are you talking about, nonna? I've gained weight with this pandemic.

Ivano: Nonno, see how easy technology can be? We can see each other all the time like this.

Matteo: *Iéssi*, ma ogni volta devi portare il *compiútero* qua. È troppo lavoro.

Ivano: It's no problem at all. Così possiamo vederci.

Giulia: *Dázza náisi. Ái láichi véri máccia. Tenchiú.*

Chiara: Nonna, have you been going out?

Giulia: Ma che *gó áuti*! Io e tuo nonno andiamo a buttare il *garbíggio evridéi.*

Ivano: But you could go for a walk.

Chiara: Just the two of you.

Matteo: *Iéssi, uí gó* a camminare. Ma tua nonna mi fa impazzire quando usciamo.

Ivano: Ma why?

Matteo: Non vuole prendere *l'elevéta* e quindi mi fa scendere le scale a piedi.

Giulia: (*interrompendo*) *Bicósi íssa nó séfi* prendere l'elevéta. Sono solo quattro *flóri.*

Matteo: (*elencando*) Mi fa mettere la *máschera* e i guanti e gli occhiali da sole.

Chiara: Why sun glasses?

Giulia: Così il virus non entra negli occhi.

Chiara e Ivano ridono.

Giulia: *Uái iú léffi*? Così dicono di fare alla TV.

Matteo: Poi quando torniamo, mamma mia, cosa mi fa passare!

Ivano: What do you mean?

Matteo: Mi fa salire a piedi per evitare *l'elevéta*.

Chiara: That's tough, nonno, but the exercise is good. Do you hold on to the railing to help you climb the stairs?

Giulia: *Óffa córsa*. Ma con i guanti!

Matteo: Poi quando arrivo al nostro *flóro*, mi devo riposare perché sono stanco, ma tua nonna non mi fa sedere sulle sedie nella *ólla*.

Giulia: E no! Sono sporche!

Ivano: (*cercando di aiutare il nonno*) Nonno, e tu ti appoggi alla parete so you can catch your breath.

Matteo: *Aiuchírinmi*! Non posso toccare niente.

Giulia: Certamente! La *ólla* è piena di germi!

Matteo: Poi arrivo alla porta del nostro appartamento, entro e mi devo spogliare alla porta. Tua nonna non mi lascia entrare.

Giulia: (*fiera di sé*) Io metto una továglia alla porta come un tappeto prima di partire, così quando torniamo ci spogliamo sulla tovaglia e poi lavo tutto.

Matteo: (*indicando con le mani*) Tua nonna è diventata *crési*!

Giulia: *Ái nó crési*. Voglio essere *séfi*! (*indignata al marito*) Invece di ringraziarmi, mi prendi in giro.

Chiara: Holy shit, nonna! That's so much work for you. So much to wash.

Giulia: *Aronché*. Meglio essere *séfi*.

Ivano: If that makes you feel safe, nonna, you go ahead. But I don't think you have to do all that work.

Matteo: (*incredulo*) Ha tolto tutti i tappeti di casa così non portiamo i germi da una parte all'altra!

Giulia: Ho visto alla RAI che fanno così in Italia.

Matteo: Speriamo che questo *coronavirus* finisce presto!

Ivano: So, nonno e nonna, do you think we could do this zoom every week?

Chiara: Yes, it was so nice to see you.

Ivano: It's nice to see you from the window when we bring your shopping, but… (*viene interrotto dalla sorella*)

Chiara: (*interrompendo*) but we like to see you face to face.

Ivano: (*interrompendo*) and this is the best way to do it right now.

Giulia: Certo, bello di nonna. Mi piace questo *zúmmi*. Facciamolo un'altra volta.

Matteo: (*guardando l'orologio*) *Ochéi* ragazzi, fra poco c'è il mio *sció*.

Ivano: Ok, nonno. You need to log off and then I'll come to pick up my computer.

Giulia: *Lagáffa*? Che cos'è?

Matteo: E come si fa?

Ivano: Put your finger on the track pad and *púscia* il *bottóne* rosso che dice leave.

Giulia: *Uátta*?

Chiara: (*ridendo al fratello*) I wanna see you explain this, genius.

Ivano: Nonna, sotto tutte le lettere c'è una *bóchisa* grigia. You see it?

Giulia: (*tastando*) Questa?

Giulia: (*frustrata*) *Óli scítti*! Non si muove!

Chiara: (*cercando di calmare la nonna*) You don't have to push hard, nonna.

Ivano: That's right. Just touch it gently.

Matteo: (*fissando il computer*) Ecco, guarda che si muove *aghénni* la freccia.

Giulia: (*indaffarata*) Mamma mia! Sono tutta sudata!

Matteo: Muoviti che provo io. (*Matteo tira fuori la lingua quando cerca di spostare il cursore*) *Lemisí* se posso farlo io.

Giulia incrocia le braccia frustrata.

Matteo: Ecco! *Aigári*. (*indicando alla moglie*) *Lúcca*! Si muove. (*Giulia sbruffa*)

Ivano: Way to go, Nonno!

Giulia: (*ai nipoti*) *Bái, bái*! Salutatemi a mamma e papà. E *nó forghétti* di venire domani che vi faccio trovare il mangiare.

Ivano: Perfect. See you tomorrow. (*lancia dei baci ai nonni*)

Chiara: *Bai, bai* nonni, I love you!

Matteo e Giulia lanciano dei baci ai nipoti e salutano gridando. Finisce la chiamata Zoom

Bianca Lakoseljac

Confessions of a Reluctant Narrator

My dear reader:

Day 1.
It is with a heavy heart, under most unjust circumstances, under duress of the worst kind, that I am forced to write to you.

You see, here in my sphere, (at least I'm not reprimanded for rhyming) I've just been demoted. Yes, demoted. Now I'm sure you're getting some idea of where I stand, or more accurately, no longer stand. And the first task assigned to me by the new boss—oh, what a heartbreak it is to find yourself bossed by a newbie—is this job.

Bare with me my dear reader . . . or should I say, *bear* with me? I get punished if I use the wrong word. All part of my training. They're a bit behind the times here. Capital punishment is still alive and well. Have I just asked you to undress? With me? Did I just confess to being naked? Oh, my. Anyhow, no harm done. We come to this world naked and we leave naked. Who'd know that better than me? Don't tell anyone I'm writing naked. Although I don't mind if you'd like to read naked. I can always look the other way—unless you're a gorgeous woman with a big heart.

I have a strange feeling coming over me, infusing every nerve and bone and muscle. Pardon me; I just remembered that I no longer have nerves or bones or muscles. No, not even anything like those jelly-glutinous-cartilage bits you crunch in your teeth when you eat roast piglet. You know, that flexible tissue that lines joints and gives structure to the nose, ears, larynx, and other parts of the body you like to chew on because you think it's going to keep your own joints flex so you could twist yourself into a pretzel as if you're still a youngling.

I gave that up (I mean my nerves and bones and muscles) when I entered this phase of my journey as we say here in my sphere. Ohm,

I get giggles every time I rhyme. I get giggles as if someone's tickling me? I love it! It's like eating chocolate-dipped strawberries topped with ice cream, fudge syrup, whipped cream and sprinkles and not gaining an ounce. At last, I could do so. Except that here, only the boss gets to eat. Talk about injustice! So rhyming is about the only fun thing they don't punish me for.

As I was about to say, that curious all-knowing, all-seeing sensation is infusing every part of me and I feel all effervescent and light-hearted and not just great, but *otherworldly* great.

Am I digressing? I'm here to tell you the story about beautiful Helena. And a gentleman; perhaps not exactly a gentleman. Should I give you a sneak preview? No, better not. Or you might decide to take off and then I'd be in trouble. The way they punish here? Let me tell you … Oh, oh, here she comes, the boss lady. The story, I better write down my story before it sizzles out like a drop of sweat on a hot grill.

As if getting demoted is not enough. I wouldn't want them to give this job to someone else. Did you hear that? I think I'm beginning to like this job.

Nooo! Press the delete button! That gibberish about getting demoted and my job. Repetition is not allowed!

Day 2.

It's me, your narrator. Who else?

I think it's time for me to tell you, off the record, what I am doing here; that I am not, actually, your omniscient narrator. I was hired for the position of an omniscient narrator. You know, the all-seeing, all-knowing eye, a God-like storyteller. Yep. Good old me. Dream job. Except, as I've told you yesterday, I've been making so many mistakes, I got demoted.

Now, they call me the unreliable narrator. Some call me the reluctant narrator because I hesitate to give them what they're looking for.

What are they looking for? Ah, everyone's looking for something. They just don't know what that something is. But they know *it is* something. So I leave them to figure it out for themselves.

By the way, did you know that paradoxically, 'good old me' is actually younger that me? You see, this job can be fun!

You want to know who the boss lady is, don't you? But of course you do. She's a grand lady, alright! Man, that silky purple hair flowing down her back, those gorgeous glowing eyes like that of a puma, they see right through you. Rumor has it she is nocturnal, so no funny stuff under the cloak of night. Her skin is like Silk of Siam—just google "Silk of Siam" and you'll know what I mean. And not a hint of makeup. And why would she? You can't improve on perfection. I'm giddy with love, like a teenager. I'm jumping up and down, doing back flips, just for her. But she's oblivious to my gymnastics. To her, I'm just a bubble, a transparent one at that, with a hint of blueness, a bit like Man O' War; like a jellyfish I've seen on Miami Beach, in my previous life. Not a pretty sight. I'm just a blue bubble with a mouthpiece enduring my punishment.

What for? I might as well tell you. You see, in the sphere that you're now in, my dear—you do realize that you're on a journey? Am I giving away some secrets? I was... how do I explain... I was a womanizer. Kind of like Casanova. Oh, yes Siree! And *loved* every minute of it. I loved so many women my heart grew as big as a watermelon. And then one day the watermelon burst under some shrapnel. You guessed it—a jealous husband. With a tiny little heart, the size of a mint candy—so tiny he had no love at all, not for his poor wife, and not even for himself. After he killed me he turned the gun on the poor woman. She survived, luckily. Then the poor bastard turned the gun on himself; and *didn't* survive. So you see, he's committed the worst crime of all. He'll never get out of his hellish sphere we call here, a soul-forlorn-wish-you-were-never-born. Dante will never let him out of the seventh circle of Inferno. If you don't believe me, just look at Blake's illustration of Hell, *The Wood of the Self-Murderers: The Harpies and the Suicides*. I bet my nemesis is there—see if you can spot him.

But to my demise, my mortal enemy has spies working for him with squinty little, sneaky little eyes, everywhere. So the first time I slipped, you know, gave into my fractured watermelon heart and had a thrust with a gorgeous, I mean irresistible goddess of a woman (oops, delete the word, goddess; that could be blasphemy, here), he found out. And snitched on me. There were consequences. And, here I am, lost my Casanova f...ing amazing arm biceps every woman with a big heart would die for. All that barbell curl, push-ups, pull-ups, day in and day out, for nothing. They turned me into this bubble of jelly. Need I say more?

It's been six months since gorgeous Helena entered this sphere we call just one level below Heaven. And there she is: in her prime. You see, one benefit of passing on from your world to mine according to the Great Design, and not messing up anywhere along the line like I did, is: you get to reclaim that prime time. Your body parts at their best! No muffin tops, no bat wings, no smoker's face. None of that.

And Helena? No trout pout on her face, my friend. And those sweater puppies, to die for! All real home-grown goodness. No plastic fillers for her. She must've followed the Great Design with the precision of the best plastic surgeon in Hollywood.

Day 3.
Now, I hand over the narration to lovely Helena. Here in Purgatory, we all know that she needs to get things off her chest. She's going through rough times, poor woman. Even I don't know how things will turn out for her because I'm not omniscient. Not yet. I am in training: taking a course on how to be an omniscient narrator.

Rather than getting fired—yes, literally being set on fire to burn in Hell—I was given a second chance to be an omniscient narrator. Under boss lady's supervision. There are rules I must learn. A whole branch of philosophy about morality: concepts such as good and evil, truth and lies, ethics, justice, virtue, the list goes on. The Seven Deadly Sins? If that were all. But, nooo! There are many different schools of thought and sub-fields of study.

And this story is my thesis of sorts. There will be an oral exam. Yes, you're welcome to observe. Just remember whose side you're on. See you there!

Darlene Madott

Concetta's Christmas Panettone

"I'm not showing my face today, *sorella mia.*" Concetta says to Francesca, over the phone. "I'm still in my flannels. Turn the box upside down. The expiry should be on the bottom." And when Francesca reads the expiration date to Concetta: "So, Easter. We have until Easter. Besides, doesn't matter the expiration date. The *panettone* will outlive us all."

Vito had specifically asked Francesca to deliver the *panettone* to Concetta *before* Christmas. Vito is Concetta's not-so-secret admirer. Between waves of Coronavirus, Francesca has picked Concetta up at the subway station, masked and with the windows of her Honda Civic open and driven them over to Catania Bakery—Concetta's "happy place" since Concetta can't have the *real* Catania, in Sicily. The Catania of her youth, where Concetta had fallen in love, had a child. You wouldn't think the smell of a bakery by the name of her home town, the sight of *prosciutto di Parma*, the olives, the cheese, could inspire such joy! But that was the thing Francesca loved about Concetta, along with her sister solidarity over their respective wounds—the joy Concetta took in small things, the whoosh and scent of an espresso machine, the unexpected gifts of Vito.

Concetta and Vito—an improbable pair. Francesca had watched it happening, the wondrous oddity of it. For Concetta towered over Vito, with her tangle of dark Sicilian curls (now dyed), her red turtle-neck sweater, her broad, masked face, which couldn't hide the dancing eyes full of laughter no COVID mask could conceal. Vito looked up at Concetta; adoringly, his little hands patting his round, diabetic *panza*, in the white baker's uniform, spouting a silly flow of playful sentences which made Concetta laugh like a schoolgirl. "Good day, Ladies, out for your morning stroll?" (at 4:00 o'clock in the afternoon), or "How was your breakfast of tadpoles and toads?" and always, on each of their visits to Catania Bakery, Vito would gift Concetta something, as she approached the cash with her *tesori—cannoli, biscotti*—telling the girl behind the plexiglass, "Put this on my tab." Francesca saw "the look" pass between the girls working the till and remembered back to the days when Vito's parents were still living, the wild arguments that would make the Bakery customers blush, such as when Vito helped himself to a plate of pasta and lamb from the hot table and sat at the coffee counter, eating in silence while the words of his parents pummelled him for his uselessness. "*Disgraziatu! Vattini e stattini a casa invece di farti vedere dalla gente cca mangi comu nu porcu.*" But now they were dead, and Vito's shift happened when his older brother wasn't there—his ungenerous older brother, Salvatore, the responsible one, who managed their inheritance—the one who wouldn't give you a free *biscotto*, no matter how much you spent on weekly purchases. Whether the gift was Vito's to give or otherwise, Concetta always got her gift.

Then, on the 11th day of advent, Francesca came alone to Catania Bakery. Vito inquired, "Where's your friend? Are you seeing your friend before Christmas?" That was when Vito gave Francesca Concetta's Christmas *panettone* to deliver. Francesca insisted he write something on a Catania Bakery card and spelled Concetta's name for him, which Vito wrote in a shaking hand, as if afraid to make a spelling mistake, "Concetta, *Buon Natale*," and signed the card simply but with flourish, "Vito".

The day following Concetta's undelivered gift, the 12th day of advent, Francesca witnessed her own little miracle. Francesca had been listening to the radio, discouraged that the earliest appointment for her booster would put her into early February, doing her breakfast dishes in a desultory way, wondering why she didn't just leave them in the sink and do them all collectively after dinner and who was around to see dirty dishes, anyway, what did it matter if she left the kitchen spotless, when she learned of a pop-up clinic announced on the radio. Deciding to brave the line-up, she bundled herself in layers: Marino-wool socks inside her winter clip-ons, snow pants, a down-filled vest, her down coat, the one she wore in Iceland, the last time she and the man she had loved travelled together, which still bore the stain from when she'd brought him a coffee at the airport and not secured the lid properly, so that when he took a sip and the coffee spilled down his front, he'd hurled the coffee cup across the airport floor and it had splashed on impact not far from where she'd been standing and why couldn't she keep these thoughts from coming... her pink hat and muff, with the hood pulled up, with its fur trim covering most of her face, and then a large woolen Afghanistan scarf wrapped around her neck and covering the rest of her face. She grabbed the book she was reading with her thermal lobster-claw gloves and headed out the door. Her bicycle had a basket on the back, in which she had her bag with her health card, vaccination certificates, and the book. She flipped one leg over her bicycle, and headed for the mall where the pop-up clinic was happening.

Francesca planted herself a solid six feet behind the man in front of her, and opened her book. "The octopus has a body. But the body is protean, *all possibility* ... The octopus lives outside the usual body/brain divide," its "brain" on every surface and in every sucker—"embodied consciousness."

"WOW," she wrote in the margins, when a voice said to her, *Close the book. Something miraculous is happening. Look around yourself. Bear witness.* She closed the book and looked around. The man standing behind her immediately engaged her in conversation. What was she reading?

By the time the line started to move, they had both given each other a taste of each other's stories. He told her about his partner of 17 years he'd lost to cancer, some 10 years ago.

"You know how they say it takes one month to grieve for every month of the relationship. Well, it was almost to the day, 17 months after he died, I had a dream. I woke to my partner's voice telling me to close the book on my grief, to get out there and meet someone with whom to share my journey."

That's when he'd made a decision to go on a dating site, and his first time was also his current partner's first time. And then, they put two-and-two together about the serendipity that had led them to meet, how they had both *known* the deceased partner.

"We were brought together by his angel."

"Well, that rule of thumb hasn't worked for me." Francesca told the stranger about the heartache she'd suffered some years ago, which was still fresh in her now.

"About four years ago, he suddenly ended *us*—a *typed* letter in my mailbox in the middle of the night."

"I'm sorry," the man in the COVID-clinic lineup said to Francesca. "I hate to generalize, but some men just don't understand themselves—why they do anything. It is not a reflection on you or your love for him or your capacity to love again. In the few moments I have known you, I can tell you are a loving and loveable person. People come and go. But the love remains. The love remains—in all its wondrous forms and varieties."

He took out his iPhone and took a selfie of them together, and sent it to the e-mail Francesca trustingly gave him, as they moved forward in the line, divided into groups by the vaccine they were to receive—she Moderna; he Pfizer.

Francesca cycles home. What was Concetta's still-open wound? Francesca doesn't really know. Nothing Concetta will ever talk about. Francesca only knows it has something to do with her now-adult son, or the man who wouldn't or she wouldn't marry, back in Catania, who she described as "very old-world in his attitudes and expectations." Whatever it was, it hasn't affected the pleasure Concetta takes in *prosciutto di Parma, carciofi, melanzane,* or a good *pecorino* cheese—nothing the sweetness of Christmas *panettone* will not salve.

When Francesca gets home, she pulls off all her layers in the basement, where she keeps her bike and a change of indoor clothes, and goes upstairs to make a hot cup of tea and check her e-mails.

The photo has arrived. There they are in the picture, bundled against the cold and double-masked for COVID, smiling hugely, Francesca can see, notwithstanding the many layers and masks, they are bravely smiling for the camera. The stranger has dark dancing eyes, just like Concetta's. The e-mail photo carries a single word in its Re line: LOVE.

So easily missed, the day's little miracle, had she kept her face buried in her book, had she not confessed her pain to this total stranger …

Francesca bundles up again and gets right back on her bicycle.

When she arrives outside Concetta's apartment, she takes a photo of Concetta's Christmas *panettone* in the basket of her bike. She sends her friend a text, along with the photo.

"Meet me at the curb. Love shouldn't be made to wait until Easter."

Anna Mercuri Maiolo

Moving Heaven and Earth

August 20, 2024

"By the sweat of your brow you will eat your food until you return to the ground, since from it you were taken ..." I know these words by heart. Book of Genesis 3, 14–19. I've heard the priest speak these words before. But this time I'm sitting in the front pew. I am within reach of the coffin resting on its bier. This time, *my* dad is in the coffin. The priest's sermon is about *my* dad. My dad is gone.

It's early morning, and Dad has already had his mug of coffee with a biscotto soaked in it. He puts on his baseball cap, and as he steps out the back door, he makes the sign of the cross. He does this every morning.

He is a little slower now, but that won't stop him from working on his garden, reviving the winter soil. His heirloom seeds, like tiny green soldiers, wait patiently for the miracle of life.

I'm only 90 years young, he thinks, a*nd a little sweat never killed anyone. I was born with a pick and shovel in my hands. Let me get started on turning this soil.*

He hits the hard and crusty earth with his shovel. The deeper he digs, the moister the soil. Deep in and shovel out, repeating the motion like on autopilot—except when taking breaks to catch his breath. He wants to take off his warm Canadiens hoodie, the one his grandson handed down to him, but he won't because he knows that's the easiest way to catch a cold. *I better not take it off, or I'll never hear the end of it from Caterì,* he thinks.

From the corner of his eye, he notices a squirrel doing acrobats to reach the bird feeder placed in the apple tree nearby.

Che faccio con stu scoiattolo. The squirrel is hanging upside down enjoying the bird seed it jiggles out of the feeder. Dad stomps his shovel on the ground to shoo it away.

The squirrel scurries in the opposite direction, only to return to what seemed minutes later. Dad pauses and pulls out his perfectly ironed handkerchief to wipe his brow.

The garden pest is back, he chuckles. *Vattene.*

While Dad toils relentlessly turning the soil, the playful teasing between them continues. The squirrel gives Dad the welcomed rest he needs between each shovel load. His physical strength is deteriorating. He just refuses to admit it.

All morning, Mom has been in the kitchen preparing the usual feast for a man who needs his food served at noon on the dot. Pots and pans clatter as she's trying to get organized for the minute her husband, the head of the household, walks in.

"*Non ci la faccio più,*" she thinks. *I'm tired. When will I ever rest?*

"*Viene mangia,*" Mom yells from the back porch. "It's ready".

Like a farmer coming in from a day's work, his boots are caked in mud, his hands are covered in dirt. The wheel barrel is still full of earth, but he's tired now. *I will do the rest tomorrow,* he says to himself. He is proud of his hard work in his little backyard paradise.

He lays his shovel and pick on the side of the house and wipes the sweat off his brow.

"Okay, Caterì. Fammi lavari i mani." He bends to turn on the garden hose to scrub his hands clean.

He dries his hands on an old towel hanging from the fence. He slowly climbs the few steps leading to the kitchen screen door and he takes a deep breath.

"Che bel profumo, Cateri. *Cosa hai cucinato?*" He has no idea what she's made for lunch, but Dad's nose knows the aroma of her cooking. She can make any meal delicious. And he's hungry. *I better take off these boots before she ...*

"Take off your boots before you come in," she says in her stern motherly tone. *Ma ti devo dire tutto?* I don't want you to dirty the kitchen floor. Do I have to tell you everything?"

That's the way she is. Dad smiles.

He lets her speak to him this way because he loves her and he knows that she likes to be in charge, but she'll do anything to keep him happy and well fed. *Oh, I am a lucky man.*

Boots off, he enters the little kitchen. He takes a peek in the covered pots on the stove before he settles into his armchair at the head of the table.

"You asked for chicken, sausages, *due patate,* and some *verdura* today, no? *Tutti i tuoi desideri, li ricevi,"* she says annoyingly as she ladles out his food. "Whatever you desire, you get."

Mom doesn't come to the table until she has set aside some food. She gently covers the filled plates with a clean kitchen towel. *"Chissà, potrebbero venire dopo,"* she mutters. "In case one of the kids comes over."

"*Ma Caterì, vieni sediti.* The food is getting cold," Dad complains. "Come sit down."

She finally sits down. Dad pours her a glass of wine, and they eat. Except for the sounds of their forks scraping their plates, they silently enjoy the peace between them. They are deep in their own thoughts, respecting each other's space, knowing each other's habits.

Mom finishes her meal long before Dad. She stares at him, amazed at how he can shovel it in. *Where does he put it all*? She waits there patiently until he drops his fork on the plate with one hand and wipes his lips with the other.

"*Hai finito?"* Rolling her eyes, and suppressing a smile, she starts collecting the empty plates near her.

"That was a good lunch today, Caterì. *Abbiamo mangiato come dei rei."* Dad pushes his empty plate away. "We ate like kings!"

He gets up to put his dish near the sink.

"Leave it there; I know you want to look like you're helping, but you don't know how to wash dishes. *Fai la mossa. Ti comporti come se sapessi cosa fare,*" Mom says.

I only wanted to do a good deed, he thinks, shrugging innocently.

"*Okay, come dice tu,"* he says as he walks to the refrigerator. "Whatever you say, Caterì." He grabs a crispy red apple from the fruit drawer.

There is no point arguing with her. In her mind, she's always right and if we argue, what would be the point? She's the queen of the kitchen but I am the king of the earth. Let me go eat my apple. Then I'm going to go check if there's any mail.

Whistling his rendition of "O Sole Mio", he returns from his walk to the mailbox.

"Well, no bills but the *giornale* came. *Da vero,* it's Wednesday today, all the specials start tomorrow," he says to himself. "I'm going to look at this and then I'm gonna go check on my little tomato plants."

He settles himself at the dining room table and carefully pulls out the weekly flyers from the PubliSac. He scours each page and circles all the *speciale della settimana*.

"The watermelon is on sale at Bonanza, seven cents a pound! What a good deal" he says. "*Vale la pena*."

Of course, when Dad puts something in his head, he shakes heaven and earth, like salt and pepper shakers, until he gets what he wants.

The next day, I pick him up and drive him to the Bonanza grocery store in the West Island.

All the way there he repeats how excited he is at the thought of getting a huge watermelon for a couple of dollars.

"*Chissà, if they are sweet. Chissà, if they have seeds. If they are the big watermelons, for sure they have seeds. Anyway, the seedless ones aren't as good. Ma, insomma, at this price, I'm gonna buy two. Vale la pena.*"

For years after that, we'd laugh about that day. Instead of just buying the watermelon, he had filled his cart with other *speciale*. His seven-cent a pound watermelon cost him well over a hundred dollars.

***

The priest's words awaken me for a moment as he says,"*Con il sudore del tuo volto mangerai il pane; finché tornerai alla terra.*" My mind stops at the word *terra,* and I slip back to another time when Dad got his way.

"Hi Dad!" I say.

He doesn't even look up.

"*La terra*, it's on sale at Maxi—99 cents for a big bag," he replies. "Let's go get the earth."

"I know where this conversation is going," I mutter under my breath and roll my eyes. He doesn't drive, and although he rides his bike everywhere, he certainly can't carry that bag of earth home.

"Dad, I'll try to go get you a few bags of earth before the *speciale* is over. But those bags are heavy."

"*Va bene,* yes, they are heavy for you. Maybe *Toni tua*, my best son-in-law, can do it? Then when the tomatoes grow, you can pick all of them for your family, okay?" He gives me a wink.

And by the end of the week, Dad had all the earth he needed because he asked each of his children and grandchildren for the same thing, using the same technique. A little charm, a little wink, a little joke, a huge smile—who could resist denying him his earthly pleasures?

***

From dust to dust, the priest recited in prayer. My mind wanders to this past spring. The buds on the trees were just about to pop into beautiful baby green leaves, though winter's cold breath of death still lingered.

My sisters and I were taking another bite size chunk of cleaning out my parents' home, trying to make sense of what to do with the embroidered sheets in Mom's trunk and the pickled jars in the *cantina*. We decided that my brother Johnny can figure out the contents of the shed, or 'a shack-a' as my dad would say. All their prized possessions were not necessarily ours, but we tried to make those famous "keep, ditch, give away" piles every time. Emotionally draining, yet slowly and surely, we were getting things done. Selling the old house was the next step.

I parked the car in front of my parents' house. A ton of topsoil had been delivered and dumped on the driveway. A peculiar sight that left my sisters and me totally confused, considering Dad had passed away a few months back.

"Where, in God's name, did all that black earth come from?"

"I have no idea, Jo. Maybe Johnny ordered it?"

"Why is it on Dad's driveway? It doesn't make any sense."

"Ya, Rosa, that is weird. Why would Johnny order all that topsoil when nobody lives here anymore?

"Here he comes. Maybe Johnny has the answer, he usually does."

"No, I didn't order any earth. I passed by earlier this morning, and I saw it. I thought maybe one of you girls did."

"What the heck are we going to do with it now?"

"I guess we have to shovel it into Dad's wheel barrel and bring it into the garden, right?"

"Maybe we should plant a few tomato plants and some beans, while the house is up for sale?"

We stood there, looking at each other, dumbfounded.

Suddenly, a gust of wind interrupts our thoughts. It sounds like a belly laugh coming from way up above the clouds.

The topsoil swirls playfully around us. I can't help but smile.

Yes. Dad always gets what he wants—even from heaven.

Rosanna Micelotta Battigelli

*Nutella** ... *Worth Its Weight In Gold*

I admire mother and daughter teams who go shopping together, or out to the occasional movie and restaurant ... They are comfortable in their respective roles, yet there exists another dimension to their relationship. They can *play* together, and have fun while they spend an afternoon engrossed in heavy-duty retail therapy.

Shopping with *my* mother, I recall, chuckling, was not always what I would call therapeutic. If anything, I felt I would greatly benefit from therapy *after* a few hours of shopping with her.

Don't get me wrong—I loved Ma—but sometimes, she could be a bit too much. Despite being small in stature, she took up a big part of my life, even more so after Dad passed. Not that I minded, most of the time. Case in point, we often cooked together: first, because I knew she was lonely, and second, I was determined that she pass on to me every Calabrian dish she had learned from *her* mother. If we were not cooking together, we'd often be watching cooking shows, sitting side by side in the matching *poltrone*.

I blame Ma for getting me hooked on Iron Chef America. There was one episode where eels were the featured item, and Ma's eyes lit up. She recounted how they used to enjoy them back in the old country and she laughed when I cringed, declaring that I could never eat such a snake-like creature.

And then there were the comedy shows. They brought laughter into her life—and mine—and our grief over the loss of Dad was assuaged for a while. *The Golden Girls*, *Everybody Loves Raymond* (Ma called it *Everybody Love Raymon*), and even the older ones, like *Bewitched*.

But I digress. It's shopping with Ma that tested my patience.

One Sunday, the grocery store was packed with the after-Mass shoppers navigating their carts with post-eucharistic vigour. *Holy Rollers*. Having done their spiritual duty, they could now proceed with grocery duty. My mother, oblivious to one and all, took her time. I expended a considerable amount of energy helping her guide her cart around to avoid collisions as she fished out the biggest watermelon from the bin, chose the best bunches of rapini, and loaded up with olive oil and tomato *passata* on sale, and generally anything that she felt needed replenishing in her cupboards, basement kitchen, and in her *cantina*. I knew that if a world crisis occurred, I could flee to Ma's place; we'd have everything we needed for months.

Afterwards, Ma and I went shopping for gifts for some relatives in Italy. First we went to a department store where she occasionally bought gold when it was '*haffa price*'. There were no specials on, but she looked through a number of bracelets and chains, earrings and pendants. "How much *is*?" she asked over and over in her faltering English, which came out more like "How much *eez?"* Ma then pointed to the crucifixes. One had a tiny body of Jesus on a simple cross, and two were so thin that they looked like criss-crossed nails. "I take that one for my nephew," my mother said, choosing the former, and then decided on a thicker one for his wife. "Now, something for the children …" Ma's eyes lit up when she spotted another crucifix. Again, a satisfied nod.

Three down, one more to go, I thought, checking the time. With any luck, I'd be home in time for a late lunch.

The delay came when she tried to decide on earrings for her 16-year-old great-niece. "I no like," she declared when I made several suggestions. Exasperated, I said, "Ma, you're 78 years old and you're trying to buy earrings for a 16-year-old. Trust me, she's going to like these." I pointed to a pair that consisted of various sized intertwining loops.

"I dunno," she murmured. "They no shine like 14-carat gold … Okay, I take," she said finally.

When I returned home, my head was pulsating with the beginning of a migraine. I trudged into the kitchen and wearily opened the fridge, hoping to find something to give me a miraculous boost of energy. Salad? No, it looked as wilted as I felt. Organic carrots? No, it would take too much energy to munch them. I sighed, closed the door and shuffled to the pantry. My eyes scanned the shelves desperately; I needed *something* that would restore me.

Ahh, of course! My eyes rested on an extra-large, 750 ml jar of pure restorative … Nutella! Chocolate *and* hazelnuts. I was too weak to resist. I grabbed the jar with a sudden spurt of energy, reached for a spoon and then plopped myself into a chair, deciding to forego toasting a slice of bread (it made the Nutella melt into gooey heaven) for an instant boost.

As the creamy brown mixture made contact with my taste buds, enclosing them in a velvety embrace, I shut my eyes in satisfaction. I deserved this reward, I reasoned, for surviving the morning. *Exactly the therapy I needed ...*

Later that evening, Ma called to tell me that the chain for her nephew's wife was not long enough.

"Ma, it fit me okay," I sighed.

"But it was hard to open and close."

I *had* struggled with the clasp. "I have fat fingers, Ma. And she's smaller than I am. It'll fit her perfectly."

"There's a sale on gold tomorrow. I want you to bring me downtown. I want to get a new chain."

"Ma, there's nothing wrong with the one you have, for God's sake."

"Ah *Madonna*, don't get me upset," she warned.

My mouth snapped shut. Her underlying message hit me like a *caciocavallo*: *Don't argue with me, because I'll end up getting heartburn and maybe another heart attack ...*

I moaned inwardly. Italian mothers *always* know how and when to push that guilt button. "Fine," I heard myself muttering.

The next morning it was cloudy and humid. "These knees," she complained in our dialect as she stepped down awkwardly from her doorstep to the ramp. As her ice-tipped fingers closed around my arm, I began my usual silent incantation to God to help me deal with Ma's excruciatingly slow pace, the result of two debilitating heart attacks and advanced osteoarthritis. Her cardiologist had warned her that she could no longer manipulate any stairs. This had just about killed my mother; she, like many Italians, depended on their basement kitchen for frying veal cutlets, and making sausages, lasagna and tomato preserves ...

I stopped suddenly. "Ma, did you remember your spray?"

She nodded, and I uttered yet another prayer that she wouldn't get heartburn, for which she would have to follow a protocol: *Spray once. Wait five minutes. If the heartburn persists, spray again. Wait another five* *minutes. If it still hasn't gone away, spray again and call 911.*This whole business scared the red blood cells right out of me, especially whenever I took Ma to see the doctor or to get blood work done. Or go shopping. I imagined scenes of congested traffic while she was spraying her third shot of nitro . . .

At the mall, Ma spotted the gold vendor. "He always make me good deal," she murmured.

The vendor smiled and remembered my mother, who made a point of telling him that she hadn't come by for a few years because of her heart attacks. "My heart no good," she shrugged, and after his concerned reply, she began her exploration of his wares. "How much? Is 14-carat? *You give-a-me good price?* I buy lotsa gold here, remember?"

Finally, *finally*, she found a tricolour gold chain she liked. She hesitated when he revealed the price. "I pay cash," Ma lowered her voice. "How much?"

The vendor sighed and dropped the price. Ma gave a triumphant smile and pulled out a wad of bills. I exchanged a grin with the vendor.

The next day, I went over to help Ma pack up the gift boxes. When I opened the box with the chain for her nephew's wife, I was surprised to see that the tricolour gold chain had been replaced by the original chain, the one that she thought was too short and too hard to open and close.

"The *tri-colore* one is better for a *young-a* person," she said casually. "I give it to one of the granddaughters for Christmas. Come on, after we finish, we watch *Everybody Love Raymon,* okay?"

I opened my mouth and then closed it. If Ma was happy, that was all that mattered. I smiled and nodded. As I cut a length of white ribbon, I said, "Hey, Ma, do you have any Nutella?"

* *"Nutella is a trademark of Ferrero S.p.A". Used by permission.*

A version of "Nutella* . . . Worth Its Weight in Gold" was originally published in *Product of Italy, Made in Canada: An Immigrant's Love Letter to Food, Family, and Resilience,* by Rosanna Micelotta Battigelli (Latitude 46 Publishing, October 2025). Used by permission.

Carmelo Militano

The Return

I looked out. Below was the city. It spread out wide and flat to the horizon in every direction. Streetlamps glowed a dull yellow or white. The suburban streets empty and surrounded by a still eerie combination of light and shadow. The green foliage of oak and elm trees burned a dark green.

I was returning to visit my mother. My mood, like the city at nightfall, taciturn.

The city at this height appeared empty of people except for the toy-like movements of cars.

The plane began a slow descent. I could make out the pale blue flickers of a TV in a home.

The last remains of light splashed pink, red, against the soft belly of large clouds, the yellow distant horizon glowed, the sky a series of polished shades of blue each one darker than the next.

My mother's arrival was different; her face pale, grim, and registered relief when she stepped off the train at Union Station and mustered up her dignity. Ignored again the cold and her fear of the future. Her fate, she decided, a sacrifice from the Old Testament.

What did the city look like to her I ask myself?

The wide downtown streets were no doubt smudged with packed ice and snow. Electric buses connected to black wires above popped and crackled blue flashes of electricity when they took a curve. Everyone wore heavy winter coats, hats, scarfs, gloves and winter boots. Winnipeg, February, 1959 was cold.

She was amazed at the snow tossed and turned by the wind, how the cold felt like a sharp slap against her face.

She held my hand tight on the platform as people rushed past her while she scanned the crowd for a familiar face.

Later it became a bitter day in her memory. But there was a moment-after a familiar face showed up- not my father, when there were smiles all around at successfully crossing an endless grey sea, passed by rail through kilometres and kilometers of silent snow-covered forests, watching day after day a never changing weak grey winter sun the colour of an ancient Roman coin she once saw as a young girl in the museum at Palmi.

Her journey began on a bright sunny Italian morning; air soft warm and supple on her cheeks, scent of tangy sea salt in the harbour. The calm pleasant blue Mediterranean sang in the distance; small waves curled and winked shiny satin bits of sunlight.

On the third day out, dolphins gathered and playfully leaped out of the water near the ship; the dolphins a welcome distraction and wonder from her dread of open water, from leaving home.

***

My mother stopped talking when she was told she had cancer; she vanished as a mother, wife, daughter, sister, to a place far and distant from the here and now. My father and I, the doctors and nurses, it seems were present only as ciphers. Still, every night she kissed her fingertips and then placed them on the cheeks of the portrait of the Virgin Mary above her bed. She then shouted good-night to my father from her room.

After my father died, I found a small silver coiled purple Hilroy notebook where she wrote to God and St. Anthony of Padua.

She told God about her need to call and remind me about coming over for lunch. She reminded God and herself she had to give my sister some advice about her new baby, to remain calm when the baby cried. She said nothing about her cancer even though it was incomprehensible. She told St. Anthony her life was chosen and endured. She asked to be forgiven for sometimes questioning God's love and mercy. She no longer wished to be a sacrifice to God or man. The trip across the Atlantic was never spoken about again.

I used to visit her in the hospitable before she was sent home.

She lay on her bed silent, hands folded, the machine monitor attached to her flashing numbers and beeping every so often. I did not know how to penetrate her silence. Instead, I respected her withdrawal from the world and sensed her bewilderment about God's absence, her silent disapproval of my father and his repeated disappointments.

I silently looked out of the hospital window at the trees along the banks of the Assiniboine River. The trees stretched upwards as if dark shadowy supplicants, and like the two of us, one evening after another, they said nothing. Eventually their foliage returned, a summer breeze gently moved through the lean green leaves and still we continued to say nothing to each other, and not knowing why, I respected an unknown sacred silence about death on her doorstep.

We both knew she was dying.

I continued to look at the blurred outlines of my reflection on the hospitable window, and unlike in films, neither one of us were ever able to offer words of hope or comfort nor could I bring myself to say platitudes. I was unable to make small talk about anything in the hope I could coax her out of her silence. I respected her privacy, her disappointment about her marriage, the cancer's return and spread. I told myself my quiet presence in the bland coloured hospital room was enough.

We remained apart and isolated on our continents of grief unable to talk but what was it we feared?

***

There is a small colour photo of her framed and pinned on the white marble door of her above ground crypt; her smile is wry. Her entire face expresses a combination of happiness and something vaguely impish or ironic. The photo was taken on the day of my wedding. It is different from the other dour black and white photographs of departed Italian immigrants.

I talk to her today the way we used to talk before the cancer. Ma, I tell her this July is a hot one. It's good for the garden. The basil and tomatoes love the heat. What are you making for lunch Sunday? How is Papa?

Have you talked to your sister lately? I worry about her health, she replies, and I don't know where your father disappears to all day!

She then sighs at the steaming pot in front of her on the kitchen stove.

I try to remember the sound of her voice. The rhythms of her Cosoleto dialect. Nothing.

I do remember some days dropping over only to find her alone watching TV.

I sat on the beige sofa and she sat on her blue Lazy-Boy arm chair and together we watched the antics of penguins on a nature show. I loved her smile; the amazement and pleasure she took in their animated wobbly walk, the way the penguins slide or plopped into the open patches of Antarctic water; we ignore the obvious question where does my father disappear to all afternoon.

~ It is late, another July sun is setting. The interior of the mausoleum is cool and silent and filled with a sickly-sweet scent. I continue to try to talk to her like we did in the past before the cancer. I tell her photograph I love her. Pause. The low hum of an air-conditioner is the only reply in the room.

I walk out empty, trying to ignore the return of the small ripples of regret, the permanent unforgiving silence, the truth we both ignored and were unable to say.

***

The next day was not hot as promised and as is typical of the city's climate the temperature dropped ten degrees. There was a wind probably from the north-west and it blew microscopic rain drops in thin urgent slants; the air and light blurred grey; the grass burned an incandescent green.

I drove down Sargent Avenue towards the respectable West End, past Giovanni the Toscano's old grocery story my father's friend at the corner of Spence Street and where in the summer the two of them would sit on the wooden steps, a battered white and green 7-UP sign behind them and smoke and talk both gone now. I drove past what was once Enzo's Sports Bar and avoided, past what is now the Dollar Store but used to be a Woolworth's Store and where Gwen and I looked in awe at the album cover of Sargent Pepper's Lonely Hearts Band for the first time.

I avoided taking a quick drive past the old house on Langside.

I felt myself pulled back to a time and place where longing and ache-neither go away no matter what happens in one's life- mixing not so much with memory and desire but with a memory how reasoning at the age of ten was not all that much different than reasoning at fifteen except it seemed you could finally do something about getting what you wanted.

You see I have been avoiding this look backward and what follows when you move with your memory back to a time and place when you were a boy, followed by a teenage boy, followed by ... well you know what I what I am saying, you arrive here and now with a consciousness resembling a disorganized old and new antique shop- mirrors, old books, photographs, dark furniture, and broken watches of every make under glass-coupled to my aging strange athletic body of seventy aware the time is almost all gone and there is nothing left to do but try and make sense of it all and yet knowing full well the best you can do is name a place, remember a building, locate half Rembrandt shades, a scent or song, the chiaroscuro faces of your youth grinning or staring blankly all under glass, again.

The street was wet and grey that afternoon and black puddles hugged the curbs. The sky above me one wide low wrinkled grey comforter.

I parked in front of her house on Banning Street and looked at the white veranda. It was a little worse for wear after fifty years and the wet wooden steps wet glistening in the late afternoon light. We had sat on those very steps, smoking and talked and talked.

I remember little from those long conversations. I do know we talked about our relationships, our selves mysterious and elusive and at least for me I recall my longing to be someone else simply by virtue of falling love and to kiss deeply and slowly everything dissolving the antics of a boy she liked in school, Alex my friend and now my rival, our mutual love of pop music, especially the British progressive rock band *Yes* and of course *The Rolling Stones.*

***

Winnipeg, Thursday, January 1, 1948

The *Winnipeg Free Press* reported—on the front page no less—that on December 23, 1947 that government liquor stores did $139,000 in sales beating all previous sales records since government control began twenty-four years ago.

It was also reported many new years resolutions had been broken "before the sounds of revelry had died away Thursday morning." And girls who had been chasing men throughout 1947—Claire Everett was among this unnamed group—found "their pursuits legal with the dawning of 1948." One unknown young woman set the record straight by discounting reports that Winnipeg girls had taken advantage of the new leap year early to propose.

We women just don't work that fast, she declared with a wink. We're slow but thorough.

Claire announced with a half-smile.

At midnight the recorded temperature was 9 below Fahrenheit but bottomed out at 13 below but by noon, Thursday, New Year's Day the temperature had edged itself back up to around zero.

The forecast for the first day of 1948 was for clear conditions before becoming cloudy by midafternoon, which was around the time Frank finally decided to shave after drinking three cups of coffee as he wrote to his family in Calabria or rather more specifically his mother who he knew was worried about his hasty exit across the barren and wide and endless grey ocean always stirring, vast and reckless, the ship a vast rocking cradle unable it seemed to him to ever move in a straight line.

He conjured up in his mind's eye the small piazza behind his grandmother's house overlooked by the low two-story commune or city hall. He imagined the small bar on one side of the piazza and the clatter of small espresso plates, cups, and spoons.

The radio droned on in English as he shaved in front of the spotted mirror in his small room on Logan Avenue announcing winds will be south west at 25 miles per hour and the high for the day will be 15 below.

The radio broadcaster with tongue in cheek announced that some New Years resolutions were reported already broken before the sounds of revelry had died away on Thursday morning. Frank did not smile. He was new to this country, this city, and after six months was barely able to scrape together a few sentences.

Michael Mirolla

An excerpt from the novella How about This . . .?
Published by At Bay Press, September 2025
Excerpt reprinted with permission

II. Back to 2044 AD [0111000 B-AI]: Here Come The Foundlings[1]—Surprise! Shock! Double Surprise!

Of late, it being a form of springtime in both the fast-crumbling city and its barely-hanging-on suburban outliers, the feral alley cats [rumoured to be escapees from gone-right GMO lab experiments with an interest in synthetic testosterone as a way to improve elite soldiers' kill ratios and billionaires' sperm counts—and vice versa] have manifested particularly ardent/feisty attitudes. Especially on the increasing number of muggy, sluggish, mogrified evenings when one looks out the window to find more than a hint of Prufrockian fog dancing around the base of overwrought street lights[2]. Giving them [the street lights, that is] the appearance of being the only real objects in the multi-verse as they

1. The long history of foundlings for readers who find such trivia useful: While the first foundling hospital in the English world was started in London by sea captain Thomas Coram in 1739 AD. [https://en.wikipedia.org/wiki/Foundling_Hospital], Florence's Ospedale degli innocenti [where children were left in a basin by the front gate] came into being in 1427 AD. [https://en.wikipedia.org/wiki/Ospedale_degli_Innocenti]. Do foundlings still exist in the first century B-AI? See V. Vinge & H. Bates, "Testing orphaned AI programs: Towards an adoption process to ease stress and anxiety among high-level language foundlings: Of stray bits and unimposing qubits," *The Journal of AI Pediatrics*, V. 2, N. 2, 2069 AD [011111 B-AI]. [Please note: ethical considerations required the researchers to only aggregate data for statistical reasons without identifying individual orphan code that both fails and passes the Turing Test.] So did you find such trivia useful?

2. "The yellow fog that rubs its back upon the window-panes . . ." Just thought we'd throw that in to make the connection obvious, having too often been accused of either obscurity or elitism.

invite hara-kiri attacks from pesticide-resistant mayflies who insist on being on the bright side when immolating themselves. [Most often perishing into the stomach cavities of super-geckos before any immolation can take place.]

So the wailing at her back door—which has become an almost nightly occurrence—comes as no surprise for El [short for Elspeth, a tall pyjama-clad woman in her mid-to-late 30s with close-cropped hair and a distinct lack of make-up on a pleasant, round, well-nourished (as they say in murder mystery morgues) face]. To the point where she has developed a ritual that consists of: [a] pushing with her butt against the spring-loaded, outward-opening back door; [b] stepping out while one foot keeps the door from slamming shut behind her; and [c] quickly splashing a bucket of cold water into the night in the hope the shock will dampen, if only temporarily, the toms' desire [for either battle or sex].[3]

But, as the bold typeface header would indicate, on this particular evening, El seems the one in for a shock when she flings the door open and prepares to douse the freestyle feline frolickers.

So, for the record, here's how El would have prepared her story in case of a possible investigation [criminal or simply bureaucratic]—and also how she explains events to herself and to her partner [scheduled to make a grand entrance in Section III]:

"I was expecting snarling cats. Or maybe in the clamouring throes of lustful amour with one or two paramours, one of whom I'd come to identify as Sir Eglamour. What else could it be? Howling cats yesterday; howling cats today—isn't that what inductive logic tells us? But there. There on our backyard deck underneath the motion sensor detector. There was the real source of the wailing which had in the meantime stopped. Infants. Two of them side-by-side in a stroller. Two infants tightly wrapped in blankets [they used to call them swaddling cloths,

3. Incidentally, this is the same repellent she threatens to use on Jehovah's Witnesses who refuse to take the first hint. [El shouting she's a flaming atheist and has given blood among other fluids and celebrates a whole bunch of pagan rites including roasting Latter Day Saints alive to be used as cucumber sandwich fillers.] But that's normally at the front door of her suburban bungalow and a story for another day.

no?] that were a combination of pink and blue. Like whoever had done the wrapping couldn't make up their minds. Two infants side-by-side in a mauve-coloured, ultra-modern, altogether spiffy, triangular-wheeled two-seater tandem stroller.[4]

"I must admit to a double take, an exaggerated double take, followed by the removal of a hand from across my mouth and furtive glances to ensure no neighbour was surveilling. Sorry, I mean, watching. Too much Elizabethan Age research. Joking, of course, as the word was first used in 1884, long after the Elizabethan Age. Anyway, I hesitated for a moment, trying to decide what next to do. But what could I do? What choice did I have? I wasn't going to leave them on the back deck in the damp and dark. Possibly to be mauled by hungry and/or horny cats. Possibly to die a slow death from starvation. So I touched the stroller again to make sure it wasn't an hallucination, then wheeled it into the house, back-heel kicked the door shut behind me and suddenly realized I hadn't been breathing the entire time. Had been holding my breath as if it was going to be my last. So I took a deep one. In out. And then I took several more.

"I didn't say: 'Be still, my beating heart!'[5] But my Fitbit Ultra-Versa V24.2i smart watch, the one I got as a 10th anniversary gift from my ever-loving and thoughtful partner, did tell me that the beat of my heart had jumped rapidly: 'Pulse rate at 118, sweetie. Time to relax.

---

4. For anyone looking for an even more complete description of this tri-wheeled item, don't bother as none will be provided. However, this may be a good time and place to talk about the number three and its significance in the history of human belief systems: from feminine triads in Greek mythology to the Christian Triune Trinity to *Harry Potter*. Or maybe not. Maybe it's never a good time to point out the non-rational in fetish thought patterns. Might lead to infection and viruses that cannot be expunged.

5. Although, as a professor of 18th century English Literature [with a minor, of all things, in Computer Science which she puts to good use], El knows full well the history of that phrase and its first appearance in William Mountfort's play *Zelmane, or, the Corinthian Queen* [1705 AD]: "Ha! hold my Brain; be still my beating Heart." While some critics have argued that the play was actually written by Mary Pix, that is not generally held today. See: "Mary Pix's nebulous relationship to 'Zelmane'." *Notes and Queries*, vol. 41, no. 2, 1994, p. 186+. *Gale Academic Onefile.* Coincidentally [or perhaps not so coincidentally], El's doctoral thesis was titled "From Sulpicia to Mary Pix: A Matrix Database Points of Contact and Overlap Approach to Proto-Feminists in the Augustan Eras."

Take five.' As you know, or maybe you don't, I've always been one to obey sensible requests. Especially when they're voiced in the melodious and calming tone my partner uses when I'm harried or acting headless. So I pulled up a chair from the kitchen table and sat myself down before the stroller. But I still couldn't believe it. And so I almost immediately jumped up again and headed towards the bedroom so I could wake my sweetie and share the news. Only to remember, as I was about to open the bedroom door, that my partner was out of town meeting one of the more difficult clients [a cattle prod manufacturer who insisted on face-to-face meetings despite sophisticated holographic possibilities for fear his competitors have compromised his electronics] and wasn't due to return until mid-morning.

"So I went back to the stroller, looked around and then peeked in like I was still having trouble believing what I saw. What was before me. I touched the stroller. Shook it gently and felt it rocking on its silent, heavy-duty springs. Definitely not a mirage. I looked in. Two babies. I shook my head hard back and forth and eased myself once more into the chair, at the same time shuffling it closer to the stroller. Maybe for fear it might vanish if I didn't stay close. If I didn't keep my eye on it. And that's where I remained in a sleep-wake dream state—and admitting to a massive smile on my face much resembling some Cheshire Cat[6]—for the rest of the night.[7]

"And that's it. That's the story of how these two babies ended up in our house. It was like a dream. A dream wherein all my wishes came true. A dream that washed away all my disappointments and frustrations. One that I hoped and prayed [metaphorically speaking, of course,

---

6. Bet you didn't know the Cheshire Cat suffers from schizophrenia and alters "reality around him": https://www.medicinanarrativa.eu/so-much-inside-alice-wonderland-for-medical-humanities. Perhaps, more interesting, the Cheshire Cat has even infiltrated scientific analogy—from eyesight illusions to RNA, quantum mechanics to astronomy: https://en.wikipedia.org/wiki/Cheshire_Cat#In _science. Hey, there's even a series of galaxies called The Cheshire Cat: https://earthsky.org/space/the-cheshire-cat-group-of-galaxies. Supermassive black holes, galaxies about to collide — oh what fun.

7. So, you may well ask, why didn't El hit the 911 button on her smart phone the moment she discovered the package on the back deck? Not sure at this point and not willing to risk giving anything away. But perhaps what happens next might help.

as my belief in higher beings extends only as far as generative artificial intelligence[8]] would still be there in the morning. At which point I knew that, as much as I dreaded it, a decision had to be made and the authorities would have to be informed."

8. See, Tijn van der Zant, Matthijs Kouw, Lambert Schomaker, "Generative Artificial Intelligence," *Philosophy and Theory of Artificial Intelligence* [2013 AD (01010111 B-AI), Vol. 5], 107–120.

Delia Petrucci-De Santis

The Balcony

I wasn't even two when my mother died. Sometimes, when my Auntie Laura came for her short visits, I wondered if my mother looked like her. A girl in my class at school looked just like her sister who was three grades ahead. Auntie was prettier than most young women I knew.

I wished she could spend more time with me when she came to visit so that I could ask her everything about my mother.

I asked my father why she never stayed very long . . . but he just grunted.

Auntie Laura lived in Rome. I had heard a relative once say that she had two boyfriends. Maybe that was why I had never heard my father ask her to stay longer. He didn't look happy to have her around. But I liked her; she always brought me pretty dresses. I knew she was the one who had bought me the pink crib when I was born.

Supper was over one evening, and there we were on the balcony off the kitchen. I was sitting on Papa's lap, and I stayed very still to not make him spill the wine from his glass which he always filled to the brim.

"Ha, *vino è vita*," he said, downing the first half of the glass. "Wine is life." Whenever he said those words, he almost looked happy. But I knew he wasn't happy. And that's why I started doing something silly.

"Papa, be still," I begged, trying to open his left eye.

"Gina, stop it. What are you doing? And don't forget, that's the only good eye I have."

"I just want to look. I won't poke you." I lifted the top eyelid and pulled down the bottom one.

He shook himself. "Listen, if I go blind, there will be nobody to look after you."

"Auntie Laura will take me with her to Rome."

"As if I would let you go with that woman."

I didn't say anything for a long time, then I *told* him. "You know what she always says?"

"What does she say?"

"She wishes you were dead instead of my mother."

He shrugged. "I am not really surprised—your aunt has never liked me, and I don't like her. She wanted your mother to be like her, but your mother was nothing like her. Your mother was beautiful in every way. But tell me, you little imp, what did you see in my eye?" And he gave me his usual sideways grin.

"A little black hole in the middle, Papa," I giggled.

"Ah, a little black hole." He pinched the front of his neck. He did that a lot. As if he wanted to stretch his Adam's Apple. "A little black hole," he repeated. "Well don't tell anyone. People will think that a half-blind man shouldn't be looking after a little girl. And your aunt will come here figuring she can take you away from me ... but I will never let that happen, not even over my dead body."

"Papa," I said, getting off his lap and relishing a good pounding on his chest.

"You always think I am silly ... and—I don't like it when Auntie Laura wishes you were dead." And I went to stand by the railing pretending to look down into the courtyard, waiting to hear what he would say.

"Come back here," he chided, setting his glass on the little table beside his chair.

I obeyed, and I let him put his arms around me tight. And as he did that a strange sound came out of his throat. I could tell he was sad, and maybe he even had tears in his eyes. I didn't want to look up into his face. I pulled away from him and ran to my room.

I threw myself on my bed, and without knowing why, I began to sob into my pillow. I squeezed the pillow hard for a long time. When my sobs stopped, I sat on the edge of the bed, drying my face and swinging my legs. After a few idle moments, I suddenly brought my braids to the front and slowly and carefully, I began to redo the ribbons on the ends—my father could never get them right. I worked at it until I got them to look perfect. I started to feel better. I also felt strangely different. But I didn't know just how. But then slowly I started to wonder about a lot of things ... did my father still miss my mother ... and what it would be like to miss someone you loved, and that person was gone forever …

My mother had been dead for four years. If only even a faint memory of my mother would come to me but it never did. I wanted to feel her loss as Papa did. I wanted to feel the sadness of not having her there holding me close … and if only I could hear her voice, remember her singing to me, for Papa said she always sang me to sleep. But most of all, I wondered what it would be like to call her name. And for the first time, I heard myself say it aloud: "Mama."

Then suddenly I jumped up. I went to see Papa. He had fallen asleep in his chair. He always rested for a while after supper before cleaning up the kitchen. I wanted to tell him that I really didn't want to go live with Auntie Laura. Ever. I would always stay with him. But I didn't want to wake him up—he needed his rest. He worked long hours in the general store we had downstairs. I would tell him later.

I headed for the kitchen and I began to clean up the way I had seen Papa do. I cleared the table and put things away … and then I decided to start washing the dishes. It felt so good to have the water run over my hands. I scrubbed and rinsed the plates over and over to make sure no speck of food was left on them. I stood and admired the clean dishes air drying on the rack and decided washing dishes was not as hard as I had always thought. It was even fun. I was starting to feel like a big girl.

I didn't go back to the balcony. I waited for Papa to come inside and be surprised. I knew what I had done would make him happy … and maybe he would tell me that I was starting to look beautiful, as my mother was … and that I would grow up to be like her, gentle and wise.

Joseph Pivato

They Were Here Briefly

The Roman poet, Horace gave us the expression “Carpe Diem,” that is, “seize the day,” good advice because we only get a few opportunities in life to accomplish what we set out to do.

In this short essay I will look back at some of the Italian-Canadian authors who have supported the Association of Italian-Canadian Writers over the years. I begin with Pier Giorgio Di Cicco (1949–2019), who edited *Roman Candles* in 1978, a seminal anthology, and produced 18 books of his own poetry such as *The Tough Romance* (1979) and *Virgin Science* (1985). His work helped to establish the existence of Italian-Canadian writing as a vital part of Canadian literature.

At the 1986 Vancouver writers’ conference he spoke in favour of founding the AICW. Over the years he encouraged many other writers such as Mary di Michele, Gianna Patriarca, and Mary Melfi. In 1985 Giorgio entered an Augustinian monastery north of Toronto and subsequently became a priest. In 1990 he did attend the third AICW conference in Ottawa organized by Francesco Loriggio. Fr. Giorgio served several parishes in the Toronto area. For about 15 years he had stopped writing, only to resume again in 1999. His next book *Living in Paradise* appeared in 2001. He was appointed Poet Laureate of Toronto in 2004. In 2011 I edited the academic volume, *Pier Giorgio Di Cicco: Essays on His Works*, which included contributions from members of AICW. Fr. Giorgio continued to write until he passed away in December, 2019 at age 70. In 2022 Giovanna Riccio and George Elliott Clarke established the Pier Giorgio Di Cicco Poetry Award in order to recognize poets in our community.

The founding mother of the AICW was Dore Michelut (1952–2009), who published *Loyalty to the Hunt* (1986), *Ouroboros: The Book that Ate Me* (1990) and edited *A Furlan Harvest: an Anthology* (1993).

She published a book of Renga poems, *Linked Alive* (1990) with Black writer Ayanna Black, also published in French as *Liens* (1990). Her essay, "Coming to Terms with the Mother Tongue," (1989) was anthologized in several collections including our own, *The Anthology of Italian-Canadian Writing* which I edited in 1998. Dore helped me organize the second conference of the AICW which was hosted by the Mariano Elia Chair at York University, Toronto in 1988. Her work with Friulan women writers encouraged them to publish. As a result, Rina Cralli had her Friulan poems appear in many publications in Canada and Friuli. In 2015 I edited a bilingual collection of Cralli's poems, *From Friuli: Poems on Friulan with English Translations* which was well received at a big book launch at the Friuli Centre in Toronto. Rina passed away in December 2021 at age 92. Our friend Dore never got to see Rina's historic collection since she passed away in 2009 at age 57.

Dino Minni (1942–1989) was one of the original organizers of the 1986 Vancouver conference along with Anna Foschi and Genni Gunn. Since 1964 he had published many short stories and book reviews in literary magazines in Canada and the USA. His own collection of stories, *Other Selves*, appeared in 1985 and *Ricordi: Things Remembered* (1989) was an anthology edited by him. His essay, "The Short Story as an Ethnic Genre" was included in *Contrasts: Comparative Essays on Italian-Canadian Writing* (Guernica) which I edited in 1985. His interview with Frank Paci was featured in the journal, *Canadian Literature*, 106 (1985), the issue devoted to Italian-Canadian writers.

After the 1986 Vancouver conference Dino and Anna Foschi collected the papers and published them as *Writers in Transition: The Proceedings of the First National Conference of Italian-Canadian Writers* (1990). It is interesting to find that among the 28 short essays included in this historic collection authors raised topics that we are still discussing in this decade. Are we still writers in transition? My essay was entitled, "Nothing Left to Say: Italian-Canadian Writers," Pasquale Verdicchio's, "The Intellectual Ghetto," Genni Gunn's, "Avoiding the Stereotypes," and Antonio D'Alfonso's, "Where Do We Go From Here?"

Dino Minni was born in the Molise region of Italy. His family emigrated to B.C. and he grew up in Vancouver. At the age of 8 he was diagnosed with Muscular Dystrophy and soon was confined to a wheelchair. He was quadriplegic and had limited use of his hands, but was able to use an electric typewriter. He demonstrated a courageous spirit and much creativity. In July, 1989 Dino lost his long battle with MD and passed away in his sleep at age 47.

Robert F. Harney (1939–1989) was a professor of history at the University of Toronto and a major scholar of Italian-Canadian studies, an academic area which he established at the UofT. Bob was a supporter of Italian-Canadian writers and anyone interested in exploring the immigrant experience. In 1978 he co-edited a book with Betty Caroli and Lydio Tomasi, *The Italian Immigrant Woman in North America*, which included poems by Mary di Michele, Pier Giorgio Di Cicco and Rosario D'Agostino. He published many articles such as "The Padrone and the Immigrant," and "Chiaroscuro: Italians in Toronto, 1885–1915," followed by "Men Without Women: Italian Migrants in Canada, 1885–1930." Some of his work was translated into Italian and collected in the book, *Dalla Frontiera alle Little Italies* (1986) which won several prizes. He also published other books such as *Little Italies in North America* with J.V. Scarpaci in 1981.

Bob was co-director of the Ethnic and Immigration Studies Program at the UofT. When I went on sabbatical in 1984–85 Bob invited me to be a Visiting Research Fellow there and thus, I was able to work on *Contrasts: Comparative Essays on Italian-Canadian Essays,* published in 1985. Bob had an Italian grandfather on his mother's side. His major research and writing project was to produce THE history of Italian settlement in Canada. However, fate intervened. In 1989 Bob had a major heart attack and later underwent a heart transplant. In August 1989 Bob died of complications from the operation. He was 50 years old and his Italian-Canadian history project was never completed.

Alexandre Amprimoz (1948–2012) was an extraordinary writer who published in French, English and Italian with 25 book titles. He was born in Rome and earned degrees from universities in France and Canada. He taught French in Manitoba (1980–87) and then at Brock University (1987–2012). He published poems, stories and essays in over 100 literary journals. He also translated the work of French authors into English. His creative writing revealed two different personalities. His French work, especially his poetry, demonstrated a more formal style, while that in English was more playful and experimental. The stories in *Hard Confessions* (1987) focus on unusual events, fantasy, coincidences, magic realism and the absurd. *Against the Cold* (1978) is a collection of poems that take us around the Mediterranean. His French titles include *Chant Solaire* (1978) and *Bouquet de signes* (1986). His *Too Many Popes* (1990) is a satire. He published several essays on Italian-Canadian writing in both English and French and contributed the article, "Death Between Two Cultures: Italian-Canadian Poetry," which he co-wrote with Sante Viselli (U. of Winnipeg) for *Contrasts* (1985). He passed away suddenly at age 64.

Antonino Mazza (1949–2017) was a writer, translator and instructor in Italian at Carleton University in Ottawa. His own books include *The Way I Remember It*, poetry (1992) and *Urban Harvest*, fiction (2004). He translated Mario Duliani, *The City Without Women* (1993), and Pier Paolo Pasolini, *Poetry* (1991). He edited *Immigrant Songs: The Poems, Fiction and Letters of Saro D'Agostino* (2012). He passed away in 2017 at age 68.

Venera Fazio (1946–2017) was a very active member of the AICW serving as president and other positions on the executive. She published one collection of her own poems, *The Fabric of My Soul* (2015), a title inspired by her many years working as a weaver of colourful fabrics. She also published, *Sweet Lemons: Writing with a Sicilian Accent* (2004), co-edited with Delia De Santis, and *Sweet Lemons 2: International Writing with a Sicilian Accent* (2010) co-edited with Delia De Santis. In 2016 Venera and Delia co-edited, *Exploring Voice: Italian-Canadian Female Writers.* To honour her many contributions to Italian-Canadian authors and Canadian literature generally, members of the AICW established the Vera Fazio Poetry Prize.

There are several more authors who contributed to Italian-Canadian literature and need to be mentioned here. Giovanni Costa was an Italian language poet who passed away in Quebec City in 2011. Anna Carlevaris (1954–2012), a Montreal art historian, contributed an essay to the volume, *F.G. Paci: Essays on His Works* (2003), which I edited. Gianni Grohovaz (1926–1988) was a Toronto Italian poet and journalist. Barbara Godard (1942–2010) was a writer, editor and translator who contributed an essay to *Mary di Michele: Essays on Her Works* which I edited in 2007.

Montreal writer Filippo Salvatore (1948–2023) published 14 books in Italian, French and English, several with Guernica Editions. Toronto writer Corrado Paina whose 17 books are in Italian and English passed away in 2024.

When Emma Pivato was working on her memoir, *And Along Came Alexis* (2021), she reminded me to look back at the forty-year history of the AICW. The result is this brief essay about brief lives.

Anthony Portulese

Duty of Care

The government's new laws are clear, there would be no exceptions. Burning her would bastardize his beliefs. But Nonno can't bear to have her in the dirt. Pummeled beneath cold mud and rock. Their departed friends not by her side to keep her company. Slowly devoured by maggots and vermin. He clutches his cross and begs his wife's forgiveness. In a whimpering rage he's forced to relent, and relinquishes her to the crematorium.

***

"*L'avet' lasciat' lì a morire*!" bellows Nonno at Zio and Papà after the orderly confirmed her test results. "*'A vostra madre*!"

He's distraught. Never able to say goodbye, not properly. The satellite signal is terrible in the hospital. We all huddle in the kitchen, over a tiny screen that keeps lagging without mercy. They install an iPad at the foot of her bed. We can see ICU nurses ensconced in PPE. Masks and face shields. Gloves, gowns and goggles everywhere. Soldiers on the front line of battle, their armour in dangerously short supply. War is being waged in our hospitals and nursing homes. The mortal enemy decimates our meager defences. Invisible and insidious. Lingering and lethal. But they fight for our families. Our supposed leaders have failed us.

***

"*Vieni balla' cu'mme, principino mio*," she commands with her Neapolitan accent, aggressive and tender. She pulls me off the couch. The raspy tunes swirl through the cozy air. My cousins laugh at my clumsy feet. I try not to turn green and to keep down my spaghetti dinner. But I laugh all the same. It means I'm full, that I'm fulfilled. She twirls me under her arm. I can smell her perfume.

She doesn't understand any of the words to Elvis' songs. She hums and vowels and belts the notes, and continues to dance throughout the first years, because dancing is all she can control. She never has a say with the money, or with the business, or with anything else. With each hemorrhage it takes her longer to relearn the steps, but she manages each time to learn anew. But then the jumpy melodies make her throw wineglasses in a panic, and so the speakers are silenced. The pills to keep her calm make her forget how to walk, and so the dancing stops for good.

***

We cannot even hold a service. Nonno wants her funeral at Madonna della Difesa, where they were wed. It's a rather poetic plan from such an unsentimental man. Their marriage could end in the same church where it began sixty-two years earlier. But none of that is feasible anymore. Houses of worship are closed during the shutdown. Temples of love and warmth warped and gnarled into cesspools of contagion. When we embark on our journey from the funeral salon, Nonno stifles his sorrow and sits in silence. His sunglasses cannot conceal the tear on his nose that catches the daylight. He stares out the window onto the streets they had walked in their youth. He looks down at his wife. He cradles her urn like a newborn child.

***

We notice her trinkets mysteriously disappear after check-ins and cleanups, so we can't let her wear jewelry. First it was a designer sweater, then it was her good jeans. A few bracelets gone, then her wedding band vanished. Stripped of her treasures, her heirlooms pilfered for profit.

***

I try to plug in the turntable. No light comes on. Not serving its destined purpose, taking up space and a bother to behold. We hadn't turned it on in ages, and maybe it had just wasted away from the neglect. Like her, alone in a corner, sitting in a chair, day after day, heartbeat after futile heartbeat, until the heart beats no more. Until her skull cracks open and her rotting brains spill onto the sterilized floor.

***

We bring her one of my sister's old dolls. It's more for us, I begrudge to admit. It reminds me that, if not she, there's still somebody in there. And knowing that is enough. It's not enough, but it's sufficient to keep me coming back. Mamma sways the doll in front of her and sometimes she smirks and chuckles. Maybe she thinks the doll was her. Maybe she thinks it was me. Maybe she thinks something, thinks anything. What a twisted perversion of nature, for a child to witness their parent regress to infancy.

But I had always known she loved poppies. She would wear their colour in the fall when it wasn't in fashion. The cushions on the couch and the slippers she stitched were always that one shade of red. And in the summer, only the brightest and flashiest flowers decorated their garden. I fill her room every week with only the reddest geraniums, until she starts to eat them. Then we put plastic plants on the highest shelves. I bring her the reddest tea-towels to fold and press, to maybe make her believe she's a young woman again, sweating at the sewing machines. Until she topples over, reaching for a red rag, and breaks her hip.

Bleeding and bedridden, no one can operate for days, so they blast morphine into her veins. The physiotherapist is on vacation for a month without another to spare, so they condemn her to crippledom. Contribute to society your whole life, and this is your reward in kind. Confined to a wheelchair, crying yourself to sleep, festering in your feces, never knowing why the people in blue pyjamas keep rolling their tired eyes at you.

***

Turning the corner, we observe an entire congregation of neighbours and bystanders, of cousins and acquaintances. We pull over and roll down the windows. Puffy red eyes glare into the car from all around, their facemasks sodden with sniffles and tears. We nod and offer thanks. Nonno ignores them all. It's midday rush-hour, but you can hear their muffled sobs with exquisite precision. The wind rustles through the leaves like wayward spirits of generations long past. A bright red realtor sign screams VENDU into the ether of black suits and dresses.

***

"Please, *signora*," beseeches Nonno of the nurse over FaceTime, his heavy voice quivering. "You can, you can take her hand? I no want her all alone. I . . . I no want her be scared."

She's no longer conscious, but her eyelids often flicker. A large plastic pipe impales her throat. A vicious gag taped over her mouth. Machines push and pull breath in and out of her lungs. We can hear the hoarseness in her quaking chest. Tubes slither all over her blanket. They poke and puncture her gaunt arms. A helpless little fly caught in a web of plastic wires. Whenever she jolts, we freeze. Maybe she's about to awake. Maybe she's about to slip away.

The nurse strokes her damp hair, and Nonno blubbers a lullaby into the phonemic. Full of love. Of devastation. The notes tremble through his teeth. Heartache bleeds from his lips. He's almost ninety and doesn't care about his health. He wants to be there, in the final moments. To complete his husbandly duty. But we force him to stay away. To keep him breathing, but no longer living. My father looks to his brother. Doubt seeps through them. Was it worth it? Should we have let him go to her? No, we cannot lose them both. But haven't we though?

***

I want to keep the records and bring them to her room. Maybe we can set up a new turntable, what a treat that would be. Maybe they can rekindle a tap in her toes, or a trill on her tongue. The others had accepted the emptiness in her gaze. I stare time and time again into the crystal balls under her brow, hoping the fog will clear. But as I see my tears reflected in those opaque eyes, I realize I'm no one's little prince, not anymore. There she lingers on the precipice of oblivion, a goddess in a hospital gown, a queen without a shimmering crown.

***

Wreath in hand, the hearse driver marches up the front stairs and places the flowers at the doorstep. He gestures the sign of the cross and bows his head. An Italian custom, but a mental image I never bothered to paint. Not for my family. The calla lilies billow in the breeze below the brass knocker. It hits me at last. An oncoming train of unstoppable reality. Nonno signed a lease in assisted living. He refuses to go back into that house, crushing my delusions. Waking me from my dream of denial. I'll never again scuttle up those steps. I'll never again be welcomed through that front door. This chapter is ended and ripped from the book. Childhood is over.

***

So here we sit, in the slippers she had knitted, sheltered from contagion, forced to watch from afar, connected and divided by a pixelated screen. My arms nestle our patriarch, smelling her spaghetti, swallowing our sobs. Wondering if we'll ever dance again, waiting for Nonna to die again ...

Anna Romano Milne

Chameleons

Giulia Longano reached for the gold *Madonna* charm on her necklace and bringing it up to her lips, gave it a little kiss for good luck. She was just about to tear open her Grade 12 report card and was hoping that all of her hard work had paid off. It was the summer of 1985 and Giulia was already making plans to attend university the following year. The column of straight A's provided validation that she was on the right path. The next step was to find a summer job and earn enough money to pay for tuition. After dropping off a few resumes, she received a call back from Steinberg's Grocery. The store was across town, but the pay was decent, and Giulia was excited at the prospect of making new friends. It didn't take long before she became close with one of the other cashiers.

Melissa McLeod was so different from everyone else in Giulia's immediate circle. She went to a public high school and was already in Grade 13. You could tell that she was someone who would be more comfortable in a sports jersey rather than the polyester red and white Steinberg's uniform. With blue eyes and short blonde hair, she was someone that Giulia's mother would describe as a real *Canadese*.

Melissa's house was a convenient place to hang out before and after their shifts. It was five minutes from the store and Melissa's parents never seemed to be home. Melissa and Giulia watched movies, played music, and even tried cigarettes. If they were invited to a party, they would get ready at Melissa's place. Giulia was feeling like a new thrill awaited everyday.

Melissa was also grateful for her new friend. Having fun in the city was great, but what she cherished the most was spending time with Giulia at the McLeod family cottage. After a day of swimming, sunbathing, and playing cards, they would collapse into Melissa's double bed. Despite their exhaustion, there was always an eagerness to talk for a few more hours.

'Did you have fun today?' Melissa asked as the clock approached midnight.

'Well ya . . . you are so lucky to have this place to just relax on the weekend. Saturday mornings at my house are all about *le faccende*.'

'*Le* what?' Melissa asked, intrigued.

'Oh sorry—the chores—laundry, dusting and cleaning toilets. Then Sunday morning we have to go to Mass and after that, the two-hour lunch.'

'Right. Your house is always spotless. But I would clean a toilet or two for your mom's lasagna'.

Reaching over to turn off the bedside lamp, Melissa added: 'It's kind of boring when it's just me and my parents out here. I am happy you love the lake so much. Maybe it will keep bringing you back.'

As Giulia closed her eyes and nestled into the soft duvet before drifting off to sleep, she responded, almost imperceptibly:

'It's not just the lake, Mel.'

With every conversation, the two friends learned a little more about the other. They were both keenly aware that if they had gone to the same high school, they would have never contemplated talking to each other, let alone becoming such good friends. Giulia had been labelled as the brainy "WOP" with the hairy arms and Melissa was the party-loving jock, likely headed for community college.

And yet, here they were. . .now practically inseparable and feeling incredibly lucky to have met and gotten to know what lay beyond the simplistic high school labels.

As the months passed, Giulia began to question what was going on between her and Melissa. As an only child, she was no stranger to one-way conversations with herself. *Is this normal? Sure it is. Every teenage girl has as many sleepovers as their parents will allow. What is it that mamma always says? "The Canadese like to eat and sleep at other people's houses." So maybe this is a Canadian thing.*

Across town, Melissa was having a similar conversation with her reflection in the mirror. *I have never met anyone as touchy-feely as Giulia. What is it that Dad always says? "Those eye-talians, always hugging and kissing. . .a man needs a little space!" So maybe this is an Italian thing.*

The double kiss on both cheeks upon arrival and departure was as routine to Giulia as taking your shoes off at the door. Now in her last year of high school, she and Melissa had adopted the familiar greeting. Kiss on the cheek: one side and then the other. Right and then left. Quick and effortless, like a good habit.

Until one day, Giulia lingered a little longer as she moved from right to left. And then another first for Giulia. At once a surprise and entirely expected, their lips touched in a delicate abundance. So soft and yet so powerful that Giulia's knees buckled.

'You good?' Melissa asked softly.

'Oh, I'm good. You?'

'Yup.'

The following weekend, Giulia took in the familiar landscape on the drive home from the cottage. On that sunny Sunday, she thought that the trees looked different somehow. They were bursting with leaves, making them look taller, rounder . . . fuller.

Not taking her eyes off of the view, Giulia asked Melissa:

'Were there always so many shades of green?'

Melissa looked at Giulia and agreed that if there were so many greens before, she hadn't noticed until now.

The excitement of those early days was dampened by the hard truth that their romance needed to be kept secret. While their upbringing had been radically different, Giulia and Melissa agreed that their relationship would be unthinkable to everyone they knew. Unless they were alone, they would need to continue to play the role of best friends. At home, their telephone calls focused on typical topics for two friends, just in case their parents might pick up the phone elsewhere in the house and overhear their conversation. When they were apart, they put pen to paper to express their feelings and exchanged pocket-sized letters during their Saturday shifts at Steinberg's.

As Giulia's high school graduation approached, a boy in her class asked her if she wanted to be his date for prom. She was surprised by the interest. Derek Knobel had been a good study partner, so she thought that there would be no harm in accepting the invitation.

'I don't get it G. Why are you bothering with Derek?' Melissa pressed.

Giulia answered in her usual logical way: 'Don't you think it will look weird if I don't have a date for prom? This will be good. Derek is the perfect decoy.'

Melissa saw the benefits and played along whenever she heard Giulia talking to friends and family, expertly working in the phrase "my boyfriend Derek" at every opportunity.

Giulia's mother and father liked Derek. It didn't seem to matter to them that he wasn't Italian. Derek came from a good family who lived in a nice part of town. He was headed to university to pursue a teaching degree. He wanted to be a math teacher at one of the local Catholic high schools. *Perfetto.*

On one of her daily morning calls to Giulia's *nonna*, Signora Longano was sharing the good news. Giulia could always tell when her mother was speaking to her *nonna* as their language of choice was their dialect.

'Shein, shein, se chiama Der-ick. Nu ragazzo serio e educato ... da na bella famiglie.'

Pulling the telephone cord as far as it could reach, Signora Longano brought Giulia a piece of hard bread to dunk in her coffee. Pinching Giulia's cheek with her free hand, she expressed her approval:

'Brava Giulia ... a trovato nu bel giovane.'

As Signora Longano walked away to hang up the telephone, Giulia mumbled as she took her last sip of coffee:

'Ya sure ... a real prince charming who can't kiss worth shit.'

On her way to school, Giulia wondered why it was that kissing Derek felt the way it did. Every single time, it was a collision of teeth and tongues, topped off by a prickly upper lip and the metallic taste of aftershave. Was this how every guy kisses?

She thought of the lyrics she had heard her mother singing at the kitchen sink ... *Con un bacio piccolissimo, you made me fall in love.* Was that how it worked? Can you fall in love with someone because of a good kiss? Or do you fall in love first and then all the kisses are awesome?

A week after their high school graduation, Derek and Giulia said their goodbyes. He was leaving town to spend the summer tree planting in British Columbia. Giulia was relieved that she was able to end her relationship with Derek without too much drama. With her first year of university on the horizon, she didn't need an additional commitment.

With Derek out of the picture, Giulia and Melissa settled back into a familiar chameleon-like existence ... always on guard for anything or anyone that might threaten their secret and treasuring those moments when they could be true to their feelings.

One afternoon, the pair headed out to visit Giulia's cousin Enzo. He was building a new house and had invited the girls to the job site. The house was at the wood framing stage. No walls yet, but it was easy to get an idea of the size and layout of the rooms. Giulia and Melissa were getting a tour of the second floor when Enzo's pager started to buzz.

'I will be right back,' Enzo said as he flew down the steps to fetch blueprints from his truck.

Always ready to seize an opportunity, the duo quickly scurried into one of the framed-up closets to steal a kiss. While the studs were somewhat more densely arranged in closet formation, it was hardly an effective hiding spot. They didn't get caught and laughed about their "closet" for days to come.

As Easter approached, misfortune befell the Longano family. Giulia's mother was diagnosed with kidney cancer and her health began to rapidly deteriorate.

Between school, work and taking care of her mother, Giulia couldn't spend time with Melissa. They did manage to connect on the phone almost every night, though not much was said before Giulia would fall asleep with Melissa still on the line.

Once she was admitted to hospital, Signora Longano spent most of her time asleep. The reality of what was happening only sunk in for Giulia once her mother stopped speaking. While it was not clear if she was still able to hear, the doctors advised that even for patients in a semi-conscious state, it was best not to speak about death and keep the conversation light.

The one-way dialogues with her mother were a struggle for Giulia. She came up with the idea of making a mixed tape of all of her mother's favourite singers: Robertino, Claudio Baglioni, Claudio Villa ... they were all there. She set up a small cassette player by her mother's hospital bed, turned the volume down and pressed "play". The nurse complimented Giulia for the thoughtful gesture but still, she felt like the songs were a weak substitute for her own words.

Despite the doctor's advice to pretend everything was normal, she held her mother's hand and attempted to cram in nineteen years' worth of gratitude into one conversation.

'Ma ... I don't know if you can hear me. *Sono Giulia*. I hope that you are not in too much pain. I just need to tell you a few things.'

Giulia paused, hoping to feel her mother's grip tighten.

'I have so much respect for you ... for the sacrifices you made for your family ... coming to a strange land to marry daddy ... working so hard ... always putting your family first. *Grazie ... ti amo assai assai.*'

Tightening her grip, Giulia braved one more wish for her mother: '*La Madonnina ti accompagna.*'

Giulia's mother passed away a few days before her 59th birthday. A week after the funeral, Melissa went to visit Giulia and her father. Having well understood the custom of not showing up empty handed, Melissa arrived with a dozen homemade oatmeal muffins and a packet of Lavazza coffee.

The visit in the kitchen was brief, Giulia's father only being able to say: '*Grazie Me-Lisa, Grazie.*'

Giulia and Melissa headed down to the basement to have some time on their own. Sitting on the couch, Melissa spoke up first: 'Your dad looks pretty rough. What's with the beard?'

'Ya, it's hard for him ... he says he has no reason to shave anymore.'

Giulia's voice cracked and she began to cry. 'I miss her so much, Mel.'

Melissa did her best to comfort Giulia with one of her warm and tender hugs.

When they let go, Giulia wiped the tears from her face and locked eyes with Melissa. They moved toward each other for a kiss. As their lips touched, they were immediately startled apart by a loud banging noise coming from the laundry room.

On their feet now, they moved quickly to investigate. The double concrete sink adjacent to the washing machine was overflowing. The dirty water was sullying the sink's white lace skirt hung by Giulia's mother to conceal its ugly rusted-out legs.

Melissa had not taken her eyes off Giulia as she stood paralyzed watching the watery pigment spread across the canvas of white lace.

And then, with a nervous urgency, Giulia grabbed Melissa's arm and whispered: 'Oh my God ... she knows.'

As Giulia loosened her grip, Melissa immediately understood what needed to come next.

The following day, Giulia was in the backyard, in front of the brick fireplace her father had built to accommodate the annual roasting of red peppers. She placed Melissa's letters on the bulky metal grate. She hadn't even bothered unfolding them.

Pulling a glossy white matchbox from her pocket, she ran her fingers over the gold embossed words "Bride and Groom". It was a sophisticated font, no doubt chosen by a beautiful bride to complement a delicate *bomboniera*.

'I just need to get this done,' she said to herself impatiently.

Striking the match, she threw it onto the pile of secret words and watched the flame rise. The mangle of foolscap paper and blue ink burned quickly.

She may have fooled everyone hanging out with fake boyfriends and hiding in closets with no walls. But there would be no fooling an angel in heaven.

Giulia waited for the fire to settle down into ashes, and then walked away.

Daniel Scarcello

Orecchiette

On Friday night, I had a dream about Nonno Frankie. I walked into his house and there was a Japanese folding screen in the middle of the family room. He sat behind it, on the couch. It was so hot in the house; the heat was almost unbearable. When I walked past the screen, I must have surprised him, because he stood up very quickly, and as he did, his pants began to fall down. Embarrassed, he scrambled to keep them on. In broken English, he told me why the temperature was so high.

"*Nonno sick*," he said, clutching his belt.

The next morning, my father called and told me that Nonno had gone to the hospital the night before, because he found blood in his urine. As he explained what happened, I could see Nonno in my dream, struggling to keep his pants on. When I got off the phone, I just sat for a while on the edge of the ottoman, stunned.

Nonno was sent home later that day, and I went to go see him. When I got there, all the lights were off. Nonno was upstairs, which was unusual, since he spent most of his time in the garden. He stood at the top of the staircase waving at me, and I wondered why he wasn't coming down. Then I realized he probably felt too weak. I didn't want him to think he *looked* weak, so I started hopping up the stairs quickly, not even giving him the chance to take a step down.

The first thing I noticed was that the folds in his grey sweater were baggier than usual, as if he'd lost weight since the last time I'd seen him. Halfway up the stairs, on a small landing, Nonna Ida called me from downstairs, and I stood there talking to both of them. From that spot, I just happened to catch sight of something caught in the folds of Nonno's sweater: a single ear-shaped pasta, one *orecchietta*.

Nonna must have made *orecchiette* with *rapini* and *salsiccia*, and the pasta must have fallen from Nonno's fork without him realizing it. I glanced at it for a split second, then looked away.

Nonna was holding up two Fortino's bags full of documents she wanted me to bring up for her. It was hard enough for her to get up the stairs without having to carry anything; she basically had to crawl on her hands and knees. I ran down and grabbed the bags. On my way down, Nonno moved a bit, and the *orechietta* fell to the floor. Facing Nonna, who wanted to know if she could throw away any of those documents, I pretended not to notice. On my way back up, Nonno bent down, picked up the *orecchietta*, and slid it into his pocket.

After Nonna crawled up the stairs, we all sat in the upstairs kitchen. It felt odd sitting up there; we never used that table. A few minutes later, my father walked in and joined us. He walked up to my Nonno, pinched his cheek playfully, and then stuck his hand into his shirt pocket, pretending to see if he had any cash on him.

Nonna Ida asked my dad to take a look at the documents. My dad took one of the Fortino's bags and dumped it all out on the table.

"They're all old bills!" he said. "Look at this! Property taxes from twenty years ago!"

My dad looked at me and smirked, dumping all the envelopes back into the bag. As he slid the papers across the table, two prayer cards, buried in the pile, popped out. I picked them up and opened them. They were the funeral cards for my other two grandparents on my mother's side: Nonna Lavinia and Nonno Gianni. They both died ten years before. I couldn't remember the last time I'd even looked at those cards.

When my parents got married, my four grandparents became the best of friends. They would even spend their winters together in Acapulco.

More family than family, as Nonna Ida would say.

Those prayer cards, combined with the fact we were eating on the second floor- a drastic change for us- reminded me of the first time I went to Nonna Lavinia's house and saw a hospital bed set up on the main floor, where the dining table used to be. The shock of seeing it there brought tears to my eyes. Because I didn't want her to see me cry, I went straight to the washroom. When I came out, I sat next to her bed. Then my Uncle Carlo walked in. I saw the look of shock come over his face. Right away, he headed for the washroom.

At the table, Nonno Frankie adjusted his pants, and I could almost feel the *orecchietta* squishing together in his pocket. I opened Nonno Gianni's prayer card, and read the poem written inside it:

Do not stand at my grave and weep.
I am not there, I do not sleep.
Do not stand at my grave and cry
I am not there. I did not die.

Then, in an uncontrollable wave, I felt the tears coming on. I stood right up, holding my stomach, as if I had to go to the washroom, then I bolted for the door. When I closed it behind me and turned on the light, I looked down at the toilet and saw a drop of blood on the tiles. Then I looked at myself in the mirror, wiping the tears from my face. When I realized that, by running to the washroom, I did the exact same thing Nonno had done, hiding the *orecchietta* in his pocket, I smiled at myself.

Renée M. Sgroi

Journeyed: an attempt at a narrative

This is a story about my mother, about movement. A journey of muscles, ligaments, tendons propelling a body forward in an attempt at motion. This story, as all stories, attempts to reach a destination.

Starting points. My mother arrived in Halifax in December of 1957, aged eleven, along with my widowed Nonna and aunt, who had sailed from Calabria and (like so many during those years) arrived at Pier 21. From Halifax they traveled to Toronto to reunite with the rest of their family. My mother's story, this story, begins with a voyage that becomes my story. A story about walking, about love, about limits. A story about Parkinson's.

Levodopa. Carbidopa. Selegiline. Sinemet. Amantadine. A cocktail of drugs to "titrate" a patient. To balance them into some kind of homeostasis. To keep the body, as a ship, on an even keel. My mother's voyage through Parkinson's was never steady, never smooth. An experiment in drugs, one microgram too much or too little. An experiment in definition, the line between Parkinson's and Parkinson*ism* as thick as a rope used to tie a ship to its dock, as thin as a strand of my mother's hair.

What I know of Parkinson's begins with a story. One day, when I was around four or five, my Papà Vecchio, my paternal grandfather, walked to my house—one of the few pleasant memories I have of him. From his pocket, *caramelle*. I don't remember what he said. What stands out is that he was mobile. He walked. For the rest, he remains an old man, hunched over in his chair, hands atop a cane he eventually could no longer use, a mumbling, barely audible person, one hand grasping a dampened handkerchief to wipe the drool constantly sliding from his mouth. Papà Vecchio had Parkinson's.

In 1817, James Parkinson published an article on the "shaking palsy" that outlined the disease that now bears his name. Parkinson linked the disparate symptoms that, up until that time, doctors thought belonged to different illnesses. He wrote: "The submission of the limbs to the directions of the will can hardly ever be obtained in the performance of the most ordinary offices of life. The fingers cannot be disposed of in the proposed directions, and applied with certainty to any proposed point. As time and the disease proceed, difficulties increase."[9] Reading Parkinson's article is like reliving the progress of my grandfather's illness. The startling clarity of medical observation is not a discovery but a precise rendering of what I already know.

What I didn't know was that James Parkinson himself took long walks, allowing him to gather the various symptoms into one, singular diagnosis. My mother sometimes walked. Parkinson's patients must retain as much movement as possible to stave off the inevitable. Yet growing up, my family didn't amble. We stayed put. We went to school, to church. We worked on improving our lives, our selves. We learned to live alongside neighbours: families of immigrants and their children, just like us.

Observations. The passage to my mother's Parkinson's diagnosis was a case of missed observations. Doctors hadn't seen the signposts, hadn't walked with her enough to notice. Once, when I was five, I walked with my mother in hospital, after she'd given birth to my younger sister. Hooked up to a saline drip after an emergency C-section that involved a rapid blood transfusion and near death, Mom held my hand as we walked. Her steps slow, measured. I could not imagine then how she would one day return to that kind of pace, that kind of gait.

Witnessing my mother's decline was a journey to a place I didn't want to visit. I read medical journals, magazine articles, anything, as if searching for a holy grail of answers. In *Awakenings,* Oliver Sacks wrote: "It is necessary to say at the outset that the shaking or tremor is by no means a constant symptom in Parkinsonism, is never an isolated symptom ... If tremor is present, it tends to occur at rest and to disappear with movement or the intention to move."[10]

9. Parkinson, James. "An essay on the shaking palsy." 1817. *The Journal of Neuropsychiatry and Clinical Neurosciences,* vol. 14, no. 2, 2002, pp. 223–36.

10. Sacks, Oliver. *Awakenings.* 1973. Vintage Books, 1990.

The intention to move. Mom always intended to move. The house we grew up in was semi-detached, near a hydro field and rail line. She wanted to move to a socio-economic class she hadn't been born into. After thirty-three years in that semi-detached, Mom finally achieved her dream: a detached house. The one with granite counter tops, a finished basement, the second kitchen my parents had always wanted. A showpiece to reflect that she'd finally arrived, made it in this country, forty-four years after landing at Pier 21. But because of Parkinson's, my mother's house eventually became impossible for her to navigate.

Mom became child-like. She shuffled when she walked. When she ate, she wore a bib and waited to be fed. My own maternal patterns kicked in as I spoon fed her yogurt and puréed food. Parkinson wrote: "when the food is conveyed to the mouth, so much are the actions of the muscles of the tongue, pharynx, &c. impeded by impaired action and perpetual agitation that the food is with difficulty retained in the mouth until masticated; and then as difficultly swallowed."[11] I hear Parkinson speak to me as if he knew my mother, could identify her by name.

Nothing in life is guaranteed. Dad thinks his father developed Parkinson's because of chemical exposure from factories he worked in when he first arrived in Canada (exposure to coal-gas and manganese poisoning may later result in Parkinson's). As perhaps today, when Papà Vecchio arrived in 1949, there were few protections for immigrant labourers.

As for Mom, she was fortunate not to work in factories. But that hydro field. The scientific community is split as to detrimental effects from exposure to electromagnetic fields. Our family knows of at least three women who lived on that street and developed dementia or Alzheimer's. Women who mostly stayed home and raised children. Women like my mother. Was our house a thirty-three-year-long incubator so that by the time my mother finally moved to her detached dream, the timer of disease had already been set?

Questions. Fragments as questions. What is my role in recording this illness? What is my role in writing about my mother? Ian Brown,

---

11. Parkinson, James. "An essay on the shaking palsy." 1817. *The Journal of Neuropsychiatry and Clinical Neurosciences,* vol. 14, no. 2, 2002, pp. 223–36.

in *Sixty,* describes his late father's decline as a transformation into "Otherness".[12] My mother declined, but *I* am the one who is other, who is subsequent, after. Bereft. Where does her story end and mine begin?

Neapolitan author, Erri de Luca writes in, *The Day Before Happiness*: "A writer has to be smaller than the subject he is describing. You have to sense the story running away from him every which way, and him capturing only a part of it."[13] A woman's story, my mother's or mine, running in all different directions: to Parkinson's, to immigration, to childhood, memories, to the movement from one story to another.

In his poem, "The Rose," William Carlos Williams writes: "It is at the edge of the / petal that love waits."[14] A story about a rose: when I was young, my unmarried aunt and uncles lived with my Nonna in a house on our street. "Home" was a street-crossing between two fixed points. I was playing at Nonna's house the day I later walked with my mother at the hospital, the day my beautiful mother gave me a rose from a bouquet at her bedside.

Rose petal remnants. We all lose our mothers one day, as my own children will one day lose me. My eldest, whose middle name is my mother's, went to university and still lives in Halifax, a city she chose. Sometimes I wonder if the city chose her. My children and I have visited Pier 21, now the country's immigration museum, several times. Each time I say, for the umpteenth time, *this is where Grandma came to Canada,* as if it was some kind of miraculous journey. And perhaps it was. My 50-something year old Nonna traveled to Canada with two young daughters. I'm a 50-something year old mother who travels with one daughter to visit the other in Halifax. The ironies of our travels are not lost on me. My eldest carries my mother's name as she walks to the landing place where my mother's story, or mine, or ours, begins.

We are at the edge of the rose petal. One month shy of her seventy-third birthday and twelve days before her passing, my mother took her last, shuffling steps to the ambulance that transported her to the

12. Brown, Ian. *Sixty: A Diary of My Sixty-First Year.* Random House Canada, 2015.

13. De Luca, Erri. *The Day Before Happiness.* Translated by Michael F. Moore. Other Press, 2009.

14. Williams, William Carlos. "The Rose." *Selected Poems,* edited by Charles Tomlinson, New Directions Books, 1985, pp. 44–45

hospital. Twelve days in a hospital bed are about the same duration as a transatlantic voyage to Canada.

I am not my mother's story; my mother's story is my inheritance. I walked with my mother; I witnessed something of her journey. At the edge of a petal, a passage. Love and remembrance, a rose, a *ricordo*. And story: movement and its absence, absence and a need for movement.

Maria Pia Spadafora

I pastelli morbidi di Licia Canton

(traduzione a cura di Maria Pia Spadafora)

«Mi piacerebbe provare con i colori» dissi a Susan.

Susan tirò fuori gli acquerelli, i pastelli morbidi, i colori ad olio e grandi matitoni colorati.

«Quali vuoi utilizzare?» Mi chiese.

«I pastelli morbidi.»

Quella fu la mia scelta. Ero entusiasta di provare qualcosa di nuovo.

«Sai cosa sono?» Susan mi domandò, avvicinandomi la scatola dei pastelli morbidi.

Non li avevo mai provati, ma li avevo acquistati ai miei figli alle scuole elementari per le lezioni di arte. Ricordo di averli dovuti comprare in un negozio di colori specializzato ed erano molto costosi. Ma alla fine dell'anno erano stati usati pochissimo per le lezioni di arte. Che spreco, avevo pensato.

«Scegli un colore» mi disse Susan, mentre mi mise davanti un foglio bianco A3.

«Blu reale» dissi, prendendolo dalla scatola. Un colore che rispecchia come mi sento questa mattina: controllata al contempo piena di vita. Preoccupata tuttavia fiduciosa.

«Chiudi gli occhi» mi ordinò Susan.

Chiusi gli occhi e seguii le istruzioni. Iniziai a fare delle forme senza alzare il pastello dal foglio.

«È un buon modo per iniziare» disse Susan incoraggiandomi.

Una sorta di scrittura automatica, pensai. In questo modo avevo ricominciato a scrivere di nuovo. Quando Susan me lo aveva suggerito circa un anno fa non pensavo funzionasse. Ma ci ho provato lo stesso, non avevo nulla da perdere. Ero in uno stato di depressione tale che non avrei mai pensato di riprendermi e indossare di nuovo colori vivaci.

Non pensavo sarei riuscita a scrivere un altro racconto o un articolo. Ma l'ho fatto. Ed ero orgogliosa di quel primo racconto. Il racconto del mio ritorno. Le parole erano scivolate sulla pagina una alla volta, molto lentamente, dopo numerosi tentativi e tante lacrime.

Con gli occhi ancora chiusi, la mia mano destra si muoveva a volte lentamente altre veloce, dando vita a forme di colore blu di ogni genere. Dopo ciò che sembrò un lasso di tempo molto lungo, ma forse solo pochi minuti, Susan mi chiese di aprire gli occhi.

«Guarda cosa hai disegnato» Susan sorrise.

Osservai un motivo casuale, forme e dimensioni diverse che non mi dicevano nulla. Persino il cuore che ero sicura di aver disegnato non si distingueva tra le forme alla rifusa. Il cuore era per l'amore presente nella mia vita. C'è di sicuro molto amore nella mia vita. Ed è grazie a quell'amore che affronto ogni giorno. Quell'amore che mi dà forza e speranza. Avevo disegnato il cuore, per cui doveva essere lì. La speranza.

Mi chiedo spesso perché sia così depressa nonostante tutto l'amore che ricevo, tutto l'amore che mi circonda ogni momento, tutti i giorni. Che ne sarebbe di me senza tutto il sostegno che ricevo? Come affronterei la giornata?

Come fanno gli altri? Quelli che non ricevono questo sostegno e amore. Come fanno ad andare avanti? Mi abbatto così tanto nonostante tutto l'amore che mi circonda.

«Scegli un altro colore» Susan mi disse. «Adesso devi riempire gli spazi bianchi.»

Scelsi il fucsia per riempire il bianco tra le forme. Un colore brillante e deciso, vivo e moderno. Si fa notare e non è affatto stancante. È un colore di tutto rispetto.

Susan mi diede la possibilità di parlare o semplicemente di restare in silenzio mentre coloravo gli spazi vuoti tra le forme.

Non rimasi in silenzio.

Le mie labbra si muovevano alla stessa velocità con cui sceglievo di muovere i pastelli morbidi lungo gli spazi bianchi del foglio. L'ora era volata.

Inconsciamente, ogni qual volta cambiavo colore, cambiavo anche argomento. O era il contrario? Mi stancavo dell'argomento o del colore? O erano semplicemente quelle pause che mi permettevano di proseguire?

Prima di ogni incontro con Susan avevo sempre paura di non avere molte cose da dire per occupare i sessanta minuti di seduta. Tuttavia, ogni volta sembrava che un'ora non bastasse.

Cosa dovrò dire per un'ora? Il filo conduttore era la delusione.

Ero delusa dalla situazione in cui mi trovavo, dalle scelte professionali, da me stessa. I miei genitori mi avevano sconsigliato di intraprendere la carriera artistica. Ero stanca delle persone che chiedevano il mio aiuto, i miei servizi. Ero avvilita dalla mancanza di rispetto professionale che ricevevo. Per qualche ragione sembrava normale chiedere a scrittori, traduttori, editori di lavorare gratis, a titolo di favore.

«Un uomo aveva bisogno della traduzione pronta per ieri» spiegai a Susan. «E quando gli ho inviato il preventivo, mi ha detto che avrebbe fatto la traduzione da solo.»

Poi alcune persone, miei presunti 'amici', mi hanno mandato a loro volta degli amici pretendendo che offrissi consigli e servizi gratis. Sono rimasti sconvolti quando hanno realizzato che li avrei fatti pagare per il mio lavoro. Come pensano mi guadagni da vivere?

«Tutti i miei figli aspirano a una carriera artistica» dissi a Susan. «Vogliono diventare scrittori o registi. Non vogliono lavorare dalle 9 alle 17. Non vogliono un capo che gli dica cosa fare». Sospirai.

«Forse i tuoi figli troveranno un modo migliore per farlo» Susan mi suggerì. In altre parole, pensai, magari loro avranno successo laddove io non l'ho avuto. Forse. Forse.

«Grazie, Susan» dissi quando terminai la seduta con i colori. «Spero di avere un racconto da leggerti la prossima volta.» Perché scrivere è la mia arte. Mi rammarico spesso di non avere un racconto nuovo da condividere ogni volta che vedo Susan. Dovrei usare le sedute di terapia per recuperare lo slancio per la scrittura. Dovrei fare i conti con il mio trauma, raccontandolo attraverso la scrittura.

«Concentrati su questa cosa, fanne il tuo obiettivo» mi disse Susan. «Scrivi di questa seduta.»

«Va bene, lo farò. Immagino questo sia il mio compito per casa: scrivere della seduta. Tornerò con un racconto la prossima volta» le promisi.

Volevo mantenere la promessa, prima di tutto per me stessa. Ma non ero molto convinta quando gliela feci.

Subito dopo la seduta, rimasi in macchina per scrivere tutto all'istante.

Guardai nella borsa e trovai la penna Swarovski che mi aveva regalato un'amica di vecchia data quando andai a trovarla a Roma dopo trent'anni.

Niente carta. Diedi un'occhiata in giro per tutta la macchina. C'era un porta fazzoletti dietro il sedile passeggero. Uffa! Pensai di scrivere sui fazzoletti o di strappare la scatola e scrivere sul cartone. Poi, vidi sul sedile passeggero un sacchetto regalo marroncino. All'interno il mio primo libro: una collezione di racconti. Era un regalo per un'amica con cui avevo riallacciato i rapporti dopo un po' di tempo. Aveva ispirato uno dei racconti.

Aprii la carta regalo, lasciandogli i cordoni dei manici, e appiattii la carta marroncina. Comprerò un sacchetto nuovo, dissi a me stessa.

Scrissi velocemente su tutti e due i lati della carta marroncina utilizzando la raccolta di racconti come supporto.

Quel sacchetto regalo con i miei scarabocchi, parole a malapena decifrabili forse l'inizio di un racconto, rimase sulla scrivania del mio studio nel seminterrato per più di due settimane. Ogni volta che mi avvicinavo alla scrivania, c'era qualcos'altro da fare. Mi diede il tormento ogni giorno. Devo scrivere la storia per Susan, per me.

Un giorno creai un nuovo documento word e scrissi il titolo, *Pastelli Morbidi*. Eccolo. Dissi volutamente ad ogni componente della mia famiglia di non toccare il sacchetto da regalo strappato e tutto scarabocchiato. Nel caso in cui avessero l'urgenza improvvisa di riordinare la scrivania, cosa altamente improbabile, ma è sempre meglio prevenire che curare. Qualcuno potrebbe notare il sacchetto strappato ma non la scritta blu su di esso.

Poi la mattina dell'appuntamento successivo con Susan mi affrettai a scrivere la storia. Mi sedetti alla scrivania due ore prima dell'appuntamento e decifrai quella scrittura illeggibile. Pare che sia motivata solo quando ho a disposizione poco tempo. Ce la farò? Mi domandai. Certamente.

Poi mi feci un caffè e mi sedetti a scrivere le note del sacchetto marroncino, ricordandomi di aver creato un file word con il titolo. Non sempre mi ricordo. Ecco perché ho più di un file sotto lo stesso nome per alcuni dei miei racconti. I miei file sono un disastro. I miei racconti sono in disordine. Io sono un disastro. Ma, dopotutto, è per questo che ho bisogno di Susan. Vorrei che fosse mia amica.

«Perché non la inviti per un caffè?» Suggerì mio marito, dopo avergli detto per l'ennesima volta quanto Susan fosse eccezionale.

«Non posso farlo» gli risposi. «Sarebbe strano.» Speravo lui dicesse il contrario.

Due settimane fa, dopo la seduta dei colori, sapevo che l'unico modo per mantenere la promessa sarebbe stato quello di scrivere di nuovo in macchina subito dopo la seduta. Sapevo che era improbabile che accadesse una volta riassorbita dalla mia realtà. C'erano lavori di traduzione da terminare e scadenze da rispettare, le mail a cui rispondere, le telefonate, il bucato, la spesa, le colazioni, i pranzi, le cene, feste di compleanno, la Festa del Papà, un marito e i figli, quattro genitori anziani ... che si impossessano di ogni mio momento libero per scrivere. Ma so, anche mentre scrivo, che è colpa mia. O meglio il mio non 'adoperarmi'. Potrei benissimo dire che non sono disponibile per nessuno di loro. Come quando ho un'emicrania e non posso far altro che rimanere distesa sul letto al buio. Dipende da me, proprio così. E sono sicura che se facessi più di quello che voglio, più di quello che devo fare, allora avrei probabilmente meno mal di testa. Perché le emicranie sono provocate dalla pressione, pressione che aumenta quando guardo la lista delle cose da fare e capisco che le priorità personali continuano a essere schiacciate in fondo alla lista. Sempre.

«Buongiorno» Susan aprì la porta. «Come stai?»

«Benone! Ho una storia da leggerti oggi».

2002
AICW BRESSANI
PRIZE WINNER

David Giuliano

Chapter Five: My First Home

[Pages 25–29 of *The Undertaking of Billy Buffone,* 2021. Latitude 46 Publishing]

In those earliest of my childhood memories of Billy and I, in the season of dandelions, I am still wearing my pyjamas, and am walking across the front lawns on our side of Miles Street. I'm wearing socks but not shoes. It must have been early in the morning because I remember the grass being thick with dew. My socks are wet. Through our neighbours' open windows, I can smell coffee and toast, can hear the clatter of breakfast tables being set.

Three yards down the street from ours, Billy is sitting on the wet grass in front of his house, basking in the early sun. He is wearing short pants and no shirt. His smooth legs are crossed in front of him. We called it sitting Indian style, never making the connection to Pickerel River First Nation, only twenty minutes away. Billy's legs are already turning brown, even though summer is just starting. His belly is round. His eyes are closed. The drops of moisture glittering on the grass, and the dandelions, give the appearance that he is floating on a green pond of yellow lilies. A prayer-bell of peacefulness encircles him. I am drawn by the soundless bell, toward him.

I stopped a few feet away, waiting for him to notice me. I stepped closer, circled him. I got close enough to smell the baby shampoo in his hair. If he heard me approach, felt me breathing close by, he was undisturbed by my presence. His eyelids remained soft and closed, his eyelashes dark and full. His hand hovered over the cap of a single dandelion, among the hundreds dotting our yards, allowing the slender yellow petals to touch the centre of his palm. It must have tickled because, as his hand almost imperceptibly moved above the flower's golden crown, his eyelashes fluttered and his lips tipped up in a smile.

I continued to watch him, waiting for his eyes to open. When they didn't open, I knelt down on the grass beside him, closed my own eyes and swept my hand around at my side. A dandelion caught between my fingers and was decapitated. I wiped its milky sap on my pyjama pants.

I winked an eye open to locate one particular flower, and closed my eye again. This time I slowly lowered my hand until I felt the glowing, energy of it in my palm. I was not so much touching the petals as sensing their warmth, cupping its life force in my downturned hand. It was as if light entered my hand, trickled up my arm and spilled into the empty cavity of my chest. Tears rose in my throat and moistened my eyes. Some of the light from the flower spilled out of my eyes onto my cheeks.

The sound of my father's roostering and slamming disappeared down a dark and closing hole. The cry of seagulls, the gentle morning surf down at the shore, and the warmth of the sun washed over me, over us. It was as if Billy and I were safe, together in a sphere of serenity, a place defying words I didn't know then, nor have found since. Something unspeakable held us, and in that moment, we became best friends.

It is difficult to say how long we sat there on his lawn. An hour? A minute? The mysticism of childhood defies the violence of chronological time. I learned, later, that the Greeks called this qualitative measurement of time, kairos time.

By unspoken agreement, we simultaneously unshuttered our eyes. Billy smiled a sleepy smile, took my hand, led me along the warm concrete walkway to the back door of his house, and into his mother's kitchen.

Billy's baby sister, Mary, would have been about a year old then, and was buckled into a high chair at the table. She and Billy had the same smooth skin, round faces, the same dark chocolate eyes and black, lamb's wool hair. She was wearing a flannel nightshirt and was eating pieces of cinnamon toast that Mrs. Buffone had cut into quarters. Her fingers and face were sticky with butter and sugar, and tinted by the cinnamon. She smelled of baby, and exotic scents, unfamiliar to me.

After that first day, on countless mornings, afternoons and evenings, Billy and I sat at his mother's Formica table eating fresh macaroons, or biscotti and drinking sweet tea cooled with cream.

At my house, I awoke most days to the sound of the back door slamming. When my father was on dayshift, he left for the mill at 5:50AM. After night shifts, he returned at 6:10AM. It was less than a ten-minute walk down to the mill, even drunk or hungover. In my father's case, not much time elapsed between those two inseparable states of alcoholism. On the days he did not work, or was on evenings —so at home during the early morning hours—I slept lightly, rose at the first hint of dawn, and crept out of the house. I pulled the door closed behind me, slowly releasing the knob, so it would latch soundlessly. I dreaded the consequences of awakening the sleeping beast.

I crossed the grass to Billy's house, as if travelling from the hostile planet of the Mad Collins to what, by comparison, seemed a fairy tale world, within which I hoped to one day reside. If the kitchen was dark when I arrived at the Buffone's back door, I sat on the stoop to wait. I cradled their quart of milk—delivered earlier in the morning by Mr. Leveret—in my lap.

As soon as I heard Mrs. Buffone's slippers on the linoleum inside, I tapped on the aluminum door with the bottle and held it up to the screened window for her to see. "Well," she would say and put her hands on her hips, "who shrunk my milkman?" I had to avert my eyes, because there was so much kindness in her voice that it embarrassed me.

"It's me," I'd say, shuffling my feet, "Matt." Mrs. Buffone would laugh, and hold the door open so I could deliver the milk. "Oh, it's you, Matthew!" I beamed with pride carrying the heavy glass bottle, and at being fully named while doing so. She and Mr. Buffone always called me by my full name, Matthew. Mr. Buffone pronounced it, "Machew." When I think back to those bottles of milk, heavy and slippery with condensation, I realize what an immense act of trust it was on Mrs. Buffone's part to allow the four or five-year-old me to carry them into the kitchen clutched to my chest. I never dropped one. Her love, I think, provided the necessary strength. That, and the trust that, even if the bottle dropped from my arms, the glass splintered, and milk washed across the floor, it would have in no way diminished her love for me.

On mornings when Billy wasn't yet awake, I would clamber on all fours, up the narrow staircase, to lie beside him on his bed. Early on, he shared a room with Mary. She was often awake when I arrived and, without lifting her head from her mattress, would watch me through the wooden slats of her crib.

Sometimes I fell asleep next to Billy. Sometimes I grew impatient and ran the tip of my finger along the top of his velvety ear, until he yawned and opened his eyes.

Mrs. Buffone made us porridge, with as much milk and brown sugar as we wanted. On Sundays, we had pancakes with corn syrup. Mr. Buffone sat on the counter smoking, drinking black coffee, and urging us to "Mànge, mànge. You be big boys!"

Billy's mother scolded his father, "It's eat, Angelo! This is Canada. You are going to confuse the heads of these boys! They have to go to the school soon. What will the other children think? What will the teacher say? She will ask, 'What? Are you peasants from the hills of someplace?'"

Mr. Buffone would hop from the counter to strike a dramatic pose, raising his arms and shouting, "Yes! I am a peasant from the hills someplace!" He laughed and, seated back on the counter, pulled Mrs. Buffone to him. She would make a show of struggling against his hugging arms and his legs wrapped around her. He pressed his lips to her ear and murmured, "*Non resistere al mio amore, tesoro*!" Billy and I didn't know what Mr. Buffone was saying, but we would cover our ears and plead for him to stop.

When they were alone, or didn't want us to know what they were saying, Mr. and Mrs. Buffone spoke Italian to one another. The tenderness in the round tones of their voices was as foreign to me as the words themselves.

"It was like my second home." People say that about the home of a childhood friend: "Theirs was like my second home." When they say it, they mean they felt as comfortable, as welcomed, and as cherished as they did in their own home. They mean, in this second home they experienced the same ease of familial patterns, safety, the same unbreakable bonds of family ties. They mean, there is no strangeness to the smell of this second home. Its inhabitants are blood. This second home is where one spends as much time as they do in their own home. If all those things are true, if that is what people mean when the say "It was like my second home," then the Buffone's house was like my first home.

Their home was where each year, on the first day of school, my photo was taken in front of the rose bushes that kept pace with my growth as they climbed the cedar-rail fence; where a mother licked her thumb to wipe jam from my face, or to tame my unruly hair; where a father showed us how to straighten bent nails and supplied us salvaged boards with which to build our forts in the trees at the end of our street; where teasing was rare, and what teasing there was, was kind, good-natured, and more often than not, self-deprecating; where my birthday was celebrated every year with Billy's; and where they knew me well enough to give me books as gifts, rather than a second-hand shotgun, as my biological father did the Christmas I was thirteen.

Billy and I were like brothers. The Buffones were my family. Their home was my home.

2022 VENERA FAZIO POETRY CONTEST WINNERS

Silvia Falsaperla

A Car Ride to Sicily: A Memoir

(for Venera Fazio)

The AICW conference at Padula was over and the next day would be ferragosto—when Italy goes into standstill and Italians flock to the seaside. Padula, a town in the southern region of Campania, mostly meanders on a hill, difficult for a traveller to get to and difficult to exit.

Most conference attendees already had their exit plans, but with few trains operating on August 15, the official start of the summer holidays, *le ferie d'agosto*, I was stranded. I had asked several attendees at the breakfast tables of the Hotel Certosa for a car ride out to a train station, but some had plans to linger in Padula for another day or two, and one couple had too much luggage to stow away in their little car to accommodate me. Finally, a godsend, as word got to me that Venera Fazio, Delia De Santis, and Venera's husband Dwayne, Sicily-bound like me, had rented a car and had room for one more passenger.

We set off the next morning, bidding Padula goodbye and the conference attendees to their ferragosto destinations. I had met Venera and Delia only once before at the 2014 conference in Montreal. At the Padula conference, housed in a building that was part of the greater complex of the Monastery of San Lorenzo, Venera did not read her poems—Licia Canton read them for her. Venera sat next to Licia on the stage, wearing a bandana. It was my impression that Venera had a brain condition that did not allow her any sustained vocal effort. The poems were soulful, sad, quasi-religious. Although I did not know then that Venera was of Sicilian heritage, which I share with her, there was something intimately familiar about her: her gentle demeanor reminded me of my cousin Luisa, herself soulful, and religious. I pondered her name, Venera, and wondered if it derived from Venus, or the Madonna, or a Saint Venera—the Madonna and saints are fulcrums of veneration in Sicilian Catholic worship. Licia had earlier announced that she would be reading from a collection entitled *Sweet Lemons.* As she held the slim book open in front of her and read, I saw that the front cover featured an illustration of lemons—to me lemons evoked Sicily, the ubiquitous lemon trees of Sicily. Surely, I imagined, the book was Venera's tribute to her (and my) first homeland.

I felt comfortable sharing a car ride with Venera and Delia. As we sat back in our seats relieved of conference fatigue, I did not feel any pressure to impress them with brilliant conversation. There a pleasant stillness and humility about them, a harmony forged by years of friendship and literary collaboration. They worked well together in service and dedication to AICW, as two sisters of a religious order, Venera as poetry editor and Delia as prose editor for the Association's many anthologies, for which they were honoured at the conference with two gifts of beautiful glass plaques. I sat beside Delia in the backseat while Venera sat next to Dwayne at the wheel, the GPS device between them. At ferragosto the highways out of Campania and into Calabria were empty, the mad rushes of vacationers had already fled to the beaches. As we rode down the lower leg of the Italian boot, pillars of cactus pears, in clusters or solitary, covered the many kilometres of the arid roadside slopes. I watched Dwayne at the wheel who surprisingly seemed at ease driving on foreign soil, as if he had made this car journey a few times before, going to Sicily as to a second home. I joked with Venera about Dwayne being a Sicilian Irishman and he seemed pleased with the moniker, silently conveying a love for Sicily and his Sicilian-Canadian wife. Then the sea emerged. We were at the toe of Calabria, at the port of Villa San Giovanni, where huge state ferries swallow up trains, cars, and passengers and ferry them across the Strait of Messina. I had made the crossing many times.

We boarded the ferry docked at port still seated inside the car. Once Dwayne parked the car on the ferry's car-designated platform and a Sicily-bound train was in turn swallowed up and sectioned off in the bowels of the ferry, we climbed up the narrow stairway to the passenger lounge. The aromas from the ship's bar pleasantly assaulted the senses: espresso coffee, granita and brioche, and the refined deep-fried scent of arancini. I had come home. The ferry lumbered on the heavy sea, sure of its route, repeated countless times in the course of a day. Crossing the Strait of Messina has always been an emotionally-charged moment for me as the ferry advanced closer and closer—the bright rounded elevated coastal land is like the arms of a waiting mother. I am sure Venera felt the same way. I was happy to make the crossing together with a fellow Sicilian, her loyal friend Delia, and her honorary Sicilian husband. I bought a celebratory arancino from the bar as tradition demanded. Then I stepped outside on deck, the ferry lumbering, cutting the sea, the same wine-dark sea mythic Odysseus had crossed over two thousand years ago. Messina emerged golden, the gold statue of the Madonnina of Messina harbour, protectress of sea ships, seafarers, tourists, and homecomers, drawing nearer and nearer.

The ferry docked and we climbed down the narrow stairway to the open-air car-park platform and got back into the rented car. We then exited the ferry and finally set foot on Sicilian soil. Venera and company were heading to her village of Bafia in the province of Messina. My destination was Aci Castello, a seaside town where my aunt lived nearby, north of my native Catania. Dwayne drove to Messina train station along *lungomare*, then past the azure sea and the tall statue of the golden *madonnina* atop a column that extended skyward from a round-walled fortress. I caught one word of the Latin inscription written on the wall of the fortress, *benedicimus.* (The full inscription reads *Vos et ipsan civitatem benedicimus* which translates to "We bless you and your city.") It filled me with comfort and expectation.

I opened my little white sling purse slung across my chest to retrieve the pre-paid calling card and the pink lined index card on which I had written all my necessary contact numbers, including my aunt's, but couldn't find them. I searched and rummaged with mounting anxiety.

I told Venera and Dwayne that I couldn't find my calling card or contact numbers, as I proceeded to check the floor of the car and between the car seats—I could have absentmindedly put them in my pants pocket instead, forgotten about them, and they had slipped out. I felt a little embarrassed for causing a fuss and worried about catching my train and my poor aunt waiting to pick me up.

We arrived at the train station and Venera and Dwayne seemed unperturbed and determined to find the missing cards. We all exited the car and Dwayne proceeded to check inside of the car. He flipped seats and checked between the seams. He opened the trunk and removed all the suitcases and checked between all the nooks and crevices.

Tall, lanky Dwayne then got back inside the car and again flipped the car seats, overturned the floor mats, when at last he found the cards stuck deep between the back seats, where indeed they had slipped out of my pocket in the moving car. Heroic Dwayne would have gladly taken the car apart rather than to see me stranded and helpless.

I took my suitcase and set my backpack on my back. Venera then accompanied me inside the train station. She did not want to drop me off and quickly leave. Instead, she walked me to the ticket booth, made sure I had purchased a ticket to Aci Castello, and double-checked my train's departure time. Once I was safe and accounted for, Venera hugged me like a loving sister, her green eyes and smile reminding me of my cousin Luisa. I was touched by her concern and care for me, sweet lemons. Then she left to join the others en route to Bafia and I stood at the platform waiting for my imminent train.

I am certain Venera enjoyed the beauties of Sicily as much as I did that summer; she in the province of Messina and I in the Riviera of the Cyclops.

In December 2017, Venera died of a brain tumor. It was a tragic loss to her family, her husband, her trusty friend Delia, and all of us at AICW.

It was a pleasure getting to know her and I wish I had had more time with her. I wish I could have learned more from her the craft of poetry and its spirit, which Sicily had breathed into us.

I am thankful of my travel adventure with her and the two people closest to her. I am thankful for my memory of her, sweet lemons.

Liotrino

(for James)

the dwarf elephants once roamed
the wooded hill at the end of
the long thoroughfare

u liotru, a specimen in lava rock
with tusks stands above
the baroque-pastry fountain

the city gathers beneath
the squat pachyderm carrying
an obelisk on its back

It is lovable and loved like
Etna and Agatha, volcano and
saint

You heard its trumpet call
with its proboscis,
early in your summer stay

Inking one more tattoo
on your arm, the florentine lily
the unfurled tricolore

the flaring fire
already there as bold
symbols

the pigmy elephant now
for memory of the city
that bore your mother

the obelisk on its back
is the burden she tasked
you with

to construct your life
with virtue and courage
art-fully

Mermaiding

The rising wave
Submerges us
Salty one
Little anchovy

Be one
With the waves
Little eel wriggling

Dolphin calf
Flipping out of the water
In play
A phalanx submerges us
In watery space

On a crag by the open sea
You catch crabs hidden in the rocks
On the slippery lichen
You lose your footing

And I catch you on the bed of a wave …

Frances Garofalo

Refuge in the Garden

A tiny figure bends over camomile flowers, gently prying velvety
stems from the damp soil.
As she touches the earth, she feels her spirit and strength renew,
her lungs filling with sweet perfumes and earthy aromas.
She carefully places the delicate flowers and stems in a hand-woven
basket,
resting it on the weather-worn table by the back entrance.
A warm gentle breeze caresses the Northern Garden,
releasing the pungent essence of mint,
and the crisp tart aroma of mela rosa apples.
Fruit trees cast elongated shadows on the sun-drenched patio,
as she ties fragrant herb stalks into bundles,
soon swept away to languish in the cool darkness of the riserva,
then summoned up to brew the tisanes that evoke
the sweetness of summer, la dolcezza dell'estate.
Looking skyward, the rosy hues of the fading sun cast a luminous
glow on her face,
easing the lines etched on her forehead.
The garden is her respite from the constant care she provides.
She tends to her husband now, like she tends to her plants,
as the merciless disease robs him of his spirit and memory, bit by bit.
She lovingly surveys the garden, satisfied with its progress,
always something in bloom, something to gather or preserve,
Sighing, she turns toward the door,
Casting one last lingering look at the garden
before entering her home.
She will brew the tisane that soothes his agitated mind.
He will sleep well tonight . . .
And so will she . . .

Vignettes of La Dolce Vita in Calabria

Sun-drenched landscapes dotted with fragrant fruit trees
evoke memories of picking figs from tips of gnarled branches
under the caress of Mediterranean breezes,
the first bite met by the sweet flesh encased in the humble fruit.
Visiting Nonna Francesca in her ancient stone house, perched upon craggy Calabrian hills,
watching as she picks wild blackberries, deep purple jewels plucked from spiney stems.
Inhaling their sweet aroma, as honeyed juices run down my fingers.
Basking in the laughter of children, charmed by Nonna—an ephemeral moment captured in time ...
Posing for photos, holding cherry branches loaded with tart fruits picked by gracious relatives
sharing their best with visitors from afar,
savouring their perfumed sweetness to satisfy a nostalgic craving
for memories of roaming the hills of one's youth.
Simple breakfasts of *pane con latte*, sweetened with sugar and a splash of robust espresso in warm milk,
prepared for grandchildren by Nonna.
They now recall the rustic dish with affection, craving the warm caress of her weather-worn hands ...
The sweet life—*la dolce vita*,
offered up by the rugged landscape for the foreign visitors
rediscovering the country of their ancestors.
Sweet offerings assuage the pain and tears
of family torn from their homeland
by cruel poverty and suffering.
A brief reunion to meet long-lost family and strengthen tenuous bonds,
savouring a fleeting moment of unity
before being separated again by distance, language and culture.
The sweet memories will linger ... until they meet again.

Chocolate, Honey and Almonds

Honeyed confections filled with almonds,
recipes passed down by ancestors
to celebrate special occasions
and welcome family home with a sweet flourish.
Dark chocolates with robust flavours piled high on ceramic platters
pique the appetite and satisfy the sweet tooth.
Simple pastries transmit Nonna's love
for children and grandchildren,
a conduit for her abundant affection
She can never do too much for them,
shielding them from the harshness of life,
creating memories that surround them with a protective aura,
gently guiding and encouraging them
as they grow up and forge their own path.
She whispers lovingly in their ears . . .
"Try another sweet, tesoro, for Nonna . . ."

Gilda Morina Syverson

Cinque Terre

One photograph after another:
Vernazza, Manarola, Corniglia,
Riomaggiore, Monterosso al Mare,
Vernazza again, Manarola again,
each village again and again—adjusting light,
picture plane, size, color, exact placement
capturing the beauty with every tweak

from peaks where I look down
into colorful tones of pinks and brown, light
yellows, lime greens, musty orange and ochre
buildings, jagged water pounding against
the shore, boats rocking side to side
on rough seas keeping all visitors off
ferries traveling back and forth.

Roads stay open for walking
and peering down into each village
where locals live in tall, narrow
houses next to cerulean blue, white,
red and any-other-color of-the-rainbow
boats that take over walkways

where strangers come and go and come
and go again. Each photograph is a reminder
of the romantic towns and fishing
villages on the steep shore in the northern
region of Liguria—the Cinque Terre

tucked away in the rugged-cliffed
mountainous area shaped by isolation
of night when sleep fades and takes
me back to memories of ancestors
and my country of origin.

Stairways, Doors and Immigrants

The neighborhood is empty, immigrants
and homeless look for places to stay.
A beaten up white and gray stairway leads
to *Nonna's* front door. Never were stairs
there before, only a long pathway down
the porch to an entry way. Passing through an unlocked
door, my grandmother's not around, nowhere
to be found. I stick my head in another opening
that leads to the basement, call "*Nonna, Nonna.*"
Below, something stirs. A young girl runs
by, whirls. I call out, ask her name and where *Nonna*
might be found. Noise rises and I head downstairs
in hopes to find my grandmother in the packed basement full
of old belongings: the clawfoot table where my mother
was birthed, bookcases of Italian trinkets, a red and yellow *carretto,*
statues of saints, framed black and white photos
of those left behind. There are shelves of kitchen utensils:
knives and forks, extra-large spoons for twirling spaghetti, sipping
soup. The list goes on. Food, housed deeper in a narrow
corridor, is stored in the back cellar, from where *Nonna*
emerges, quickly moves along. I follow her footsteps
up the cellar stairs to the young girl, an immigrant child,
my grandmother has taken in. It's the child that hangs
near *Nonna* busy preparing the basement for storage and safety.
I point to the broken door my grandmother does not see
as she quickly backs away from me and down

the cellar stairs. I call after her, she does not answer.
The young girl grateful to have a home, I stand next to her
by the broken door, wondering who to call and fix
the old portal with parts no longer available.

Author Biographies

Maria Luisa Ierfino-Adornato (M.A., Executive MBA), freelance writer, AICW member, plus author of: *High Spirits*, in 2005; *McCord's Quiet Rebellion* in 2011, the sequel, *McCord's Griffintown*, in 2015; *Order Sons and Daughters of Italy, Montreal Centennial History* in 2019; and winner of the 2021 Accenti Magazine writing contest.

Gianluca Agostinelli is a Professor of English & Communications at Niagara College. In addition to teaching in China and Italy, Gianluca has taught at McMaster University, Niagara Catholic District School Board, and Brock University, where he is completing a Ph.D. in Educational Studies. Gianluca has published dozens of creative and professional works, including an academic book.

Michelle Alfano is a Toronto writer. Her personal memoir *The Unfinished Dollhouse* was selected as a Globe 100 Best Book of the Year. Her novella, *Made Up of Arias*, was winner of the Bressani Award for Short Fiction. Her short story "Opera" was a finalist for a Journey Prize anthology.

George Amabile has published twelve books and has had work in over a hundred national and international venues, including *The New Yorker*, *Harper's Poetry* (Chicago), *American Poetry Review*, *Botteghe Oscure*, *The Globe and Mail*, *The Penguin Book of Canadian Verse*,

Saturday Night, *Poetry Australia*, *Sur* (Buenos Aires), *Poetry Canada Review*, and *Canadian Literature*. He has won dozens of prizes and the Bressani Award three times.

Josie Di Sciascio-Andrews has written seven collections of poetry. Her work has won several prizes and appears in many journals and anthologies. Her latest book of poems, *Meta Stasis*, was released in June 2021 by Mosaic Press. Josie is a member of The League of Canadian Poets and the Ontario Poetry Society. She is the host & coordinator of The Oakville Literary Cafe series.

Rosanna Micelotta Battigelli was born in Calabria. Her novel *La Brigantessa* (Inanna Publications) garnered a 2019 Gold IPPY Award for Historical Fiction. *Pigeon Soup & Other Stories* was a Finalist in the 2021 American BookFest Best Book Awards and the 2022 International Book Awards (Fiction: Short Story category). www.rosannabattigelli.com

Born in Vancouver, British Columbia, **David Bellusci** is an Italian-Canadian writer and author of eight books. Bellusci's poems have been published in Australia, Canada, India, New Zealand, UK, and USA. He lives in Vancouver where he teaches Philosophy and Religious Studies. Bellusci is a member of the Writers Union of Canada.

Dominic A Buttazzoni: A lawyer and educator by training, and now, during my retirement, a full-time hockey player who simply likes to play with words. Perhaps, I won't say more, for well I know how difficult it is to judge in abstracts about one's own biography if one wishes to judge correctly.

Licia Canton is the author of *The Pink House and Other Stories* (2018) and *Almond Wine and Fertility* (2008). She is director of the documentary film *Creative Spaces: Queer and Italian Canadian* (2021) and co-founder of *Accenti Magazine.* She was president of the Association of Italian-Canadian Writers (2010–14; 2021–22). For her work in culture, she received the Italy in the World Prize (2018). She holds a Ph.D. from Université de Montréal.

Domenico Capilongo is a Toronto high-school creative writing teacher and Karate instructor. His books of poetry and short fiction were shortlisted for several awards. He recently finished a manuscript about words that were born in the 1970s. Find out more about him at: domcapilongo.wixsite.com/home

Maria Giuseppina Cesari (Giusy) lavora come traduttrice alla Corte di Cassazione e docente a contratto presso la UNINT (Roma). Dopo la pubblicazione di saggi sulla letteratura italo-canadese e italo-americana, è passata alla scrittura creativa. Attualmente sta lavorando su un romanzo ispirato alla storia di famiglia durante la seconda guerra mondiale.

Florence-born **Anna Foschi Ciampolini** lives in Vancouver, B.C. She is a bilingual award-winning short story writer, freelance journalist, translator, and co-editor of three anthologies. She has published her works in Canada, U.S.A., Italy, and Costa Rica. Anna is an AICW founding member and co- founder of the F.G. Bressani Literary Prize.

Nella Cotrupi was born in a small mountain town in Reggio Calabria, Italy. She immigrated to Canada with her family as a small child, and grew up amidst the rugged beauty of Northern Ontario landscapes. She is a writer and literary critic, having also worked as a lawyer and educator.

Domenic Cusmano is a writer and communication professional. He is co-founder and publisher of *Accenti*, an English-language cultural magazine, and of Longbridge Books, dedicated to the publication of works that celebrate cultural diversity. He is currently working on a collection of short stories inspired by his frequent travels.

Writer, poet, filmmaker and arts educator **Liana Cusmano** (aka Luca /BiCurious George) is a three-time Montreal Slam Champion and runner up in the 2019 Canadian Individual Poetry Slam Championship. Their first novel, *Catch & Release* (2022) was published by Guernica Editions. They were a 2022 finalist for the QWF Spoken Word Prize and winner of the 2024 Society Pages Poetry Contest.

Adriana A. Davies' publications include *From Realism to Abstraction: The Art of J. B. Taylor*; *The Rise and Fall of Emilio Picariello*; *The Frontier of Patriotism: Alberta and the First World War*; *From Sojourners to Citizens: Alberta's Italian History; Changing My Skin: Dark Elegies and Other Poems;* and *My Theatre of Memory: A Life in Words.*

Delia Petrucci De Santis' short stories have been widely published in literary magazines and anthologies. Some of her work was translated into Italian. She has been an executive member of the Association of Italian Canadian Writers for many years.

Sonia Di Placido is a writer of poetry, plays, literary feminist fiction, CNF articles, academic essays, and book reviews. Currently, she is completing a literary fiction novel, also part of thesis in the Optional-Residency MFA Creative Writing Program, University of British Columbia. She has published 3 chapbooks by Lyricalmyrical Press and Aeolus House Press between 2008 and 2016. Two books of poetry, *Exaltation in Cadmium Red* in 2012 and *Flesh* in 2018 were published by Guernica Editions.

Visual artist **Marven Donati (M. Verbena Donati)** was born in Italy and immigrated to Canada in 1961. She holds a BA from the University of Moncton and an MFA from the University of British Columbia. In various series of acrylic on canvas, Donati's work employs the female body to explore limits imposed by custom and tradition, as well as the impact of self-censoring and self-deception. She has exhibited in solo and group exhibitions, most recently a retrospective of her prints in Ottawa. Her paintings have appeared on magazine and book covers, and have won a number of awards. A number of her paintings are held in private collections. In 2024, at the age of 100, she published her memoir, *Unsettled*. She died at home in April 2025, two weeks short of her 101st birthday.

Silvia Falsaperla is a graduate of University of Toronto. She has published poetry and prose in Canadian and American literary journals and anthologies. She has been a winner of literary contests in Canada, read her work in international literary conferences, and her poems have been translated into Italian, Spanish, and Japanese. Her hybrid collection of poetry and short stories entitled *The Garden of Kolymbethra and Other Poems and Stories about Sicily* was published in 2024 by Legas. and a new collection of poetry is forthcoming with Ekstasis Editions. She loves dogs, to travel, and ride her bike.

Eufemia Fantetti is an instructor, writer and editor who teaches at Humber College. Her second book, *My Father, Fortune-tellers & Me: A Memoir* was released by Mother Tongue Publishing in 2019. Recently, she co-edited the award-winning anthology *Tongues: On Longing & Belonging through Language* with Ayelet Tsabari and Leonarda Carranza.

Tessa Floreano is a dual Italian-Canadian citizen living in the Seattle area. She is a published poet and author with her first historical novel, *Slain Over Spumoni*, released by Wild Rose Press (summer 2022). Her first nonfiction book, *Italians In The Pacific Northwest*, was released by Arcadia Publishing (autumn 2023).

Lucia Gagliese is the Canadian daughter of immigrants from Puglia. Her stories have appeared in *Best Canadian Stories-2021, Accentí, The New Quarterly, This Will Only Take a Minute* (Guernica Editions), *The Healing Muse,* and others. She is a clinical psychologist and professor at York University in Toronto.

Frances Garofalo of Thunder Bay, Ontario is a former superintendent, author and researcher. Her research focuses on district leaders and student achievement. She served on advisory boards, providing strategic policy advice in the areas of law and education. Her short stories and poems have appeared in the *AICW Newsletter*, *Accenti Magazine* and *People, Places, Passages* (Longbridge Books, 2018). She was recently awarded First Place in the 2022 Venera Fazio Poetry contest.

David Giuliano is an award-winning writer. *The Undertaking of Billy Buffone* is his first novel. *Postcards from the Valley,* a collection of essays, was a Canadian best seller. *It's Good to Be Here* is a memoir about cancer, the metaphysics of medicine and the power of story to heal. He has also published two illustrated children's books. His second novel will be out in 2025. David lives on the north shore of Lake Superior. www.davidgiuliano.ca

Connie Guzzo-McParland, co-director of Guernica Editions, is the author of two novels, *The Girls of Piazza D'amore* (2013), *The Women of Saturn* (2017) translated into Italian as *Le Donne di Saturno* (2019), a biography, *An opera in 3 Acts*, translated into French, and the translation of *La Dodicesima Stanza* into English as *The Twelfth Room*. Her works have received various awards, including the 2008 Concordia David McKeen Award in Creative Writing, a finalist nomination for the Quebec Writers' Federation First Book Award in 2013, and the *Premio Vetruvio* Special Award by the jury and second place award by the *Concorso Letterario Internazionale Città di Crucoli* for the Italian translated *Le Donne di Saturno.*

Nicole Haldoupis is a writer from Toronto who lives in St. John's, Newfoundland and Labrador. Her first book, *Tiny Ruins* (Radiant Press, 2020), was shortlisted for four Saskatchewan Book Awards and the Bressani Literary Prize. The novel she wrote for her MA thesis at Memorial University received the 2024/2025 Department of English Award for Thesis Excellence. She's currently a PhD student at Memorial University, a creative writing instructor at the College of the North Atlantic, and a managing editor of Paragon Press.

Elio Iannacci is an award-winning writer, poet and a long-time arts reporter for *The Globe and Mail*. He has contributed to 80 publications worldwide, including *Vogue Italia*, *The Hollywood Reporter*, *Maclean's* and *The Toronto Star*. His Master's thesis, *Queer-Diva Collaboration in 20th Century Popular Music*, was nominated for a Governor General's Gold Medal.

Diana Iuele-Colilli is an Emeritus professor of Italian Studies at Laurentian University. She is also the co-founder and co-director of the student theatre group Le Maschere Laurenziane. Diana has published in the areas of second language acquisition, historical Italian linguistics, Italian dialectology and Italian Canadian language and culture. Diana is also Honorary Vice Consul of Italy for the Sudbury (Ontario) region.

Bianca Lakoseljac is editor of *Rudy Wiebe: Essays on His Works* (Best Book Awards shortlist), 2023, Guernica Editions. She is the author of two novels: *Stone Woman* (Book Excellence Award winner); and *Summer of the Dancing Bear*; a collection of stories, *Bridge in the Rain*, and a book of poetry. She is past president of The Canadian Authors Association, Toronto. Bianca taught communications at Humber College and Toronto Metropolitan University. Her second book of poetry will be published this spring. www.biancalakoseljac.ca.

Josephine LoRe is a first-generation Canadian writer of Italian descent. Her poetry has been published in fifteen countries and five languages. She has three collections: *Unity*, the *Calgary Herald* Bestseller *The Cowichan Series*, and Alberta Bestseller *In My Father's House*. Josephine has been nominated for the 2025 Pushcart Poetry Prize. https://www.josephinelorepoet.com/

Darlene Madott is the author of nine books, including *Dying Times*, 2021. She has twice won the Bressani Literary Award, been short-listed for the Carter V. Cooper award three times, and has often been the finalist in *Accenti* magazine competitions. Her ninth book, *Winners and Losers*, was published by Guernica, 2023. Webpages: www.DarleneMadott.com; www.DyingTimes.com

Anna Mercuri Maiolo is a retired college professor, who has dedicated 35 years to the teaching of English Literature and English as a Second Language in Montreal. Anna's stories are inspired by events that magnify the banalities of the ordinary while encapsulating wisdom and reverence for tradition.

Carmelo Militano was born in the village of Cosoleto, RC, Italy. He is the author of three poetry collections—*Morning After You*, *The Stone Mason's Notebook*, *Archeologia Eros*—and five books of prose: *The Fate of*

Olives, Sebastiano's Vine, Lost Aria, Catching Desire & The Patina of Melancholy. Militano is the winner of the 2004 F.G. Bressani award for poetry. All his prose works have been short-listed for various literary awards. He lives in Winnipeg. www.carmelomilitano.com

Anna Romano Milne is a regular contributor to the online magazine italocanadese.org and a member of the AICW's editorial board. She has held several senior Canadian government positions and is an active member of the Italian community in Ottawa. Anna enjoys writing poems and short stories, often incorporating the Molisano dialect in her creative works.

The author of more than twenty published titles, **Michael Mirolla**'s publications include three Bressani Prize winners: the novel *Berlin*; the poetry collection *The House on 14th Avenue*; the short story collection *Lessons in Relationship Dyads.* His novella, *The Last News Vendor*, won the 2020 Hamilton Literary Award for fiction. A symposium on Michael's works took place in Toronto in 2023. From September 2024 to June 2025, Michael served as the Writer in Residence for the Regina Public Library.

Cristina Pepe was born in Orsara di Puglia and immigrated to Canada with her parents as a toddler. A Vancouver based writer, educator and artist, Cristina travels to Italy every year and writes an art and culture blog, *Un po' di pepe* (http://unpodipepe.ca) where she often writes about Italian culinary culture and gastronomic traditions. Cristina is a two-time winner of the *Accenti Magazine* Photo Contest and is a member of the AICW Executive.

Joseph Pivato was born in Italy and he grew up in Toronto. He has a Ph.D. in Comparative Literature from the University of Alberta, and teaches literature and cultural studies at Athabasca University. His research interest is Italian-Canadian writing and he has been keynote speaker in Wollongong, Australia, and Udine, Italy. In addition to many articles, he has published the following books with Guernica Editions: *F. G. Paci: Essays on His Works* (2003), *Caterina Edwards: Essays on Her Works* (2000), *The Anthology of Italian-Canadian Writing*

(1998), *Echo: Essays on Other Literatures* (1994), and *Contrasts: Comparative Essays on Italian-Canadian Writing* (1985).

Anthony Portulese is an emerging Italo-Québécois writer from Montreal. His nonni originate from: Bellosguardo, Campania; Scanno, Abruzzo; and San Nicola, Calabria. He holds degrees in pharmacology, art history, and civil and common law. Since graduation, he's been published in the *Rutgers Art Review* and literary magazines like *Maisonneuve* and *Panoram Italia*. He dedicates his story to the memory of all beloved grandparents lost to COVID-19 during Canada's long-term care crisis.

Giovanna Riccio is a poet, teacher and independent scholar. She is the author of *Vittorio* (Lyricalmyrical Press, 2010), *Strong Bread* (Quattro Books, 2011), and *Plastic's Republic* (Guernica Editions, 2019) which was shortlisted for the Bressani prize. Her writings have appeared in national and international publications and in numerous anthologies while translations of her work have been published in six languages.

Christine Sansalone is an associate professor in the English Literature, Media and Writing Program at Laurentian University. She is currently the president of the Association of Italian-Canadian Writers. Christine is also the co-director of the student theater group Le Maschere Laurenziane. Christine has published articles on second language acquisition, theater history, the Italian Canadian internment during WWII, cinema and literature.

Daniel Scarcello studied philosophy at the University of Toronto. His first novel, *I By Fire*, is about an author who writes a book by letting coincidences determine the plot, and in the process comes to believe God is speaking to him through his book. His blog, *A Collection of Coincidences*, is available on Substack and Medium. He currently leads a critique group at Vaughan Public Libraries called the *Writers' Room*.

A member of the League of Canadian Poets, The Writers Union of Canada, and the author of two poetry collections, *lifeprint, in points* (erbacce-press,

2020), and *In a Tension of Leaves and Binding* (Guernica Editions, 2024), **Renée M. Sgroi** was one of four finalists in *Accenti Magazine's* inaugural poetry contest. Find her online at: https://reneemsgroi.com

A native of Calabria, **Maria Pia Spadafora** is a teacher, a freelance translator and a creative writer. She translated from English into Italian short stories and poems by several Italian-Canadian writers, such as Licia Canton, Delia De Santis, Darlene Madott, and Sonia Di Placido. Maria Pia is currently the Vice-President of the AICW. She lives and works in Milan.

Gilda Morina Syverson, author, poet, artist, educator and speaker, was born and raised in a large, Italian-American family in Syracuse, New York. She is the author of the full-length poetry book, *Facing the Dragon,* and the chapbook, *In This Dream Everything Remains Inside.* Her heritage was the impetus for her first memoir *My Father's Daughter, From Rome to Sicily.*

Sante A. Viselli è nato a Strangolagalli (Frosinone). Laureato in lettere francesi, ha insegnato in diversi atenei in Canada. Professore emerito (University of Winnipeg), e chevalier dans l'ordre des palmes académiques, è membro onorario della società canadese degli studi sul XVIII o secolo. I suoi studi accademici portano sulla letteratura classica francese e comparata. Varie pubblicazioni nel campo della creazione letteraria includono due raccolte di poesie in francese: Le Pendule e Aux Lisières.